The
Trouble
with
Legends

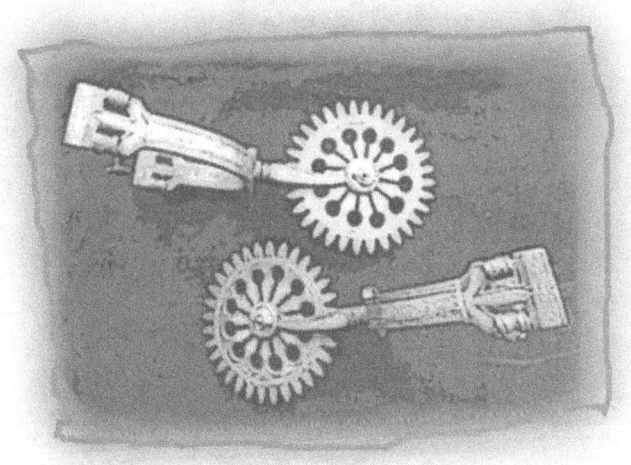

Jeninne Taylor

THE TROUBLE WITH LEGENDS is also
available as a Kindle edition from
Amazon.com

10 9 8 7 6 5 4 3 2 1

ISBN 978-1-57550-083-6

Printed in the United States of America
Cover Art by Johanna M. Bolton

THE TROUBLE WITH LEGENDS *is a work of fic-
tion. All the characters and events portrayed in
this book are fictional, and any resemblance to
real people and incidents is purely coincidental.*

Like every other teacher in the country, Maris Connelly is looking forward to the end of school and the long summer vacation.

But she didn't plan on becoming the target of an obsessed stalker. Or being haunted by the spirit of a long dead bandit. And, to make life more interesting, a new neighbor moves next door - Jim Hayden - immature, irresponsible ... not her type at all. Although he is incredibly good-looking ... but still not her type!

On the bright side, however, there is the usual Friday night gathering with her crazy, and witty, friends. Their favorite cantina, El Picaro, in the picturesque village of Sendero, California provides the group with a meeting place, a pitcher of margaritas.

Having to deal with someone lurking in the shadows as well as an ethereal bandito is enough to have the intrepid English teacher frustrated, anxious, and just a tad frightened. But surrounded by her unconventional friends and close-knit family, Maris maneuvers her way through the perilous summer. She has even more help from a couple of huge dogs, a vicious feline, and ... of all things, rattlesnakes!

Dedication:

To the Woody's gang.

Great friends and good times.

Acknowledgements:

Paula Joseph for her advice and interesting ideas.

Al and Patty Shultz with a recommendation to
remember my roots and revisit the "good old days".

Johanna Bolton for her guidance and
cobbling everything together
into one readable package.

The TROUBLE with LEGENDS

Chapter 1

The trouble with legends is that people tend to believe they're factual ... but who am I to say one shouldn't have faith in such things?

Since this was the last week of school I was letting my sixth graders explore our local heroes as well as some of the historical luminaries from the past ... Hercules, Alexander the Great, King Arthur, William Wallace and Robin Hood.

In the afternoon we would watch a film based on whatever swashbuckler I could find that wasn't considered too offensive for my students.

I'm sure most of the class had access to far more risqué R and even X rated shows at home on television, but one must mind the rules.

So, we would manage with the 1938 "Adventures of Robin Hood" starring Errol Flynn, the 1940 "Mark of Zorro" with Tyrone Power as the dashing masked avenger, and Disney's animated "Sword and the Stone."

The days before the start of summer vacation mostly consisted of trying to maintain a semblance of order and an atmosphere of learning. Sounds like a plan ... so myths and

1

legends were a perfect way to end the school year.

I could always count on one or more of my students to relay "the true story" about the hoard of coins and pouches of gold dust hidden by the freebooter, Joaquin Murrieta, somewhere in the foothills near our town.

Murrieta, the bandit hero of California ... the old myth refuses to expire. He was the swashbuckling defender of the downtrodden, a mixture of fact and folklore, a Robin Hood type, driven to crime by social injustice. Some say he was the inspiration for Zorro, the fictional character created by Johnston McCulley in 1919.

Then there was the other side of the coin that most people tend to ignore; an indication that Murrieta was a sadistic killer, preying on unarmed miners, primarily the Chinese. Humm!

Our charming village, Sendero de Robles, is nestled in the Tehachapi Mountains. It's part of the mountain communities of Badger Pass, about twenty minutes from Santa Clarita, California. The area has old west cowboy and gold rush roots.

Sendero Village maintains a year-round population of nearly seven thousand with another two thousand people scattered about the foothills and lake.

Palomino Lake is the main attraction. A thriving tourist industry caters to visitors who enjoy bucolic surroundings.

Outdoor enthusiasts camp, hike, bike, swim, canoe in the lake, and fish in the small streams that feed into Kashtuk Creek, which eventually meanders into the Palomino.

There is also thirty-seven miles of the Pacific Crest hiking and equestrian trails to enjoy or possibly get lost on. Our mounted sherriff's posse, to which I belong, rescues these unfortunate souls that veer off the beaten path.

Due to our altitude of over four thousand feet, we often get a sprinkling of snow during the winter months. Higher elevations have quite a bit of seasonal weather, which attracts visitors from Los Angeles and the San Joaquin Valley, who never, or mostly never, have the opportunity to experience such conditions.

There are two long sledding slopes and several areas that allow skimobiles to race over snow covered meadows. Not much in the way of places to ski, our mountains are more in the order of foothills rather than steep, lofty peaks.

I guess one might say we have quite a bit to offer tourists. The almost fairy-tale Spanish-style village features stucco arches, shaded walkways, old growth trees, and trickling fountains around the pedestrian friendly plaza.

Red tiled roofs, decorative wrought iron railings, carved stonework entryways invite people into boutiques, specialty stores and galleries that help support the local economy.

There are also cafes, cantinas and wine shops, which provide food, drink and entertainment to locals and visitors.

Some places cater to the early morning breakfast crowd; others accommodate those interested in an alcoholic beverage or three, have a desire to dance, and generally socialize the night away with like-minded folks.

I smiled at the thought of a frosty margarita that awaited me after school.

"No one should be that happy, we still have two and a half more days," Penny Jordan muttered and sat the lunch tray on the table across from me.

"I'm going to ignore that remark. I'm thinking about a lovely, cold, glass of booze."

"I'll have to ponder on that for a while. Okay, I've pondered. The usual place and time?"

Our usual place was a Cantina called El Picaro, around the corner from the Mission Plaza; the time was four o'clock, give or take.

Since this was mid-week I didn't plan to stay long. The established routine my friends and I had fallen into was to meet on Friday, have the "Happy Hour" munchies, a few drinks, and be home around seven-ish … or so.

"I need to borrow one of your movies."

"Which one?"

"You said something about Robin Hood? I could stand to look at Russell Crowe."

"I don't have the Russell Crowe version, you'll have to settle for Errol Flynn."

Penny sniffed. "Oh yeah, can't have the little darlings exposed to the shenanigans in the Russell Crowe interpretation. The Blob would have an emotional breakdown."

"The Blob is a quivering configuration of jelly on the best of days."

Penny quickly looked around the lunchroom. "Shish ... Fayne the Pain and Miss Borsage have their heads together at the far table. Those two, and I quote 'admire and applaud' our esteemed principal and are probably plotting something diabolical."

"It's too late for anything too awful, besides we've signed our intent to return for next year and been accepted by the district."

The lunchroom door banged open and Adam Schaffer shuffled through carrying a large box. The two women at the end of the table stopped talking and glared at the new arrival.

Adam set the container beside Penny, then nodded to the obviously curious on-lookers. "Just some technical journals ladies," he said loudly.

Fayne Dagley sniffed and arched her heavily painted on eyebrows. "You shouldn't have to be reminded that Mr. Ruiz doesn't allow school equipment to be removed."

Adam grinned. "I'm sure it doesn't apply to professional journals, but you're welcome to inspect the contents to make sure I'm not absconding with anything that could be considered "equipment.""

Mrs. Dagley huffed a little, turned away, and continued her conversation with Bernice Borsage.

Adam strolled to the refrigerator and retrieved a tote bag and sat down. "The Bitch and the Witch are always sniffing around," he said softly.

I had to clamp my lips together to keep from laughing. "Smile dearie, hope you don't have anything hidden away. I wouldn't put it past them to scurry like rats to the office and tattle to The Blob."

"Never fear ... dismantled the old junk computer last week, everything is at home to assemble into something workable for next year."

"We're going to have a mid-week drink after school," Penny announced

Adam nodded, took a bite of his sandwich, then mumbled. "In place of Friday, or is this an addition to?"

"It's a curative for what ails us," I stated.

"Maris Connelly, please turn in the book count, it was due last Friday," Bernice said as she swept past.

I frowned and tried to remember what I had done with the stupid four-page document. "I'll send it to you after lunch."

"Please do, and don't consign it to that Eric-John hooligan; he disrupts my class."

I didn't comment until both women were gone. "He disrupts my class," I mimicked.

Penny chuckled. "I'd suggest Cruz, but he would never make it there and back, you'd have to send out a search party."

"Hay, I like those guys, Eric-John may be a smart-ass, but he doesn't take crap off anyone, and Cruz ... he's in lala-land most of the time. Never know ... the boy might be the next Bill Gates."

"Hooligan. Haven't heard that term in forever. I like it. Much more descriptive than juvenile delinquent," smirked Adam.

"Maybe we should refer to Miss Borsage as a spinster

rather than an unmarried woman of mature years," Penny stated.

I chuckled "FYI-bitch is at it again."

"For your information the term "hooligan" came from a rowdy Irish family that terrorized London in the late 1800's. The original name was probably Houlihan but became corrupted over the years."

Adam and I looked at each other and gave our standard reply. "Waa-Waa-Waa."

The El Picaro is a "just right" place, been around for years, family owned and run. It has a beautiful bar with intricate wood paneling, a backlit stained-glass picture of an oak tree on one wall, and amber colored windows across the front.

I was sitting at our regular place, in the corner, relaxing upon the button back leather sofa that stretched along each wall of the room. Adjacent were reclaimed wood plank tables with a glossy bar-top finish.

The middle section displayed small round tables surrounded by wood and leather captain's chairs.

Laura Cordova placed a napkin in front of me and set down the frosty drink. "You get confused about the day of the week?"

"Not hardly."

"The rest of the gang coming?"

"Penny and Adam for sure, maybe Christian. Don't think Sandy can ditch out."

"No Dana?"

"Naa ... she had some errand to run."

Laura adjusted the tie on her apron. "Not much longer and you'll be free for the summer. Got any plans?"

"Not really. We went to Italy over spring break, so have to be careful and mind the piggy bank. How about you? Doing anything fun and exciting?"

"The usual, summer classes in theater at CalArts and working here with the rest of the family."

"I remember the college grind ... don't even want to think about it."

Laura nodded toward the door. "Chris just wandered in, I'll be back. Gotta check on the other customers."

Christian Jordan pulled out the chair opposite me and sat down. "I want you to know that Caroline wasn't thrilled when I left."

Caroline Mercer was the secretary at Chris and Penny's property management company. "You should have invited her to come along."

"Someone has to hold down the fort, it's been busy, people calling non-stop about rentals. You'd think they would plan a little better, everything around the lake has been reserved for months."

'Oh yeah. Thanks for getting a long-term tenant for the duplex."

"I thought you would prefer that rather than a week-to-week all summer long.

Just might work into something more permanent if the guy decides to go for the vacant position in the sheriff's department."

"That's right, Ron Walker plans to retire ... finally. So, my renter ... this Howard fella intends to apply?"

"His name is Hayden, James Hayden, and he's on temporary loan from Santa Clarita for the summer."

"Must have done something dumb to get the" baby sitting tourists duty" in the sticks."

Chris shrugged. "Don't have any idea ... here's Penny and Adam."

Adam slid in beside me and Penny sat next to her husband. "Hi, you made it."

"Not without incurring the evil-eye from Caroline."

Laura appeared to take our orders. "Want a pitcher of

7

margarita's?"

Penny shook her head. "Ice-tea. Have to pick up Nicole from day care.

Adam grinned. "I'll have an Old Dusseldorf, or Pendle Witches Brew."

Laura nodded. "Corona it is … Chris?"

"I'll have the same."

Laura chuckled and headed toward the bar.

Adam leaned back and sighed. "After tomorrow I'll never have to deal with Aubrey Peacock or his crazy mother ever again."

I patted his shoulder. "That's right ... ol'Aubry is graduating from eighth grade, you must be so proud."

Penny smirked. "I wouldn't count on not seeing Mrs. Peacock, I'm sure she will continue to bring goodies. After all, she did have the determination, to scale the fence, and she really really likes you."

Adam shuddered. "One would think after the sheriff's deputy escorted her off the campus in handcuffs she would have gotten the idea."

I looked at Penny and we chimed. "But Aubrey needs me!"

"Aubrey needs a different name and another parent. Can't even imagine what the poor kid will suffer in high school. They'll have to put a guard on him at all times."

I slurped a straw full of booze. "Make sure you speak to the counselors over there, perhaps something can be arranged like we organized. All of us, except for the Witch and the Bitch, made sure he wasn't victimized. Don't leave it to "Pattyfingers" to do anything."

"Perhaps I could persuade our dedicated counselor to contact the high school on Aubrey's behalf. We get along smashingly," Penny giggled.

I grunted. "The only reason you get along is that she's scared shitless of you, after your confrontation."

"It was all a misunderstanding, I didn't shove her into the wall, she sort of backed into it during our conversation. Besides I had a witness, Oscar was in the room stacking copy paper."

Christian inhaled deeply and rolled his eyes. "Leave it! No more school talk, I've managed to confirm the place in Oxnard, on the sand, for a week in August."

The drive home was less than ten minutes. I put the key in the lock, took a deep breath, braced myself and opened the door, almost making it inside before being assailed by two massive, excited, Mastiffs.

Despite the noise, and being swacked with tails, eventually forged my way through the living room and into the kitchen.

"Guys! Guys, calm down! I know you're thrilled to see me. Just let me put my purse down, and I'll feed you."

Faro, the brindle male, sat back on his haunches, while Hallie, the apricot fawn female pushed her enormous head into my stomach.

Mastiffs are huge, good natured, gentle and loyal. Benevolent behemoths that think they are lap dogs and occasionally sling drool on anybody close by.

Faro was sitting politely but doing his "feed me" dance of lifting up one paw and then the other in rapid succession, Hallie gnawed gently on my arm.

I gathered their bowls, went to the pantry where the food was kept in a large plastic bin and shoveled a quantity of dry kibble into each dish, and grabbed some "beef, bacon and cheese" canned food.

The whir of the opener increased the drooling. "Just have to mix this together and you can eat. Remember, 'patience is a virtue,' and, according to Chaucer, 'patience is a high virtue ... but virtue can hurt you' whatever that means. Have to check out the *Canterbury Tales* to find out."

Chapter 2

It was finally over; I even managed to survive the eighth-grade graduation celebration. As usual the ceremony and dinner were held at the pavilion located between the high school and kindergarten through eighth grade buildings.

The teachers were recruited as servers in the food line and on cleanup detail. Everything was over by nine o'clock, for which I was eternally grateful.

The renter must have moved in next door, but I hadn't set eyes on him, just his truck parked in the carport that separated the two dwellings. One had to be careful not to encroach upon the rather narrow space provided for two vehicles.

Sometimes there was an inconsiderate, week-to-week renter, who took his half out of the middle. I'd find it necessary to remind the person how to play nicely with others and share, by parking in back of the offending vehicle. It was always entertaining to listen to various excuses for hogging the carport, and I took my time in moving my car.

I also had a fairly decent solution to loud music booming until the wee hours. An early morning wakeup to the skirl of bagpipes emanating from my portable audio system placed outside the offender's bedroom window was gratifying.

My duplex had been built in the fifties and needed a ton of work. The refrain of "location, location, location" definitely applied to the neglected acre property. The large back yard and patio had a spectacular view of the lake, almost picture perfect.

In the three years since the purchase I had redone all the floors with tile or wood. Now I was working on the kitchen, one appliance at a time, and almost had the bathroom in shape ... almost. There hadn't been much to do in the two bedrooms besides remove the hideous wallpaper and add new color to the walls and install drapes.

I painted everything inside and out, renovated the fireplace in the living room with an efficient insert to slash heating bills and added a stone surround and mantle. The old air-conditioning unit was put out of its misery and I installed a new evaporative cooler. I could get along quite well with a "swamp cooler" and ceiling fans.

The one-bedroom rental next door had been coated over twice, and received new floor tile, cooler, and fans. With the proceeds from this summer, I planned to replace the refrigerator or the stove. The place was clean and livable; one might even call it cozy.

When I glanced at the clock on the bed stand it was ten to five. I didn't really have to make the effort; the dogs were lurking over me like a couple of vultures. If I rolled from my side onto my back the creatures took it as an invitation to maul.

Hallie weighed about one hundred and eighty pounds and Faro over two hundred; a person could smother beneath all that love.

"Can't you guys give me a break? I don't have to be up at the crack of nothingness today, but no ... you pathetic

11

beasts want breakfast, and from vast experience will not leave me alone until the deed is done."

Hallie pawed at the sheet and I could hear the thump of Faro's tail. "Fine, I'll feed you, then I'm coming back to bed for an hour or so. We'll head out to the ranch later."

The ranch wasn't really a ranch, I mean, not like hundreds of acres. The Connelly place was about sixty acres, where my family raised horses -- palomino horses.

For those not familiar with palominos, these lovely animals are different shades of gold with a white mane and tail. The beautiful horses are not an official breed themselves, but can be Quarter Horses, Arabians, Morgan, and many others. It's the color that is distinctive.

The golden hue can be difficult to produce, even when breeding two palominos together. A foal might be anything from a light chestnut, maybe a cremello or a perlino, as well as variations of gold.

A cremello is a cream color with blue or greenish eyes and a white mane and tail. A perlino is yellowish-white with light eyes and pink skin, while the lower legs, mane and tail will be a darker gold.

Palominos are popular show horses, rather taller and heavier than most, and of course very flashy.

I wanted to see the new foal that was born last week, and take a long ride on my sweet mare, while I let the dogs run amok.

By six thirty I was up and had brushed my hair and found a rubber band to secure the unruly blond mop into a ponytail. My two faithful friends were half inside the bathroom watching, and from time to time would inch forward, hoping I wouldn't notice. I could have closed the door, but they would whiffle and snuffle around the bottom and thud against it, much easier to keep it open and contend with group toileting.

I slathered aloe on my face and added some color to my

eyebrows, so much for my beauty routine. I studied the face; one might say I was a palomino ... blonde, blue-green eyes, taller and heavier than most ... forget the flashy part. Fortunately, I didn't have a long horse face; mine was sort of round with even features.

Really must concentrate on taking off a few pounds this summer.

My gray T-shirt said *OTHODOX PAGAN* across the front in large black letters, and the well-worn jeans were somewhat ragged at the bottom. The scuffed boots had creases over the upper part and probably should have new heels sometime soon. The final touch was an old gray and white camouflage boonie hat my brother had worn when he served in the Marines. I was a devoted follower of haute couture for sure.

Penny often mentioned that I bought my car for the dogs. She was partly right; the Honda's back seats folded down, as did the front passenger side, and the opening of the hatch back was quite large.

The dogs could sit close and drool down my arm or neck. I had basic transportation, no frills, and affordable ... a necessary plus.

After six years of teaching, my salary was less than a maintenance and operations employee. I knew that because I saw a district job opportunity flyer and wanted to apply for the position.

Adam said I wouldn't get hired because I was "certificated" and the situation called for "classified." I also had no experience.

That didn't stop me from being rather pissed about such things.

There were other benefits; I had two and a half months off with pay every year. Many people believed that was the case, not realizing we freeloading teachers had to set aside funds to get us through the summer. Arrangements with the

13

bank for an automatic withdrawal from each paycheck during the year was the smartest way to make sure one could survive.

I loaded the dogs into the car and headed down the hill to Lakeside Road. Someone had used great imagination in naming the road around the lake ... Lakeside. Crossed the bridge over the Kashtuk River, made a left onto San Marino Drive, traveled another mile, and turned into the dirt and gravel lane to the house.

The hounds were impatient to be set free, to meet and greet the critters that lived here.

Two shepherd-mix dogs rushed toward the car and barked enthusiastically. A couple of geese waddled and honked in the grassy area near the fence, and a huge white Yorkshire pig roused himself from under the shade of a tree and wandered in our direction.

My mother came onto the porch to see what the racket was about. "Grover, Monty! Hush!"

I opened the hatch and let the beasties out, they ran toward the other dogs and the four circled and sniffed and settled into an easy comradery. The two geese continued to honk.

"If I had some lettuce I'd feed you," I called out to the pair. My dad had named them Maudie and the Old Man about ten years ago, they roam free, and could hold their own with the dogs and pig.

Percival grunted and climbed the steps to stand beside my mom, who gave him a fond pat. The pig wrinkled his snout a few times and flopped on the porch.

I pushed through the dogs took a deep breath and grinned. "I'm free at last!"

Mom smiled. "Come to see the foal?"

"That ... and visit you and Dad, and ride Matchless."

"Want breakfast?"

"As much as I would love two or three biscuits, bacon

and eggs, I'll settle for a cup of coffee."

"Another diet ... again? I can't believe you feel dieting is necessary; you look fine to me."

"I'd look fine to you and Dad if I weighed four hundred pounds, had buck teeth and mange."

Mom led the way into the farmhouse. It had been re-modeled several times since the nineteen twenties when my great-grand parents built it. The original footprint remained -- large entry hall, living room to the right, a small study to the left and next to that, a formal dining room. Upstairs were three bedrooms and two bathrooms.

The huge kitchen and pantry had been reconfigured and modernized. There was enough space carved out of the kitchen to have a guest bathroom situated off the hall and a laundry room adjacent to the back porch.

The eating area in the kitchen looked out to the patio and back yard. A large veranda ran the length of the house and featured several rocking chairs and a lattice weave glider sofa.

Mom poured coffee into mugs and we went outside to sit in the fresh morning air.

"Where's Dad?"

"Probably in the stable. He's expecting an outside mare, a new girlfriend for "The Kid.""

The Kid was really The Sundance Kid, a beautiful stallion that had a record of producing golden offspring. The other stallion was Rio, a light chestnut with a flaxen mane and tail, my father's favorite.

"The new foal is out of Rapunzel and Rio?" I asked.

"Yes. A nice strong filly."

I took a few sips of coffee. "You started your class ... what ... two weeks ago?"

"Indeed, and will finish at the end of June. It's just the basic history of painting from pre-historic wall art to the modern era. I'm throwing in a brief analysis of the more famous works, the Mona Lisa, a Vermeer, a few by Van Gogh. Each time I teach this course I select something different."

I just had to ask. "Do you think the Mona Lisa is really Da Vinci in drag?"

My mom chuckled. "I have no idea; the portrait is supposed to be the wife of some rich merchant or even Leonardo's mother."

"You and Dad going on vacation? I'd be glad to stay, take care of the animals."

"We might go for a few long weekends. This time of year is busy; someone is bound to get lost in the mountains, and there is always the threat of wild fire. Thanks for the offer. I'll let you know ... You have any plans?"

"Not really -- go to the beach for a week, volunteer at the museum, Mr. Atkins asked if I could help out."

"Doing what?"

"The care and handling of nitrate-based photography. Those old negatives are highly flammable and can self-ignite. I guess quite a few boxes of photographs have been donated and need to be separated, inventoried, and catalogued."

"Might be fun going through old pictures. And perhaps you could get a glimpse of the *"Lady in Black Lace"* the basement of the museum is supposed to be haunted."

"Oooh ... how fun is that. Another haunted place to go along with just about every old deserted hovel around here. Like the prospector's shack, where a large, mostly transparent, old man with a white beard calls out to passers-by. Any one of the forty-five or so abandon mines in these hills, maniacal laughing in Diamondback Cut, faces peering through windows and a moving ball of red light in the Castro house.

"Let's not forget the infamous, shadowy, almost non-existent trail that turns slightly to the right, away from the Pacific Crest Hiking Trail. The path is surrounded by vegetation and the farther you go, the colder it gets and more diffi-

16

cult to breathe. And there's the feeling of someone following behind ... Some say there are human bones on the side of the trail."

My mother smiled. "There is always a glimmer of truth in every story, and you know there is something odd about the Castro house, that's the reason it doesn't stay rented for very long."

"It doesn't stay rented because it's too far from town for most folks. Quite a few people from the city decide to move to the country and don't realize how isolating it can be ... no convenience store or Burger King on the corner."

"The Castro Place isn't that far away from town. No, it's something else."

We continued to slowly rock and finish our coffee, then I collected the cups, put them in the sink, grabbed a carrot out of the fridge and made my way across the yard to the stable.

Inside was cool; the doors at either end were open as were several of the stalls exit and entrances out to a paddock. I inhaled the aroma of hay, pleasant smelling pine shavings and straw.

Each morning the occupied stalls were cleaned or mucked out, manure and wet materials removed to cut down on odors.

Dad was having an in-depth conversation with the mare, Rapunzel. "We must decide on a name for your little girl, can't continue to call her "Baby-face."

I chuckled. "I'm sure Rapunzel doesn't give a rat's ass about a name."

Dad turned around and squinted in my direction. "Good morning to the fair Maris."

As a young man my father had spent summers in Ireland with relatives in Galway, and from time to time managed a lilting brogue.

"Tis grand ta see your fine self as well," I replied with a

17

fairly decent Irish accent. "I've been thinking about a name for the last few days, how about we stick with "R" as a beginning letter, the parents are Rio and Rapunzel. One of our great-whatever grandparents from the year one was named Remy."

Dad looked thoughtful, gave the mare another pat. "Remy, not bad. What do you think Rapunzel?" The horse nudged the human with her nose and snorted softly, then looked at her foal that had wandered a short distance away.

The long legged, somewhat awkward, filly resembled her father, light chestnut, and flaxen mane and tail.

"A real beauty," I said.

"Yes, she is. You going to ride this morning?"

"Thought I'd give Matchless and the dogs a little exercise."

I picked up a halter and lead rope from the tack-room and we walked toward the pasture. There were several areas of crossed fenced permanent grass; my horse was with four other mares.

Across a vacant pasture was Rio in his own enclosure, another area contained two geldings, and the last pasturage was for The Sundance Kid.

I stood near the gate and called Matchless who came eagerly, knowing she would be rewarded with something good to eat. I snapped the carrot into three pieces and let her nibble from my hand, then slipped on the halter and fastened the lead onto the ring.

Dad had some horse cookies for the other curious ladies that crowded around wanting their share of goodies.

With the mare in tow we walked back to the stable where I brushed the golden coat and checked her hoofs. Dad brought the bridle and saddle and set them on the sawhorse.

"You pay attention to where you're going. Rattlesnakes are out. Saw one sunning himself on a rock just the other day."

"I'll keep eyes and ears open. Wouldn't want the dogs or Matchless to get bit. Why don't you come along?"

Can't. Waiting for a mare to arrive."

"Oh yeah, forgot ... Okay, see you in a few hours."

After saddling and bridling my horse, led her out of the stable, mounted, called the dogs and headed towards open country.

Chapter 3

I rode all morning. The back trails through the low foothills wound around familiar places, my brother's property, the Macias and Castro holdings ... I waved to Old Tom the care-taker of the Castro place. One could usually find him sitting in a rocking chair on the porch. He was quite the character and told stories of the good old days before everything be-came so complicated.

Tom didn't care for computers, cell phones, or the treasure hunters that could often be found digging on Castro land.

Some of the shops in town sold maps of where the old mines were located or places that Joaquin Murrieta might have buried his ill-gotten goods. Humm ... X seldom marks the spot.

The narratives told and retold in regard to the Robin Hood of old California, would find that the *truth* is probably somewhere in between.

As a child, my grandmother knew Grandma Castro, who was in her nineties and conveyed a story passed down through her family about Murrieta.

Seems the Castro place was where the outlaw and his

band pastured their palomino horses. These horses were either captured from herds that ran wild, or stolen from people who lived in the small, backwater hovels known as Los Angeles.

There was an abundance of wild horses that ran free in the early 1800's. Quite a few of them were palominos, and thus the name of our lake.

Anyway, the Castro family were friends or relatives of Murrieta and his gang and gave them aid and comfort when being pursued by a posse. One might assume that the ranch or surrounding area would be an ideal place to hide any stolen pouches of gold dust, nuggets, or coins.

The more probable story was anything stolen was quickly lavished on booze, women, and gambling. Myth and legends of pirate treasure was just that ... myths and legends. The loot was gone as soon as there was a place to squander it about.

A big reason people still treasure hunt around here is the tale of an assay office robbery in the San Joaquin Valley that netted thousands of dollars' worth of gold coins.

Supposedly, Joaquin carried out this nefarious deed, and the bandits were pursued and tracked to our small section of the universe.

The ten and twenty-dollar coins were minted in San Francisco and never circulated. In today's market, each coin could be worth as much as fifty thousand dollars ... quite a prize if located.

The only problem is, no one really knows much about this robbery, the amount actually taken, or if the loot was even gold coins. Joaquin Murrieta was often given credit for things he couldn't have possibly done, such as being seen in several places at the same time.

Another dilemma was there were four or five other bad guys called Joaquin wandering around the countryside ... a rather confusing situation.

After having lunch with my parents, I went home and took a nap with my furry friends. They had worn themselves out following delicious smells or chasing the rabbits that darted about.

The rest of the day was spent being lazy, reading for a few hours, catching up on television programs I had recorded ... and munching on a small salad. I would have preferred pizza and a beer, but a promise is a promise about shedding a few pounds.

⌘

It must have been past mid-night when I heard the banging. The dogs charged madly to the front door then on to the couch by the window and barked frantically. I stumbled out of bed to the living room window to see what was going on.

Soon there was yelling as well as banging, the commotion was coming from next door. I tried to see who was making all the noise; it was definitely a woman's voice but couldn't see her unless I ventured to the porch.

Perhaps if I turned on the outside light it might discourage the idiot who was creating such a commotion.

It didn't make any difference even when I flicked the light on and off several times. I finally opened the door and ventured outside, which wasn't easy with the dogs wanting to accompany me.

A woman who didn't seem to notice or care about the light, or me, continued her tirade.

I could make out a few words, "Jimmy ... talk to you" the door opened, and the irate female was pulled inside, and it was finally quiet.

Great! My new renter had girl troubles. If stuff like this persisted I'd have Christian evict him for violation of the rental agreement about noise at ungodly hours of the night.

I forced my way back inside -- which was a little difficult, because the dogs wanted to investigate --. turned off the porch light and went back to bed.

It took a while for the critters to settle themselves and for me to simmer down. I had thoughts of confronting the fellow in the morning but decided to wait. Hopefully nothing more would happen. Having a contentious neighbor was not how I wanted to spend my summer.

The small Sendero Museum, and Old California Frontier Village is a popular place. All the schools in the Mountain Communities visit regularly; it's part of the curriculum. During the summer there are a variety of arts and crafts activities for children, sponsored by the museum in collaboration with the school districts.

The Frontier Village has about sixteen acres where one can examine the fifty or so historical structures collected from the surrounding areas and reassembled on the property.

The history and culture of the people who lived here are preserved in the Native American dwellings, mining shacks, schoolhouse, general store, courthouse, church, assay office and others.

The inside gallery has a modest collection of fossils and artifacts -- items from the California Native American Tribes ... Kitanemuk, Yokuts, and Chumash.

The woven baskets are beautiful. Many were used for cooking. Their weave so tight and strong that food mixtures could be brought to a boil by placing heated stones inside the receptacle.

Arrowheads, bows and arrows, pottery, mortar and pestles for grinding acorns into flour are featured as well as many pistols and rifles from the early 1800's.

I once tried to make acorn flour as a class project. First,

one must collect the acorns -- try to find those that have no worms. Shell, grind, using a mortar and pestle ... really fun! Rinse with cold, then hot water many many times to wash away the bitter flavor, let dry ... and voila!

The process only took twelve days, and ended up with moldy, nasty tasting, lumpy flour that we dumped in the trash. One could starve to death!

Among the many collections are photographs of Sendero from the late 1800's and of the pioneer families who settled here. My job for the next few weeks ... after looking through the donated boxes of pictures, was to separate, catalogue, and preserve. Then add or subtract photos from the display and label everything as succinctly as possible.

I had done this activity over the years and didn't mind donating my time for a few weeks in the summer if I wasn't off to exotic places like Ragged Breeches, Slumgullion, Rum Blossom or Gouge-Eye, all real towns that had once flourished in the California Gold Rush Country.

⌘

There was an exhibit in the gallery of three rather nice paintings by Isabella Castro done mid-eighteen hundred's. And a display of artifacts from the ranch enclosed in a glass case. The family had loaned everything around 1930, I guess to make sure they were preserved.

The pictures were of the original ranch house, a corral with horses and vaqueros leaning on the fence, and a final piece of the ranch house, corral, cowboys, and in the background, Diamondback Cut.

Diamondback Cut wasn't really near the ranch buildings as portrayed in the painting. I always thought it was interesting to include it in the milieu ... guess Isabella had her reasons.

As often as I had been in the museum, I always stopped to admire the three paintings, and sometimes envied such talent. The features of the three vaqueros were mere suggestions of a face, rather vague and blurry. The horses were palominos, probably the reason I was so attracted to the scene. This morning was no different from any other visit. As usual, I paused and admired, then went on my way to the stairs down to the basement.

Mr. Atkins was waiting for me. "Maris, thank you so much for helping out. As you can see there is quite the pile."

Two tables were covered with boxes and several more containers were stored underneath. "Quite a pile is an understatement, this is going to take some time."

"I don't expect you to go through it all by yourself. Hopefully the others I have asked will show up."

I took a deep breath. "I'll do what I can. Might as well get started."

Mr. Atkins smiled, took a long look at the boxes and left.

I had decided to donate a few hours a day, three days a week, didn't want to spend my entire summer in the basement. At the same time, I wasn't going to rush, but take time and look at the pictures, as well as make sure the old flammable ones were identified and stored properly. Hopefully the photos were labeled in some way, as to who the people were and perhaps a date, instead of "Momma and Baby John."

Three hours later I had finished about half of the box. I placed it back under the table with a note on top that stated this was a work in progress and I planned to return.

There was a bathroom near the stairs. I had to wash my filthy hands, probably should have worn gloves, but gloves could often be more of a hindrance when dealing with photos that were stuck together.

25

I needed groceries, and thought about stopping at the drug store, which included an old fashion soda fountain, where I usually had a milkshake. But reminded myself not to succumb to temptation ... damn!

I could be consoled with having an adult beverage tomorrow evening with the crew. They probably had the latest gossip going around town. Like most small places everybody knew his or her neighbors' business, good, bad or indifferent.

I had been the topic several years ago, due to my short-lived marriage of little more than a year. Truth be known, the union should have terminated after three months.

We both knew it was a mistake but decided to hang on for a year ... that way the fiasco didn't look so bad to family and friends. One should always be considerate of family and friends ... wonderful!

Tony moved to the Seattle area several years ago, but he and I still keep in touch.

I parked on my side of the carport. The fellow's truck was gone. Just as I got inside the phone started to ring, and the dogs began to bark to add to the noise. The two bags of groceries were dumped on the couch near the extension.

I could hear the robotic voice announce the caller as Dana Mattheson.

"What?"

"Is this the person to whom I'm speaking?"

"No, I'm not home right now ... go away."

"Fine way to treat a friend!"

"Who said you were my friend?"

"Doesn't matter, you're stuck with me anyway. What are you up to?"

"Just finished at the museum and went to the store."

"How exciting. I cleaned the pantry, got rid of the bugs in the oatmeal."

"I thought you were going to San Diego to see your

brother."

"The plans changed. He and my sister-in-law are coming here -- should arrive in about an hour and stay the night."

I sat on a chair at the center island. "What have you done now?"

"The usual, I refuse to move closer to home so he can run my life. He doesn't like a long-distance relationship and thinks I'm under the influence of unsavory people -- like you."

"Mwahaha, come closer my little chickadee, while I cast my spell over your feeble mind, and make you do unspeakable things."

"Yes, Master ... or is it Mistress? I always get confused."

'Tell "The Pope" to go suck an egg."

"As much as I would like to do that, he does lend me money when I need it to fund our trips. Wouldn't want the "bank" to close my account."

"You pay him back don't you?"

"Of course, but it might take a few months."

I ventured into the living room and gathered up a sack. Had to put the cold things in the fridge, then went back for the second bag before the dogs tore it apart looking for a treat.

"You going to the cantina tomorrow?"

"Absolutely! Never know when I might meet a rich, wildly handsome guy, who will sweep me off my feet and take me away from this hum-drum life."

"In the years we have been congregating haven't seen anyone like that. Wait, there's Big Fat Benny. He always drops by the table to chat."

"Big Fat Benny is a" bookie" and old as god!"

I chuckled. "Like I said, a perfect match."

Dana muttered something that sounded vaguely like "moll." I responded that her *hormonal blondness* was showing, and she was watching too much Australian television on Netflix.

"Tell your brother to bring some of the "extra summer" deputies around. Isn't he still in charge of supervising the help?"

"If I remember correctly, Scott introduced a few of the guys last year. Don't want to make the same mistake again."

"I kind of liked Kurt what's-his-face. He was cute."

"He was also married."

"Yeah, there was that. Well, the relatives will be here soon, must get mentally prepared. See ya tomorrow."

After giving the dogs some "Scooby-Snacks" I went out on the patio to relax and look at the lake. A slight breeze rippled the water. In the distance one could see small boats, mostly canoes, making their way to and from the shore.

The campgrounds were full, as were the bungalows that surrounded the lake. Quite a few dwellings were built on the hillsides and on up to higher elevations.

Some of the huts were very basic, consisting of a roof, screened in walls and metal bed frames. Other places were cozy cottages with all the comforts of home.

I should be doing something constructive, the fence in the backyard required a new application of stain. The wood structure was six feet tall, the bottom five feet was solid, the top foot was lattice. The color had faded over the years. I probably should have gone with a lighter shade, but really liked the dark walnut tint. It was rich looking and a little different from the usual natural or honey oak color of most fences.

Dad said he would pressure wash the fence whenever I was ready. But becoming ready would mean getting off my backside and exerting myself, which, at the present time, I didn't want to do.

I'd think about it later ... much later.

Chapter 4

I stood fuming near my car. The stupid jerk neighbor had parked so close that I couldn't get to the driver's side door. Even on the passenger side there wasn't room enough for me to get through because one must park close to the building to make way for two vehicles. I could climb in the back but decided to have a face-to-face confrontation with the moron.

I rang the bell, banged on his door and waited. Then repeated the actions again, after a third time the door opened a crack. Two eyes squinted, then blinked. "Whatever you're selling I don't need," he muttered.

I leaned against the door to prevent the ass from closing it. "You "need" to move your truck," I said none too politely.

The portal opened a little more, the fellow was wearing only boxer shorts and a confused look on his face. "What are you talking about?"

I huffed loudly. "You parked your truck so close to my car that I can't get inside."

He closed his eyes and sighed. "I'll get my keys," then shut the door.

I paced up and down and thought if the idiot went back to bed I'd get my own set of keys, barge in and drag him to his damn truck.

Finally, he shambled outside; clothed in a t-shirt and jeans and walked barefoot toward the carport. "Sorry, didn't realize I was so close."

He looked rather scruffy; his thatch of chestnut colored hair was sticking up in all directions. I moved out of the way so he could get to his vehicle and watched as he backed out.

I was tempted to make a nasty remark as I left but managed a curt "Thank you." Hopefully this wouldn't continue, a fight over parking and bimbos yelling and beating on doors in the middle of the night, did not make for a nice summer.

I should take a deep breath and forget about it, enjoy the morning air; there was work to be done at the museum.

I parked in one of the spaces reserved for staff on the north side of the building and went through the side door. Once in the basement located my box of photographs and hauled them to a space next to the wall.

It looked as though someone else had been working; there was less congestion on the tabletops.

It must have been an hour or so later when I felt the building tremble and shake slightly. An earthquake was not unusual in this part of the country. Sendero was located around three fault lines, the San Andreas, Garlock, and smack above the White Wolf.

I would imagine we experienced small, undetectable to us humans, temblors all the time; this one was probably about a three or so on the Richter Scale.

Nothing looked damaged; no small cracks in the ceiling as far as I could tell. Probably should go up-stairs and see if everything was all right.

Mr. Atkins was wandering around, as were several other staff members looking at the walls and ceiling. No one seemed particularly frantic; most everyone lived in and around this area and didn't become hysterical when the earth trembled a little.

"I was in the basement, didn't see any problems down there."

"As far as I can tell nothing has been disturbed in here either," said the director.

I looked up to check for any fissures. "Glad it was a nice roller instead of a jarring shake."

Mr. Atkins continued to gaze upward. "Hope this is not a precursor to the so called *Big One* expected at any time."

"If these little quivers help mother earth let off steam, then keep them coming."

Mr. Atkins nodded in agreement. "I should make sure the village didn't suffer any harm."

I wandered toward the collection of paintings by Isabella Castro to see if there was damage. Everything looked fine, the adobe ranch house, the middle one with the horses in the corral, and the third image with Diamondback Cut. It was a different story with the display cabinet.

The glass cabinet contained artifacts from Spanish California that belonged to the Castro family. A leather money belt, silver incense burner, small jewelry chest with rawhide lacing, silver picture frame, carved wooden candlesticks and a beautiful set of early California spurs. A candlestick was tipped over and one of the spurs had fallen off its peg.

I would have to get a key from the secretary to unlock the cabinet and put the items back in their places.

The candlestick was set upright once again. I picked up the spur and received a jolt, like a shock of electricity going through my fingers. I dropped the silver heirloom, clutched my tingling hand and uttered a few cuss words. Then took a deep breath and with trepidation touched the spur again. Thankfully, nothing happened, and I returned it to the peg. Okay, that was unexpected, some kind of static energy in the air?

31

My hand still tingled a little bit as I glanced up at the pictures.

Something about the last painting looked odd; the picture seemed a little brighter, the shrubs around the Cut were more vivid. I stepped closer; maybe it was light coming in from the upper windows that made things more colorful.

I glanced across the room to see if the sun was streaming, but the louvers were aimed upward. Direct sunlight can be harmful to antiquities, so was happy to see they were in the usual position.

I leaned in a little more, then backed away quickly, a chill ran from head to toe. The eyes on one of the vaqueros were staring at me! That was impossible, the faces were never really clear, just indications of features. No eyes! No faces ... Until now!

I could feel my skin prickle, then took a deep breath and looked again. The eyes and now the rest of the face were very distinct. I carefully examined the other two figures, nothing had changed, just an indication of features.

Surely no one had messed with the painting. There hadn't been enough time for any cleaning to have been done, something like that was quite a process and didn't happen in a couple of days.

All righty then ... I got as close as I could to carefully examine the rather nice-looking cowboy, then glanced around to see if anyone was nearby. There were visitors, but they were across the room on the other side.

"Aren't you a fine handsome devil," I whispered.

I don't know if I expected the vaquero to reply, if that happened, I would make an immediate appointment with a shrink. Thankfully, nothing weird occurred, well, nothing weirder than a face appearing where there had once been a featureless blur, and almost electrocuted by a spur.

I moved away and to the side, the black eyes followed me.

32

This was crazy, my heart was beating much too fast, the hair on my arms was standing up and I wanted to run, but didn't.

I carefully backed away and told myself there was a perfectly rational explanation for what I had experienced. I just couldn't think of any at the moment. I should return to the basement, get my purse and leave ... have a pineapple milkshake at the drug store. It was too early for an adult beverage or two.

I'd call Penny; see if she was home, we could have a nice chat about what I had seen, and she would enjoy a treat from McClure's.

⌘

"A Strawberry Special! What do you want in return for such a delight? I'd give you my first-born child, but you'd bring her back in fifteen minutes."

"I thought about maple nut, but this vanilla ice cream, strawberry, almond, and banana concoction seemed a better idea. Where is the whirlwind?"

"Nicole is outside playing with the hose, helping me wash the patio furniture."

"I didn't bring her anything, figured we could share ours."

"Doubt if she comes inside, she's having too much fun getting wet."

We sat in the family room and watched the little blonde sprite sprinkle everything including herself with water, happy to be outside on a warm summer day.

"So ... what have you been doing?"

"Nothing much, working a few hours a day, several times a week at the museum, went riding ... oh and having a lovely time with my new renter."

"Do I detect a note of cynicism?"

I stirred the thick ice cream and took a bite. "If you call being awakened by a dingbat woman yelling and banging on the door in the middle of the night or parking his truck so close to my car that I couldn't get inside ... then I could be called cynical. More like pissed off!"

Penny moved to the screen door to check on her daughter, then returned to the couch and sat down. "Oh dear, maybe Christian should have a talk with the fellow.

"I'll give it a little more time, see what happens in the next week."

I leaned back against the comfortable cushion and took a deep breath. "I had an interesting experience at the museum."

"You mean the earthquake?"

"Well that ... something else happened after the rock and roll ... one might call it a little eerie."

Penny squeaked. "You saw *The Lady in Black Lace!* She is supposed to haunt the museum, but no one has ever seen her except for Mrs. Latimer, but some say that's because she had a drinking problem."

"It was Mr. Latimer who drank like a fish, the former director, had a rather undistinguished reputation for absconding with a few of the more valuable antiquities bought with museum funds."

Penny set her drink on the coffee table. "What was so weird?"

"You know the three paintings by Isabella Castro that hang on the east wall?"

"I've seen them, so what?"

I took a deep breath. "One of the cowboys now has a face and the eyes follow when you move."

My friend furrowed her forehead. "So what? If I recall, the guys always had faces."

"No, not real features ... not a defined nose, mouth and eyes."

34

"I guess I didn't take much notice, the pictures have always been there, year after year ... the old adobe house, the corral, cowboys and horses, the Cut."

"Well now one of the men has a face and eyes that follow you around. How is that possible?"

She once again went to the screen and watched Nicole. "I have no idea, perhaps you have just now noticed, the faces aren't very big, I mean not like a large portrait."

I closed my eyes and tried to bring up an image of the painting. "Not possible, I've studied those pictures for years, enjoy looking at them, especially the scene with the horses."

"All right, we should take another look later today after Nicole's nap. I'll call you when she wakes up and meet you there."

"Fine."

I drove home, parked without any problem from an encroaching neighbor, fought my way through the dogs and went to deposit my purse in the bedroom. I was surprised that the dogs hadn't followed to jump and wrestle on the bed; instead they stayed outside in the hall.

"What's the matter with you two, by now the bed is a shambles."

I hung my bag over the back of the chair. "Come ... Faro, Hallie." They didn't move, Hallie whined a little, not especially unusual, she did that when she wanted attention.

I looked at the huge animals, then turned slowly around to study the room. Could be they were upset about the earthquake, animals can sense things like that.

I searched for any damage, small cracks or anything different, and found nothing, except for the curtains moving a tiny bit.

The fan wasn't on, so checked to see if the window was closed ... it was. So why were the curtains rustling slightly ... why not ... hell ... everything else today had been strange. The stupid neighbor, an earthquake, antique spurs that delivered quite a jolt, a picture that changed, peculiar animals and erratic curtains ... just another day in my life.

I took one last look around, everything was in its usual place, and decided the dogs were just nervous because of quake.

Penny squinted at the painting. "You're right, the faces are just a blur, all three of them. Maybe what you saw was a trick of the light."

I got as close as I could and examined each face, which wasn't terribly difficult since there was no detail to see. "It was no trick of light and my imagination wasn't going ape-shit," I grumbled.

"Maris! Little people have big ears that pick up every-thing, especially swear words. Nicole will blurt out profanity in the most unsuitable places, which leads to embarrassing situations."

"Sorry!"

"Since we're here, might as well visit the Frontier Vil-lage, she loves the play area with the child size stage coach, wagons and train."

⌘

As soon as I came home after the visit to the museum, I went to the bedroom; the dogs followed me and romped on the bed as usual. Okay, nothing out of the ordinary, time to push the experience into some dark corner of my mind.

My dinner was a bowl of celery, carrots, raw broccoli and diet soda, had to make the sacrifice after the pineapple milkshake.

Television programs were either re-runs or ridiculous reality shows, who knew there could be so much drama in storage unit auctions. The next great thing will be dumpster diving for unimaginable treasures, like who can find the greatest amount of wilted lettuce and rotten Chinese take-out.

The gang was there when I arrived at El Picaro late Friday afternoon. Laura waved at me from across the room and would bring my booze when she had time. I didn't know if it was a good or bad thing that the serving person didn't have to ask what I wanted to drink.

I sat next to Sandy, Adam's wife. "Hey, how's the law and order business," she was secretary to the Sheriff, and always had the latest gossip.

"Never a dull moment when the tourists arrive, the usual resident crazies keep us busy too."

"Can't wait to hear the weekly happenings."

Christian began to laugh. "The De Looney's were cited again."

The actual name was De Luna; the family was always involved in some dispute with the neighbors. "What did they do this time?"

Christian chuckled. "The De Looney girls were drag racing the riding lawn mowers with the Kingsley boys, ran over Mrs. Rivera's prize petunias or whatever."

Sandy snickered. "Mr. Hawkbower was ticketed for shooting his pellet gun while patrolling the neighborhood in his golf cart, seems the squirrels have been menacing his bird feeders."

My drink arrived I savored a first taste. "The tourists behaving?"

Sandy shook her head and exhaled loudly. "Depends on what one considers behaving. A guy was transported to the clinic for burns after trying to start his bar-b-que grill with gasoline rather than charcoal lighter.

The deputies were called to intervene in drunken brawls at various camp grounds around the lake."

"Sounds like the usual fruits and nuts that come to enjoy the area," I said.

Christian made a drum roll sound on the table. "Just thought you guys would like to know there will be a new development going in across the highway at San Emidio?"

"The one with two acre lots higher up the mountain?" Adam inquired.

"Yep, going to call it Deer Park or Peak, something like that, quite high-end.

"Ohh ... there should be "deerie" names for the streets." Dana gushed.

"What are you talking about? Deerie names?" Christian muttered.

"You know like Bambi Lane."

Our gang had the ability to delve into topics with true wit and mostly nonsensical verbiage that required a quick mental sharpness and inventiveness.

Adam almost choked on his beer. "Bambi Lane! That is just toooo cute for words. All right, we have one minute to think of great "deer" monikers!"

It was quiet, which was unusual for our rather boisterous group. Adam grinned and removed his "granny glasses" he looked somewhat like John Lennon, with a short beard, mustache and light brown hair. He pointed to his wife. "Go".

"Doe-See-Doe Circle."

I was next. "Antler Point."

He nodded to Christian. "Pass."

"You can't pass." Adam smirked.

"Give me a little more time."

"I'll come back, be ready," then gestured to Dana.

"Moose Drool!" Dana announced smugly.

Penny chortled. "That's a beer made in Montana."

"I don't care, I like it ... imagine living on Moose Drool Drive."

"Fawn Dell Court," blurted Penny.

"Rutting Road." Adam contributed.

We all stared at Christian who had a wicked grin on his face.

"Buck Naked Loop," he chortled.

Chapter 5

Potato Salad! Why did I always have to bring the potato salad to my brother's gatherings? That was a stupid thought, I already knew the answer to that question; it was because Scott liked the way I fixed it. He also knew I hated the amount of time it took to prepare all the ingredients ... boil and peel the eggs and potatoes, slice and dice the celery, onion and pickles and make sure it wasn't drenched in mayonnaise. Sigh!

I was helping my sister-in-law, Rosa, pull everything together for the party. My two nephews were supposed to be distributing chips in baskets but seemed to be eating more than they poured out of the bags.

Jeffery is nine and Marc two years younger. The boys are a handsome combination of their parents. My fair-haired, green-eyed brother, blended with the gorgeous black hair and dark eyes of their mother produced children with hazel eyes and thick auburn hair.

Scott married his high school sweetheart, Rosario Macias. The Macias family lived next door ... well, the closest neighbors to our ranch. When the couple wed, each family gave ten acres of land so the two had twenty acres to build

39

their house and pasture horses.

It took a while for them to have a finished residence; they lived in a partially completed structure for years. Rosa was now a pharmacist at McClure's Drug Store and would eventually become a partner when the elderly Mr. Stanton McClure retired.

"Boys, eat less and take the snacks and dip out to the patio," Rosa ordered.

The kids stuffed a few more chips into their mouths and carried the baskets outside.

"Is my brother trying his hand at match making again? I don't recognize many of the guests."

Rosa laughed and continued to place hamburger patties and wieners on a large platter. "You know how older brothers can be, smile and be nice, you might actually meet someone special."

"Yeah, from past experience I rather doubt it. Most of these "summer deputies" are so immature; it's like being around a bunch of teen-agers. Let's not forget the lecherous married ones or the Barney Fife types.

Dana will probably find some adoring puppy-dog guy that will follow her around for the summer then head back to wherever he came from in September."

Rosa chuckled. "You never know what will happen, so enjoy yourself and have a little fun. Would you check on the ice in the tubs? Can't have the beer getting warm."

My brother was happily engaged in conversation, Dana and one of Rosa's sisters, Elena, were talking and laughing with two guys at one of the tables.

I checked the ice, fished out a bottle of beer, and sat down near my friend, who seemed totally absorbed in whatever the fellow across the table had to say.

Something about pursuing a bad guy into stinging nettle and getting impaled on a barbed-wire fence was the topic of conversation.

My gaze wandered to the three men with my brother and caught one of the group staring in my direction. It took a few moments to recognize my neighbor, what's-his-face.

Oh great! Just what I needed ... to make nice with the idiot. Not exactly how I wanted to spend the rest of the afternoon and early evening. Perhaps I could hide out in the kitchen as much as possible. Oh crap! He was wandering over!

"I was trying to make up my mind if you were my neighbor," the guy said.

I turned and made myself smile and make eye contact. "I think you may be right," ... god, what was his name?

He offered his hand. "Jim Hayden, nice to meet you in better circumstances than the last time."

"Maris Connelly, nice to meet you too," I managed to say.

Deputy Jim Hayden was a cutie, and knew it, with his chestnut colored hair, golden flecks in dark green eyes, and fashionable two-day-old dark stubble. He was only a few inches taller than I ... not my type in any way, shape, or form.

I preferred the tall, blond, Scandinavians like mom's side of the family. My uncles Eric and Garth were around six foot four.

"I'm sorry about the parking situation the other day, must have been really tired after being on duty all night."

I nodded. "One has to be careful, the carport is a little cramped."

Mr. Hayden grinned ... oh so charmingly, probably one of the devices he uses on all females.

"Excuse me, I must help Rosa, almost time to eat."

The gathering went well, I kept my distance from the *irresistible* Jim Hayden, who soon turned his attention to Elena.

Dana was busy flirting with the red haired, freckled

face, gentle giant ... Steve Mitchell. Must admit he was nice, rather shy and my friend seemed taken with him.

I indulged in a couple of beers then switched to soda since I was driving and had to take Dana home.

It wasn't especially late, maybe a little after nine o'clock when I pried her away from Steve, but not before they exchanged contact information.

"We could have stayed a little longer," Dana grumbled.

"Quit whining, he has your number, and will probably call soon."

"You have to admit he's very nice, I like him a lot."

"You two are a perfect Frick and Frack."

Dana chuckled. "He is kinda big."

"He could toss you ten feet in the air if he chose to do something like that. What are you five feet nothing?"

Dana bristled slightly. "I'm five foot two and one half."

I had to snicker. "Yeah, on a good day."

"Steve didn't seem to mind, I think he was drawn to my perky personality."

"More like he didn't get a word in edgewise, with you babbling all evening."

"I don't babble ... he's just shy … and likes my blond hair and sparking blue eyes."

"I didn't hear him say anything about your hair or eyes."

"Not in so many words, but I could tell he was interested. So, what do you think of the insanely cute Jim Hayden?"

I grunted. "Don't think of him at all, he's my renter and I have no interest in cultivating any kind of a relationship ... he's not that good looking."

Dana smirked. "Oh my ... yes he is."

There are no streetlights on this section of country road, so attention to driving is important. Obviously, the idiot coming my direction didn't care, because the vehicle barreled toward me, with high beams blinding and forced me off the road, we just missed a telephone pole!

Dana shrieked, I cussed, then reverse accelerated to a speed of about 30 miles per hour. Came off the gas, turned the wheel counter clockwise and was pointing in the direction the van was headed and tromped on the pedal.

My first thoughts were to chase the bastard down and run whomever off the road but should probably do the right thing and get the moron's plate number and report his reckless driving to the authorities.

I could make out taillights in the distance and was starting to gain on the van.

Dana finally found her voice. "My god what are you doing!"

"Going after the creep to get the license number."

There was a long silence and I could hear rapid breathing. "What the hell did you just do, and was it intentional?"

"Very intentional, it's called a J-turn, my dad taught me."

"Jesus, Mary and Joseph ... you're scaring the crap out of me ... slow down!"

"We're close, can't let the son-of-a-bitch get away! Hell and damnation the idiot is turning off ... inside the big iron gates!"

I slowed down, then stopped and watched the van go up the driveway and the gates silently close. The large structure up the slight hill had once been a clubhouse for a golf course that never materialized.

The stylish sign on the stonewall read ... *COVERDALE RETREAT* ... The community had wondered what exactly this place was supposed to be.

From what Christian had ferreted out, a Dr. Coverdale, bought the clubhouse, spent months remodeling and turned it into whatever a "retreat" might be. Speculation ran from "nuthouse" to convalescent hospital or the like.

"Well, we know where the jerk was headed anyway," I

muttered. "I can tell Scott what happened, maybe he can do something."

Dana had stopped hyperventilating. "You never told me you could drive so ... so whatever you just did."

"It's called defensive driving, kind of a technique that helps anticipate a dangerous situation and what to do when bad things happen. I've learned a few useful slides, skids and turns."

"Well damn ... you should be in the movies ... stunt driving, not wasting your talent teaching school. Imagine the fun and excitement, not to mention the hunky men."

"Yeah, Jason Statham and Vin Diesel will just have to wait a little longer to hire me as their bad-ass partner."

I was still pissed-off when I entered the house and expected the dogs to greet me in the usual rambunctious manner, but all was quiet. I called out "Faro, Hallie," then turned on the lamp in the living room.

I could see them sitting quietly on the patio, so opened the sliding glass door and spoke to them again. "What are you doing out here, see some night creature in the yard?"

Faro moved closer, stuck his nose inside then entered the room, Hallie followed behind. "I'm sure you want a Scooby Snack."

What a silly question, of course they wanted a treat ... devoured the biscuits, begged for more and drooled on my jeans. It wouldn't be normal not to have dog slobber and hair on one's clothes.

Eventually made myself comfortable on the sofa and turned on the TV, might be a movie worth watching while I had a cup of tea. Damn if the gravelly voice of Vin Diesel didn't project across the airwaves, one of the *Fast and Furious* films number twenty-five or whatever. Adore mindless car chases and fight scenes, you don't have to think deeply about the "meaning of life" or if we are alone in the universe.

It was the low growl from Faro and whine from Hallie that woke me from a confusing dream. I lay still and listened, nothing seemed out of the ordinary, nothing moved, could have been a coyote off in the distance that disturbed the dogs.

I was startled at how real the dream felt, like a feather brushing against my cheek, then a whisper, or a sigh that sounded like "*Chica palomino.*"

Did I really hear the words "*palomino girl*" in Spanish? Lovely, now I was dreaming in a foreign language at three thirty in the morning ... what next, a Pakistani murmuring sweet nothings in Urdu?

The dogs were now quiet, Hallie cuddled next to me and Faro continued to look around the room then rested his head near my feet. I would take the fur balls for a run in the morning ... much later than now ... when I rode Matchless.

My brother stopped by the next day in the late afternoon on his way home from work ... I had called him earlier.

"Tell me about this car that ran you off the road."

"It was a van."

"You didn't get the number or even a partial?"

"No, I was too busy trying not to wrap myself around a telephone pole. The van was light colored, but not white, maybe tan."

"Make, year?"

"Not a passenger kind with sliding doors on the side."

Scott wrinkled his forehead. "A cargo type, for transporting goods?"

"Yeah, no windows and opened at the back."

"How about a logo, a company name?"

"Nope, no distinguishing markings that I could tell."

Scott scratched behind Faro's ears with one hand and patted the fawning Hallie with the other. "I could drive by the "Retreat" and see if there is a vehicle in their parking area. Might be difficult to find a driver though."

45

"I know, could have been anyone since I didn't see who was at the wheel. You want something to drink, soda, tea, ice water?"

"No thanks, on my way home, but will pay my respects to whomever at Dr. Coverdale's place of business. Maybe get a look at the inside, everyone is real curious about what goes on behind closed doors."

"Think you can get the gates to open, not just anybody is admitted, or so I've heard."

"Lucky I'm not just the average bear, shouldn't be a problem for Sergeant Connelly of the Sendro Sheriff's Department. Most places, no matter how private, don't want the police snooping around, and are usually eager to cooperate in hopes we will go away."

I had to admit he was right. Scott was rather imposing, tall and solidly built, not a person to be taken lightly.

He left after being thoroughly slobbered, leaned and loved upon by my companions, I didn't slobber or lean, just hugged him and said I appreciated his help.

Tomorrow I should spend a few hours at the museum, start on another box of photographs. There was also a trunk that had come in the other day that Mr. Atkins said contained a lot of old linens and several dolls.

Thanks to the many years of volunteering I had learned how to care for fusty fabrics by gently washing them in warm water, using mild phosphate free soap, and letting them dry on a white towel.

One can remove stains with baking soda and vinegar ... lemon juice helps to whiten discolored areas ... never use bleach. I was a fountain of knowledge of things archaic.

It wasn't long before my neighbor arrived but didn't park in the carport. I peeked through the window as he walked up the sidewalk and into his house. A little while later heard a noise that could only be a vacuum.

There he was ... no shirt, clad in board-shorts, preparing

to clean and wash his truck. Goodness me, the guy was a rather nice specimen of a red-blooded American male.

I probably shouldn't be ogling; no doubt he knew what he was doing, probably just another way to draw attention to his fine self.

I definitely wouldn't go outside. There was plenty to do inside, such as clean out the bathroom drawers and cabinet. No telling how many almost empty containers of shampoo, squashed tubes of toothpaste, or dried up jars of make-up that I hardly ever wore, were languishing about.

Half way through my task the doorbell sounded, the dogs went ballistic, barking and jumping around. Thankfully my front door had an old-fashioned leaded glass window embedded at eyelevel.

Imagine that ... Mr. Bare Chest was on the doorstep. I opened the small window.

"Yes?"

"Sorry to bother you, but do you have any glass cleaner?"

The dogs were barking, milling about and jumping at the door. "If I open the door, you will be mauled, the beasts have no manners."

"Not a problem, we're old friends, I've been petting them through the openings in the lattice on the back fence."

Terrific ... he loves dogs, and probably "just adores" long walks on the beach in the moonlight. "Fine, brace yourself."

Chapter 6

The dogs plowed into Jim Hayden, Hallie grabbed his arm and was trying to drag him into the house. If he had been wearing long trousers Faro would be tugging at the cuff to help the guy inside.

I must admit the fellow was resolute and didn't bolt down the driveway. "Hey ... calm down. I know your names, but which is which?"

"The brindle is Faro, and the apricot fawn is Hallie." I was able to grab Faro by his collar to keep him from accidently knocking the man over.

"They have no manners, totally my fault, I'm a real pushover and they know it."

"Okay you monsters, I'll pet both of you." Thankfully he wasn't overwhelmed and soon the dogs were sniffing rather than jumping.

"Come in, I'll get the window cleaner."

The dogs and neighbor followed me inside.

Mr. Hayden looked around. "Nice place, like the colors, and it's not too cluttered."

"Thank you, I don't collect a lot of cutesy things ... besides books, probably because I'd have to dust them from time to time."

I'm basically a slob, which I'm sure he could tell from my attire, old ratty cut-off jeans, a stained purple t-shirt that said *Weasleys' Wizard Wheezers* and no shoes.

Through the years I have collected T-shirts with witty phrases, kind of like an on-going hobby, perhaps even an obsession, sorta-kinda.

"You a Harry Potter fan?"

"Indeed, gotta love magic. I'll get the window cleaner, when you're finished leave it on the porch by the front door, wouldn't want you to suffer the dogs again."

"Not a problem, they're really sweet, but imagine they wouldn't be so nice to someone uninvited."

"My friends ask if I'm concerned by the size of the "doggie door" anyone could get through something that size. But a would-be intruder should think twice as to what beast might be lurking ... I mean that's something I'd consider."

I went into the kitchen and found the cleaner under the sink and handed it to my neighbor.

He took the spray bottle but not before his eyes traveled over my body from feet to face, then grinned. "Thanks, saved me from a drive to town."

"As I said, just put it on the porch."

The letch was so obvious; surely he didn't think I was thrilled to be the object of such scrutiny, must work on some women though. The bold perusal of my anatomy was a complete turn-off ... how old was this moron ... thirty going on fourteen?

⌘

"So did Scott find out who was driving the vehicle that ran you off the road?" Adam inquired.

49

I shrugged. "Seems no one at the Retreat had any idea about a van."

We were at El Picaro in our usual place at the usual time. "He said a snippy staff member informed him "that no van had been on the property". Scott will return on Monday to speak with Coverdale, the good doctor divides his time between the Retreat and his office in Santa Clarita."

Penny nudged my arm. "Don't look now, but Big Fat Benny is headed our direction."

Dana just couldn't resist a whispered comment. "Got a thing for you Maris, every time he's in here he stops by."

"Hope his two "friends" Vinny and Guido stay away, those goons give me the creeps."

Christian muttered.

"Maris Connelly, nice to see you, how is your summer so far?" Benny inquired, when he arrived at our table.

"Very nice to see you too Mr. Edmonds, the days of summer always pass by much too fast." I replied to the corpulent, racketeer or whatever he was.

"How is Lesley?"

"Mother is well, teaching a class on art history at CalArts."

Mr. Edmonds stared at me for a long moment, then nodded. "Please give her my kind regards."

I said I would and watched as the three men made their way out of the cantina.

"I think he's in love." Sandy simpered.

"Not with me, more like my mother. I asked a long time ago why the man always inquires about her. Mom said they went to school together and she was his partner when they were learning to square dance."

Adam narrowed his eyes. "When did they ever teach square dancing?"

"Don't know, but obviously they did in ancient times. Benny was always quite tall, heavy, and probably a little scary, no one wanted to partner up with him. My very kind-hearted mother volunteered."

Christian smirked. "She must be so proud of how he turned out."

"I don't think the two "no necks" are named Vinny and Guido, you made that up, or is there something you're not telling us," Adam said and wiggled his eyebrows.

Christian grinned. "They must be from central casting, I'm sure I've seen them in some of the *Godfather* films."

Dana grabbed my arm. "Oh my god, he actually found the place ... and looky who he brought along. Be nice everyone, no snarky comments."

Walking into the cantina was the massive, red-haired, and probably love struck, Steve Mitchell ... with my neighbor in tow. How fricken marvelous!

Dana waved them to our table and slid over to make room. "Glad you could join us, let me introduce the gang."

Our group can be almost conventional when we must, so for the first fifteen minutes we were sorta-kinda appropriate. Then the conversation degenerated into our usual nonsensical verbiage. It was all Adam's fault.

"Speaking of the lost ark, I know where it is ... in a warehouse in Washington D.C."

And we were off. "I hope the place is humungous, Noah's Ark was about 450 feet long and 75 feet wide." I said with a perfectly straight face.

Christian chimed in. "Not that ark, the other ark with the Magna Carta inside.

"Which Magna Carta, there were many copies made, we saw one at Salisbury Cathedral."

Penny piped up. "For your information, there were over two hundred copies made in 1215, around seventeen survived over the years, and King John never signed any of them."

"Not with a quill, rather, he consented to the terms with

51

the King's seal ... I actually know the words to free the Ge-
nie from Aladdin's lamp." I bragged.

"Problem is ... you haven't found the right lamp."
Sandy transitioned quickly to the new topic.

"Wait just a damn minute, I bought a rather nice lamp
for you in Istanbul at the Grand Bazar," Christian stated.

"I believe that was where you offered to sell me to a
merchant who wanted a blond wife," Dana whined.

"We couldn't come to an agreement on the price."

Laura, our server, came to the table to check on the new
arrivals and us. We ordered another round.

Jim Hayden seemed quite amused, poor Steve Mitchell
looked confused, one had to pay close attention to the dia-
logue and be well versed in history to follow along.

"You guys are like piranhas, gotta think fast, and keep
your wits about you to stay alive in the conversation," Jim
said to no one in particular.

"That's the fun, and the reason not many normal people
survive the group when we get started," I replied.

"How long have you known each other?"

"Years ... Christian and I grew up here, several of us
met at college, and we teach together."

"You don't look like a teacher."

"What should a teacher look like, someone from *Little
House on the Prairie?*

"No, I didn't mean that, your brother said you ride in
the Sheriff's Posse, and there are the huge dogs ... I just
thought you might be someone involved in law enforcement."

"My father retired from the Sheriff's Department last
year, and my brother is doing his civic duty, so I think the
community has been well served."

I returned to the group exchange in time to hear Adam
comment. "I think there is something sinister going on at that
Coverall Retreat."

"Wasn't there a famous singer named Frank Sinister, "Dana inquired.

"The name was Sinatra, Frank Sinatra, and I think you're right about something disturbing in regards to the Coverdale ... not Coverall, place," I announced.

"Zombies, they're creating Zombies, and plan to take over the world," Adam continued.

Christian hunched his shoulders and looked around. "Not zombies, aliens, the whole place is crawling with aliens ... think about it, a mysterious doctor, a building that no one is allowed inside, who knows what this Coverslip person is really doing behind those locked gates."

"Yeah . . .an experimental laboratory to create a Frank-enstein!" Dana said with enthusiasm.

"Frankenstein was the doctor not the monster." Penny added.

Sandy looked thoughtful. "Could be vampires, vampires lurk about at night, and probably don't drive all that well."

"Why would a vampire need to drive, they change into bats and fly ... you know like a bat out of hell." I snickered.

"Hell ... did you see the latest episode of *Lucifer* ... Lucifer Morningstar is soooo bad ... but good ... in a bad sort of way," Penny sighed.

I nodded. "Love his car, 1961 or 62 Vette ... oh my, want one of those, and maybe the man himself."

Jim winked at me. "It's a 1962, black on black, Corvette convertible with **FALLIN 1** on the license plate."

Way to go deputy Hayden! He might be able to think with his brain instead of another part of his anatomy ... who knew?

Jim leaned close. "I'm still trying to figure out who is who in your little group."

"Across from you ... the John Lennon look alike with the glasses is Adam Schaffer, he teaches science and com-puter. The attractive lady with brown hair and blue eyes is his wife Sandy, she's the Sheriff's executive secretary."

"I've seen her in the office, but have never spoken to her."

"Penny, the dark blond, is another teacher, and the fair haired, blue eyed guy is her husband Christian. You probably recognize him from the property management business and you know Dana from the bar-b-que."

"Quite an interesting bunch."

"We have fun and often travel together, been to quite a few places over the past few years."

"Such as?"

"Europe, the Caribbean, Hawaii, the Greek Islands."

"Sounds expensive."

"Not if you do your homework, many times we come across some real deals."

Drinks arrived, and the conversation changed once again to what was happening around the town. Mrs. De Looney spent the night in jail for being drunk and throwing rocks at her neighbor.

Grandpa Geddes found the car keys and escaped his caretaker. The vision challenged octogenarian often drove slowly down the middle of the road, using the white line as his guide. The Sherriff's Department always brought him and the car home after he finished shopping.

A water balloon fight turned into a brawl at one of the campgrounds and a noisy wannabe outdoorsman with a loud radio had his tent vandalized by irritated neighbors ... the usual summer fun.

⌘

I finished another box of pictures, and wrote a brief statement about the family, where they had lived and so forth. Three hours at the museum passed by in a flash, but now I wanted to go home, remove the fine sprinkling of dust that had accumulated on my body and clothes, relax on the patio and read.

I stopped by the bathroom to get rid of the top layer of dirt, then went upstairs and paused in front of the three paintings to make sure all was well.

The original Castro house was as customary, the horses were the same, two of the cowboys were leaning against the corral fence as usual ... the third fellow was very unexpected ... the man no longer faced forward, he was now in profile!

I took a deep breath, the hair on my arms stood upright, and my heart raced. I closed my eyes for a moment than looked again, stepped closer and realized that I could now see the hand of one of the other cowboys quite distinctly ... it only had three fingers!

Three fingers! As in the infamous Three-Fingered Jack ... Joaquin Murrieta's partner in crime! I reminded myself to breathe, remain in control, don't freak out, didn't want to spend the rest of the summer in a padded cell ... breathe in, breathe out!

Possibly the stories were true, the Castro ranch had been a refuge for the outlaws of the California gold rush. But what the hell was going on with the painting, and why couldn't anyone else see the change? What did it all mean!

I should take a ride early tomorrow morning, go past the Castro place and Diamondback Cut. Everything had changed over the last hundred and sixty plus years, the original ranch house and corrals were long gone and the Diamondback was on my folks land.

My great grandparents bought twenty acres from the Castro family in the 1920's, which included the Cut.

Never could figure out why Isabella Castro decided to incorporate that area into her picture, the actual location was a distance from the ranch. Possibly the narrow, rugged, gap between the foothills spoke to her in some way ... artists see things differently than the rest of us non-talented beings.

55

I'd walk away, and look at some exhibits, then return to see if the figures changed positions. I took my time and dawdled in front of the stuffed animals, rather the specimens of animal species that roamed this area, which had been preserved in a tableau behind glass.

I made myself move slowly back to the paintings ... the third cowboy was now facing front again but was smiling, and Three-Fingered Jack's hand was partially hidden by the lasso.

This was a fine kettle of fish; taunted by a mysterious entity, why was I singled out for this honor? I wasn't a member of the Castro family, or exhibited psychic powers. I mean, there were times I had "feelings" about things or people, but nothing one could call an ability to experience weird phenomena.

I might be somewhat neurotic, who isn't? Psychotic, not so much, perhaps a little pathological ... compulsive ... obsessive ... humm.

Time to get out of here, nothing like a pineapple milkshake to cure a psychosis. Sitting at the counter in McClure's Drug Store was always comforting. Guess I could stand raw carrots, celery and a cup of ginger tea for dinner ... again.

The drug store was a popular place, especially during the summer; tourists enjoyed the old timey atmosphere. One could sit at the counter or go outside and plop on benches or perch on the area around the fountain. The fountain did have its drawbacks; ones backside could get wet, but soon dried in the warm summer air.

With drink in hand I meandered down the sidewalk toward my car. Tomorrow I would ride out and see Old Tom, the caretaker, of the Castro place, then have a look at Diamondback Cut. The breeze through the narrow canyon might whisper anomalous vibrations from the past ... or not.

Chapter 7

I decided to take a look at Diamondback Cut because of the discrepancy in the painting. It shouldn't have been depicted next to the Castro house and corrals. The dogs would stay at my parent's place, didn't want them to nose about in that area, too many snakes.

Before going to the Cut, I spent an hour or so with Old Tom at the Castro Ranch. Eventually the conversation turned to Joaquin Murrieta.

The band of outlaws were sometimes known as the Five Joaquin's Gang, which was something I hadn't known before, seems that five of the members had the name of Joaquin. This wild bunch was responsible for cattle and horse rustling, robberies, and murders.

The newly created California Rangers were tasked with the mission to capture or kill any or all of these marauders. Eventually the Rangers encountered a group of armed men near Monterey, Murrieta and Three- Fingered Jack were reported killed.

The severed head and hand of the two outlaws were brought to the governor as proof of their death.

Sometime later the distinctive hand and head went on tour of mining camps, preserved in jars of whisky ... a real money-making idea. The fee to have a look was one dollar, it was claimed by many, that the head wasn't Murrieta's.

In the early 1850's the Castro's had a large herd of Palomino horses and were known to have "dealings" with the Five Joaquin's. The place seemed to be a safe haven for the outlaws; perhaps Joaquin did survive and live quietly in this area with his beloved Palominos and stash of ill-gotten gains ... or not.

Tom also mentioned he had run off a couple of fellows wandering around with a metal detector a few days ago, such encounters happened a few times a month.

Treasure hunters seemed to be a persistent lot and not above trespassing and
even digging on private property.

After saying goodbye, I headed for the Cut. The rift between the hills had acquired the name for a reason; the place was full of rattlesnakes.

Rattlers live in dens, which vary from holes in the ground, or protected rock ledges to deep crevasses in the hillside. The number of pit vipers per den could be from a dozen to a hundred or more.

A snakebite isn't an automatic death sentence; a lot depends on the health of the victim and the time between bite and treatment.

The old Hollywood version of slashing the bite and sucking out the venom is hogwash. If possible, try to stay quiet, allow the bite to bleed for about thirty seconds and cover with a bandage if available.

Keep the panic down and the heart rate as normal as possible. A victim might have trouble breathing, nausea, sweating and burning pain. One should get to a hospital for doses of anti-venom, which will be given in increments for a period of eighteen hours.

I tied Matchless to a large mesquite bush away from the mouth of the Cut, then surveyed the opening. The passageway was narrow, about six feet across. One could see rocks of various shapes, colors and sizes going up the sides, and holes that could be homes for a few hundred snakes.

I wasn't partial to snakes, especially after my brother crept up behind me and draped one around my neck when I was a kid. It was a king snake not a rattler, nevertheless, the experience wasn't pleasant, Scott thought it was hilarious.

I took a deep breath and made my way down the middle of the rock-strewn path, trying to be vigilant ... listening. The warning noise of a rattler can often sound like a buzz as well as a rattle, or even a hiss. I carefully checked the ground before I took a step, then searched the sides, and paid close attention to flat outcroppings where snakes might wish to bask in the sun. After going about twenty feet detected a buzz and stopped.

This was a really stupid idea, no one in his or her right mind would continue further into the Cut. My brain was working overtime, envisioning hundreds of snakes slithering out of holes waiting for me to move within striking distance.

I took one last look around, my gaze traveled up both sides of the Cut looking for something unusual. It might be helpful to have some idea of what I expected to find, perhaps a neon sign that said **DIG HERE** or **FOR A GOOD TIME CONTACT JOAQUIN**.

It must have been after ten thirty that evening when I heard my neighbor's truck pull into the carport and another vehicle park out front on the street. I peeked through the curtains and saw a couple walk up the driveway and meet Jim Hayden and a woman.

The dogs hovered over the back of the sofa trying to see who was outside and gave a half-hearted bark or two. They didn't seem concerned and eventually made themselves comfortable on the couch.

Hopefully, the foursome next door would eat, drink and be quietly convivial. I was just out of the shower and wanted to go to bed and not be troubled by inebriated people.

My hopes were dashed when I heard a crash that could only be glass breaking near my front door. I managed to put on a robe before the doorbell rang.

Not the best time to receive callers, my hair was wet, the bathrobe was ratty-looking and the dogs were barking and waiting for the chance to greet whomever was outside.

I opened the small glass window to see Jim Hayden standing on the porch. "It's rather late for a neighborly chat."

"Sorry to bother you, but we had a small accident, wanted to make sure you didn't come outside without shoes. I'll try to get whatever I can tonight, but there might be a few shards of glass I can't locate."

All I could do was take a deep breath and be thankful the idiot was sober enough to clean up the mess. "Thanks for the warning, I'll be careful."

Jim ran his fingers through his thick hair and blinked as if trying to clear his vision. "Yeah, ah ... would you like to join us for a drink?"

"No thank you, I was about to climb into bed, been a long day."

His eyes narrowed, and he grinned slightly. "Bed ... sounds inviting."

Damn, could the man get anymore suggestive ... probably. "Good night Mr. Hayden," and shut the small glass aperture.

He must have leaned against the door for a moment then called out. "Yeah, night." I think he might have muttered. "What are ya wearing?" then chuckled.

I was hearing things; the moron wouldn't actually make such a ridiculous remark, if he did, I could now add *pervert* to his growing list of faults.

Why did I even care about his juvenile behavior, not my

problem, as long as he stayed on his side of the carport, paid his rent, didn't destroy my property and kept the noise down.

The dogs were waiting patiently for me to either join them on the couch or walk down the hall to the bedroom. "Come on, let's get some sleep."

I was instantly awake when the dogs growled. I had been dreaming ... the soft voice was speaking in Spanish once again. *"La fortuna favorece a los valientes."*

Which translates to *"Fortune favors the brave."*

What the hell? In normal circumstances I rarely dreamed at all, but, not only did I experience weird messages, it was in Spanish.

I tried to remember what other sensations besides the words ... a presence, something in the room? Perhaps ... I didn't think I was afraid, no vengeful spirit tried to smother me or crawl into bed ... besides the dogs.

There must be a reason for everything that was going on, the figures in the painting that moved about, a whisper in the night, a shadowy form. From the way the dogs behaved it wasn't just my imagination.

A hot cup of tea would be nice; I'd sit outside on the patio and think.

I was still thinking when the sky became a gorgeous pink; shapes that had been shadows turned into trees and the sun began to warm the new day. The dogs were not especially appreciative of the beautiful morning and were demanding food. Hallie was making yipping sounds and Faro kept pacing from the chair to the door.

"Hang on, you won't starve in the next few minutes."

I thought I heard sounds coming from next door, so peeked through the lattice part of the fence. Sure enough Mr. Hayden was snoring away on the outdoor chaise lounge.

Must have had a good time if the amount of beer bottles littered on the table were any indication. Couldn't see anyone else crashed in chairs or on the lawn.

I should check for broken glass on the sidewalk after feeding the dogs and putting on shoes.

The car that had parked out front was gone and I couldn't see any large pieces of glass, but swept the walk and porch anyway, didn't want slivers to imbed themselves in the paws of the great beasts.

A trip to the vet was not an expense I wished to incur, or the lovely experience of trying to control the two monsters at the doctor's office.

The staff at Dr. Baker's Animal Clinic loved my giants, but it was a chore to manage them, and keep the two from bothering other clients. Most people don't appreciate strings of drool, being whacked by deadly tails, or their pets cringing in fear of being devoured.

Later that afternoon Penny called; she wanted to get together at the cantina, even though it wasn't Friday. The group didn't need much of an excuse to meet, we celebrated Japanese Beetle Day, Improved Emotions Day, National Chocolate Month, The Washing Machine Ate My Socks Day, just to name a few.

Penny, Dana, Adam and I gathered around the table, Sandy and Christian were still working.

"My sister called this morning, she was terribly upset. One of her teen-age clients was found dead in a motel room close to Baker, California."

I set my drink down and looked closely at Penny. "How tragic, does she know what happened?"

"Claire is a social worker and deals with foster kids that have reached the age of eighteen. I don't know if you are aware, but the State of California continues to support and help them find a job, attend school or receive vocational training for those who desire further education."

"I didn't know that, but probably should because of special education students who continue to receive services until they are twenty-two."

"Was the kid on drugs?" Adam asked.

"No ... this part of the story is rather grisly. The young man had been operated on and a kidney removed. From what little details Claire could ascertain, the poor kid was left in the motel room probably to recover, but something must have gone wrong and he died."

Dana shuddered slightly. "Damn, who would do that to a kid?"

"Someone involved in the body parts trade," replied Adam.

Dana looked a little shocked. "What are you talking about?"

"It's a lucrative business buying and selling parts of one's anatomy. In very poor countries many people sell one of their kidneys to make money. Then there are the real nasty guys who kidnap, remove what they want, which results in the death of the victim, and sells the various organs to the highest bidder."

I leaned forward a little and mumbled. "You know this how?"

"Came across the information a while back, something to do with how some gangs are branching out beyond selling drugs."

I turned to Penny. "Was this kid involved in a gang?"

"I don't know, but I doubt it."

"So, what is your sister going to do?"

"I would imagine she wants more information about what this young person was doing in Baker, when he was supposed to be going to a group home."

"Don't envy her at all ... how sad."

"So, what are the boys up to this summer?" I asked Adam changing the subject to a less gruesome topic.

"Sandy has them in swim lessons, and the arts and crafts program at Frontier Village. Can't have them sitting in front of a TV playing games all day."

Adam and Sandy had two boys, Joey and David, who were involved in sports and any other activities their parents thought would keep them occupied and out of trouble.

"They probably see Jeff and Marc ... Scott said the nephews were doing something similar."

"Did Scott find anything more about the van that ran you off the road?"

"He actually made contact with Dr. Coverdale, and was given a tour of the Retreat, by the doctor himself."

Dana gasped. "How exciting we're going to be overrun by Zombies!"

"No Zombies, no alien creatures, just affluent people recovering from plastic surgery or exhaustion from their jobs. The place is an island of tranquility for those who can afford such luxury."

"Bet that ain't cheap." Adam muttered.

"Scott says the place is gorgeous, Spanish Colonial architecture, beautiful, serene grounds, pool, restorative spa treatments, which include steam room and sauna. Of course one must have an exercise room, tennis court and putting green.

My brother says attendants provide ice water, chilled towels, snacks and beverages to those lounging about in the pool area."

"Such luxury in our small part of the world. Where do the clients or patients or whatever they're called come from?" Penny asked.

I chuckled "Doubtful from around here, most likely the Los Angeles area, might be nice to breathe clean air, far away from crowded freeways and throngs of people."

"So, besides a tour, Scott didn't learn anything about a van?" Adam stated.

"No."

"Then someone is lying, the gates had to be opened, a button pressed by a human being."

"Zombies, most likely," Dana said gleefully.

"Dr. Coverdale isn't a Zombie, Scott says he has a bubbling personality, quite a character and loves to talk. I guess his hair is some interesting color, golden blond with streaks of red, and masses of curls that he constantly pushes off his face."

Penny giggled. "Now that is something I would love to see, don't think I've ever ran across a physician who looked like that. Most professionals in the medical field are rather stern looking and don't have gold ringlets hanging about."

Adam continued thoughtfully. "Could be another staff member, after all, the doctor isn't on hand every day, and I doubt he works late in the evening. The incident with the van happened after nine at night."

I nodded. "Certainly would like to know more about this doctor, wonder if my sister-in-law has any information, she works in the pharmacy. Could be she's had an opportunity to make his acquaintance or knows someone who has met the interesting sounding man."

Chapter 8

I stopped at the Farmer's Market to replenish my supply of veggies, must encourage the healthy eating plan. If one is in the know you can also support our local pot dealers Mac and Mo.

Phil Mackey and Javier Molina have been supplementing their fresh produce for about twenty-five years and continue even after Marijuana has been legalized in California.

It will probably take a while before a smoke shop opens around here. Even if that happens the price will be more than what Mac and Mo charge. There should be a significant tax on "ganja" like there is on cigarettes and alcohol.

"Maris, you're out early this fine morning," Mac said cheerfully.

I smiled and picked up a tomato. "All the good stuff will be gone if I wait until the afternoon."

"The squash is nice, same with the carrots, we have pickled beets if you're interested," Mo pointed to the jars.

"Love pickled beets, plus some orange honey, four tomatoes, carrots, and the summer squash should be enough."

The man packed my reusable bag with the requested

items and asked if I needed anything else, meaning a gram or two of "hash".

"Not today gentlemen take care, be safe," and paid for my stuff.

I also wanted to drop by the drugstore and have a chat with my sister-in-law. My mind was working overtime because of the way Scott had described the interesting looking Dr. Coverdale. I pictured a rather ridiculous fellow with blond ringlets, who chattered just to hear his own voice.

I arrived a little after the place opened, it wasn't busy yet and the ice cream counter was closed until later, which was a good thing. I waved to the young clerk checking supplies.

The pharmacy part was in the back and I could see Rosa moving about. "Hey, do you have a moment to talk?"

My sister-in-law poked her head around the corner of the shelf that had small bins labeled with each letter of the alphabet. "Hi, you're up and around early."

"Had to visit the farmers market ... and was wondering about something Scott mentioned, it made me terribly curious."

Rosa walked to the counter. "Who or what are you curious about?"

"Do you know Dr. Coverdale? The guy that opened the Retreat."

"I've met him, he contacted the pharmacy when the remodeling of the club house was near completion. Why?"

"Is he as weird as Scott says?"

Rosa laughed. "He's a different sort, one might say flamboyant, I think the man is enormously fond of himself."

"For some reason I imagine long golden ringlets hanging to his shoulders."

Rosa chuckled. "He's not that strange, but has a headful of curly blond hair, and I'm sure a professional stylist adds red highlights to make it rather colorful."

"Sounds delightful ... so what is his specialty, medically speaking."

Rosa straightened a few items on the counter. "I checked him out with the Medical Board of California, his license status and so forth. Dr. Julian Coverdale is a qualified physician ... family medicine."

"So, when Coverdale is away from his sanctuary, who's in charge?"

"A Physician Assistant, a woman named Jan Stottler runs the place, from what I understand, she's kind of a dragon."

"I was under the impression it's more like a spa than medical facility."

"I guess it's a little of both, the more nursing care, the higher the price."

"What's the going rate for recovering from a nose job?"

"The average cost per day in a California hospital runs about $2800, so I would imagine it's significantly higher for a deluxe accommodation."

I offered a low whistle. "Damn, don't think I'll be checking into the place anytime soon. Thanks for the information I should get out of here before the soda fountain opens."

Once in the car I took a jaunt around the lake, it's a beautiful drive, old oak trees provide shade, the water is a deep blue, and the rolling foothills seem to go on forever.

I enjoy it despite the hordes of people camped all over the place in tents, motor homes and cabins. The tourists keep the town going, without them the place would have a difficult time surviving.

While driving I thought about my crazy dreams and the viable painting, it would be nice to discuss it with someone. Most would chalk it up to a "figment of imagination" or a slow descent into madness.

That's it; I was teetering on the brink of insanity ...

doubtful, I don't think "nut cases" know they're crazy.

Well, I was a tad loony, aren't we all in some way? Where was my fairy godmother when I needed her?

The next best thing was my own mother, she was an artist and very familiar with art history, there should be a few tales of cursed paintings.

"Why this sudden curiosity about haunted objet d'art?"

Mom and I sat on the patio enjoying tall glasses of ice tea. "You wouldn't believe it if I told you, let's just say I've had a couple of unexplainable experiences."

My mother's eyes narrowed as she studied me. Percival the pig lumbered around the corner of the house checked out the tabletop then flopped down beside my mom's chair.

"Percy wants another apple, the greedy old thing."

"You spoil him too much, he eats like a pig."

"How perceptive of you ... and you don't spoil Faro and Hallie?"

I grinned and reached down to give the porker a scratch on the head.

"The only weird painting I can think of right now is by Bill Stoneham, called ... ah, something to do with hands. The artist painted it in the nineties or thereabouts, it's of a small boy and a life size doll in front of a window that display disembodied hands, which is kind of creepy. Different owners of the painting claim the figures move about. Want to tell me what has happened?"

I took a deep breath, then let it out slowly. "The pictures in the museum, the ones by Isabella Castro ... seem to have taken on a life of their own."

Mom looked at me carefully. "How so?"

"One of the men standing by the corral has a distinct face and changes positions, from leaning against the fence and facing forward, to standing tall and turning his head to the side."

"I'd like to see this altered picture."

69

"Don't think you can ... it only changes for me. I took Penny to check it out when it first happened, and it was back to normal. Same old cowboys, same old ... everything."

We sat in silence drinking our tea. "I'm going to stop by the museum and have a look, perhaps someone related to you might invoke something.

Isabella Castro was quite talented, I'm sure she had no formal training, and wasn't even out of her teens when she painted the triptych."

"So, you believe me, don't think I'm hallucinating?"

Mom smiled. "Very doubtful you're having delusions, unless it's early onset schizophrenia."

"There is something else to go along with the picture thing, I think there is a presence in my home, the dogs sense it too, they growl and at times refuse to come into the house or particular rooms."

Mom pushed a stray lock of ash-blond hair behind her ear. "I guess you aren't alone in being extra sensitive, I've experienced similar sensations from time to time and decided it's my grandfather letting me know he's watching over me."

I grinned. "Good to find that insanity runs in the family makes me feel much better."

Mom chuckled. "Now the question is why ... why this psychic phenomenon has decided to make itself known?"

I finished chewing on a chunk of ice. "No clue, but it's trying to tell me something, my night visitor speaks to me in Spanish."

"Spanish! Good thing you have a working knowledge of the language. What does this entity have to say?"

"Called me '*palomino girl*' and something about '*fortune favors the brave*' whatever that means."

Mom gazed thoughtfully out to the pasture. "I have a feeling your new friend is a male and must like you ... you don't seem especially frightened."

70

"The change in the painting is chilling, but the night visits aren't especially terrifying, just unsettling."

"I'm sorry I don't have an answer for whatever is going on, but I'll do some checking into haunted paintings, could be a fun addition to an art history class. People love to be scared, but at a distance."

"True. I should be going, don't think the pile of dirty clothes will wash themselves, unless my night visitor decides to help out around the house."

Mom smiled. "Haven't heard about ghosts doing chores, other than moving objects from place to place."

"Can't get good help anymore, gotta go, thanks for the tea and conversation."

I was almost home when my cell rang, it was a bit disconcerting for a brief moment, I had changed ringtones from Eric Clapton's *Layla,* to the theme from *Pirates of the Caribbean.* I didn't want to pull over or talk while driving so let it go. It was Adam; I'd contact him when I got to the house.

After starting a load of wash, set outside on the patio and called my friend.

"So, what are you up to this lovely day?"

"Been doing some on-line sleuthing."

"Find anything important Sherlock?"

"More like disturbing."

"What are we talking about, I've lost the gist of this discussion."

"Remember the conversation the other evening, Penny's sister was upset about her client or whatever ... the teenager that was found dead in the motel room?"

"Yeah, tragic, but I'm not sure where you're going with this?"

"I thought it would be interesting to do a little research."

71

"How do you research missing body parts?"

"Never mind ... what I did find was this isn't the only time something similar has happened over the last year."

"You lost me."

Adam made a huffing noise. "There have been seven other people found in hotel rooms with a kidney removed."

I didn't reply for a moment, long enough for Adam to ask if I was still there. "You're telling me this sadism has happened before ... why hasn't it been all over the news?"

"How the hell should I know, you're gonna love this, all the victims were teenagers."

"You mean to tell me that seven young people died after being mutilated, and the media hasn't been screaming it from the rooftops?"

"That's just it, only one kid died, all the others have been found alive and relatively well, just missing a body part. Never in the same geographical location ... happened all over the place, other counties ... Los Angeles County, Kern County, Imperial, San Bernardino and Ventura."

"So why hasn't anyone picked up on this?"

"Don't have the slightest idea, might be something your brother should investigate."

"I'll give him a call. Did you tell Penny to contact her sister?"

"Going to do that right now, we should probably have a meet up later."

I sat outside thinking about the conversation long after Adam said goodbye. Surely someone in law enforcement had made the connection, I mean how could something like this go on and no one know about it? Possibly because of a lack of communication between counties, I knew that from state to state there were problems, but not from county to county.

Evidently, this is a well-organized, cold-blooded group who have gotten away with mutilation, and now murder, for a long time and probably made a fortune.

I was talking with Laura at the cantina; it wasn't crowded as yet, so she had a few minutes to spare after serving my drink.

"How is school?"

"Not bad, I'm enjoying my classes, Scene Design Production is time consuming."

"When you grow up what will you be?" I teased.

"Hopefully find a job designing sets ... responsible for the visual concept of a film, TV or theatre production, would love to get an internship."

"Never give up on your dreams."

"Thanks for the encouragement. Gotta get back to work, talk to you later."

I sat by myself in the corner and waited for the gang to arrive, there were familiar faces in the groups sitting at the tables and bar. I waved to a few people across the room.

Sandy and Adam came through the door, then Dana, Christian was next, Penny hurried in shortly after.

"Had to drop Nicole off at the grandparents. So did Adam tell you what he discovered?"

Dana seemed a tad flustered. "It's all so gruesome, what people do to each other."

"Man's inhumanity to man is rampant and I've determined we are a violent and avaricous species," I announced.

Dana nodded her head in agreement. "I've often thought about why humans are that way and decided it's because this is not our native planet. I mean why do so many people have allergies? We shouldn't be allergic to our own planet ... probably because it's a dumping ground for all the undesirables in the galaxy!"

One has to realize that Dana can be a ditz; she often marches to a different drum. Like the time she decided to become a vegetarian ... for about a day. Admitting she didn't care for many vegetables, but would supplement her diet with chicken, fish and filet mignon, after all cows are vegan because they eat grass.

Becoming Jewish for less than week was an adventure. The menorah fashioned out of cardboard caught fire from the birthday candles attached with tape and she didn't care for all the rituals.

Christian loved to tease her. "So how come the aliens want to abduct us? You once mentioned you believed that people were being abducted all over the place, you'd think the little green men wouldn't have anything to do with our kind."

Dana scrunched up her nose. "Maybe they want to see why we are so violent."

Adam leaned forward in a conspiratorial manner. "Back to the original conversation please ... the reason for such acts of depravity is simple ... money, lots and lots of money. A kidney can sell for as much as two hundred and seventy five thousand dollars, a liver over one hundred and fifty thousand, a heart around one hundred and twenty thousand and one inch of skin is about ten dollars.

The human body could be harvested for as much as eight hundred thousand dollars."

It was quiet at the table; it took a minute for what Adam had said to sink in.

"So the really bad guys can make millions gathering and selling body parts to the highest bidder." I shuddered at the thought of what had happened to those young people.

Penny said softly. "I spoke to Claire and told her what Adam had discovered. After the shock, she said she was going make calls to directors of the Independent Living Programs in other counties and report on what had happened to her client.

Why haven't these acts made the headlines?"

"Possibly, because the victims were located in small

towns that don't have much of a police presence. The motels were kind of off the beaten path and the tiny communities were in different counties," Adam replied.

"I'll make sure my brother has all the information, this could be the tip of a very nasty iceberg."

Chapter 9

The call came late last night ... a man was missing. A frantic woman notified the Sheriff's Department her husband hadn't returned from his hike. A fellow named Gary Shaw was supposed to be back at their cabin before dark.

It was too late to start looking; the area where the hiker seemed to be headed was not the best place to travel after sun set.

At first light the Mounted Posse would assemble at the base camp, a staging area near the most popular trails into the foothills.

My father would trailer the two geldings we used for searching the backcountry. I gathered my riding gear; the rest of the equipment was at my folk's place. One doesn't just dash off in a mad rush; preparations were necessary in order to conduct a thorough search.

The Mounted Posse is composed of mostly volunteers who provide their own horses or mules. Members are trained in Search and Rescue techniques, first aid and tracking. Monthly meetings are held and a few times a year we have refresher courses to keep abreast of methods and communication technology.

It was still dark when I headed out. I took the road past the Coverdale Retreat, and as always, slowed down and glanced through the gates toward the building. A van was parked at the entrance under the portico, the covered area in front of the doors.

I stopped and took another look, it could be the same van that was so recklessly driven, but this one looked white, not tan, the model was the same, but the color seemed a lot lighter.

There was nothing wrong or strange about a vehicle parked in front of a building, I sighed, and thought it was time to let the incident go.

I pulled up next to Dad's truck; the horses were tied by the side of the trailer. My father was drinking from a travel mug and talking to several members of the Posse.

He smiled as I approached. "Hi, there's coffee at the Command Post."

"I could use something to get me started, had a bowl of oatmeal and an apple before I left home. Any more information on our missing man?"

"The fellow has some hiking experience but isn't familiar with this area ... so his wife reported. Didn't take his cell phone, not much reception in that area anyway."

"Glad our lost individual isn't a child, children can be difficult." I nodded to the other men. "Is this our team?"

Dad shook his head. "They're still making assignments, we have about twenty-five riders. Shouldn't be much longer, get your coffee."

I made my way to the canopy area situated by a truck with the purring generator; this sector would serve as Command Central. I found the coffee urn, filled a disposable cup and watched the activity.

Soon we would be issued maps, two-way radios and divided into groups. Hopefully it wouldn't take long to find this guy.

The general public probably doesn't realize that over the years profiles have been developed on people that go missing.

Children can be difficult because sometimes they hide from searchers, thinking they will be in trouble for wandering away. They often meander aimlessly in no particular direction.

Then there are individuals that are depressed or have mental problems, they can also hide, become difficult when found, and behave irrationally, even violent.

Hikers and walkers tend to venture farther because they are traveling in a purposeful manner. Often they are poorly prepared for an emergency, but will seek high ground to get their bearings and tend to look for shelter. They can also panic just as anyone might when lost.

I rejoined my father and soon the call went out for us to gather at the tent. We listened to the usual safety and communication instructions, were given our equipment, which included bright orange vests with yellow reflecting strips and divided into groups of four. I was teamed up with Dad, Stewart Jenkins and ... Jim Hayden.

How in the hell did my neighbor manage to qualify for the Mounted Posse?

I didn't think he could do anything but drink and look cute for empty-headed females.

I was busy checking my gear when Mr. Hayden strolled over. He was leading one of my brother's horses.

Dad greeted him like some long lost relative and introduced him to Stewart. I had to admit he looked the part of a dedicated searcher but looking and doing were two different things.

"I believe you two are already acquainted," my father said.

"We are, Maris and I are old friends," Jim remarked

with a grin.

"Yes, old friends and neighbors. I didn't realize you were interested in this sort of activity."

He adjusted his saddlebag. "That's part of the reason I was selected to help the department for the summer. I've done quite a bit of Search and Rescue."

I wondered where he kept his horse, hadn't seen one in the back yard ... oh yeah, he was borrowing my brothers mount and probably his trailer.

My father swung up on the big gelding. "Glad to have you with us Jim, better get started, we've been assigned the Old Bear Trail, and plan to search it up to the tree line."

I climbed on my horse and the four of us headed off as the sun appeared over the mountains in the distance.

The first part of the trail we could ride two by two; it would eventually narrow to a small path only wide enough to continue single file.

We rode in silence for a distance then my fellow tracker said softly. "You don't care for me very much do you?"

I wasn't prepared for such statement but had a little time to think. "I don't know you that well to make such a judgment."

He chuckled. "Oh, I think you have your mind made up, most people make an assessment very quickly ... first impressions and all that."

"Shall we concentrate on the matter at hand, which is to locate the missing hiker ... you do sit your horse well, don't ride like a sack of potatoes."

"Thanks for the compliment, you ride nicely too."

Tracking is observing and interpreting what has been observed. One must scan the environment to get an overview of the surroundings, a visual sweep of the area for tracks, litter, even bloodstains. The eyes move horizontally sweeping the foreground from left to right then back, moving the line of vision gradually.

79

This area consists of grassland, shrubs, and oaks. There are rolling hills as far as the eye can see; often the ravines between the hills have rock outcroppings.

Some of the flat land is full of dense red brome, and the knolls feature clumps of bunchgrass, lupine and sometimes a line of oak trees. The rock outcroppings can be dark colored granite to light-colored quartz.

A problem to consider is abandoned dig sites. Scores of mines have been excavated since 1849. Open shafts are a hazard and often hidden by vegetation or decayed boards, the vertical shafts can be hundreds of feet deep.

An old entrance supported by rotting timbers can collapse with the slightest touch.

The Forest Service and San Emidio Ranch have fenced off many of the known mines like Burnt Mountain, Split Rock and Three Springs, but it doesn't take long for the curious and often stupid public to cut through or tear down such structures.

Around noon we stopped under the shade of large oak trees to rest the horses and ourselves. We carried energy bars and water; I shared cut up slices of apple and dried apricots with my fellow riders.

A half hour later we were on the move again. The team had decided to split into pairs and search in opposite directions at a junction. There were several mine entrances that should be investigated on both routes.

Jim Hayden had come prepared with his own satellite phone, so there was an ability to keep in contact with each other and the base camp. Dad and I went to the left; Jim and Stewart followed the path to the right.

There was no sign of recent footprints along the narrow trail; we had been advised that the lost fellow was wearing size twelve, lightweight, hiking shoes called North Face Ultra. In the middle of the sole was the word *"Vibram"* Mrs. Shaw knew that tid-bit of information because she had purchased the shoes for her husband's birthday a few months ago.

Search and Rescue try to obtain as much information as possible on a missing person, physical description, color of clothes, footwear, backpack and so forth.

We found nothing around an old mine entrance, the nailed-up boards were still in place and there were no prints except for various animal tracks in the dirt.

Dad radioed we were heading back to the junction.

I hoped the other search parties would be more successful than we had been. While waiting for Jim and Stewart I scanned the area with my binoculars for the umpteenth time, didn't see anything but a few head of cattle off in the distance.

After meeting up again continued toward the tree line. Near the large oaks we stopped and looked back down the trail, the panorama was lovely.

Jim gazed into the distant landscape. "This is quite the view."

My father nodded. "I never get tired of looking at it, in the early spring the wild flowers cover the hillsides with orange, yellow and purple splashes of color."

I took a deep breath of clean air. "As much as I would like to stay here and admire all this beauty, we should press on. I say we split up again and go a mile or so in each direction, our hiker might have headed for high ground."

Jim took a drink from the canteen, removed his hat and wiped is forehead. "Sounds like a plan, come on," he looked at me and grinned.

I could hardly be impolite by refusing to go, so nudged my horse, and followed along after him.

After a period of time we stopped, it was getting quite rocky. Another look through the field glasses didn't show anything but more and larger rocks.

"Want to give a shout?" I said.

"Why not."

We yelled our hiker's name several times, listened and called again. Jim got off his horse, handed me the reins and started to climb. I watched as he went part way up a ravine, then back down.

"Didn't see any sign of overturned rocks, soil depressions or disturbed vegetation."

I returned the reins. "We should start back, they've had enough time to search the other side by now."

The crackling sound of the radio interrupted our conversation. Dad and Stewart had found Gary Shaw. We hurried to the location given, which proved to be near an entrance to an old mine.

My father was giving the map coordinates to Command Central as we arrived.

It was going to be a problem to remove Mr. Shaw from the rubble, rocks and timber that had collapsed on him.

I could hear Stewart speaking calmly to the trapped man, explaining that we would get him out as quickly as possible.

After securing our horses to a nearby tree Jim and I headed for the old diggings to investigate the situation.

The circumstances weren't the best; we would have to do some engineering to shore up the beam that was pinning the man under a mound of loosened debris. The substantial support timber was now on a slant, one end buried in the rubble, the other wedged precariously onto a fragile looking plank at the top.

Mr. Shaw thought his ankle might be broken, was cold, thirsty and hungry. We had to get him out sooner than later; excessive heat loss leads to hypothermia, which is very dangerous.

Before we could dig him free, the old timber must be braced, if not, the entrance could crash down.

I began to look around for a piece of wood long enough

to shove under the beam, of course nothing like that magically appeared. There were branches, but not the length required or strong enough to work.

Jim was investigating the weathered crosspiece at the entrance with his flashlight.

"Won't take much for this structure to collapse, if we try to remove Gary the whole thing might go," he said softly to my father.

"Yeah, I was thinking that too. I'm surprised it's lasted this long."

"There might be some old lumber further back into the mine we could use to prop this side."

"Can't take the risk, don't want to rescue a second person. I'll radio back to camp and tell them to send something to shore this up, a chopper should be dispatched to medevac this guy out."

Jim took a deep breath and let it out slowly. "Can't remove him without securing the beam first."

I had been prowling around and thought I saw something on the other side of the cave. "Dad come over here," and focused my flashlight toward the dark interior on the right side of the cave. "There seems to be a couple of posts laying on the ground, move a few rocks and it might solve the problem."

Stewart had managed to push a canteen toward Mr. Shaw, but when the fellow reached out more debris rained down. We all held our breath and waited.

"Don't move, stay absolutely still," my father cautioned.

Gary lay quietly until the dirt and small rocks settled. "Can't do this much longer ... hard to breathe."

"Don't talk, just inhale and exhale slowly, we'll think of something."

My father gestured for us to move further away. "Don't know how long before the chopper gets here, we have to act quickly, the guy's starting to panic."

Jim removed his hat and ran his fingers through his hair. "If we can't find a suitable piece of wood then maybe we can shore it up with rocks."

I nodded. "Something like a wall about four feet high under the plank."

"Exactly, stacked rock with a sturdy base could bear the weight for a time, long enough to get the guy out."

Stewart muttered to my father. "Will ... the fellow doesn't look so good, he's shivering even though it's warm."

"Yeah, can't do anything for him until he's removed from that rubble," Dad replied.

"I say we build a wall," Jim stated.

I nodded in agreement. "Let's get started."

Dragging large rocks isn't especially fun, in fact it's a pain in the back ... literally. According to Jim Hayden, a retaining wall has to support itself, so a solid base is needed. The base stones should be the larger stones, and the foundation as wide and relatively flat as possible.

Jim retrieved the hunting knife from his saddlebags and used it to dig down a few inches to place the first row of rocks. Then began to stack the next row, making sure the rocks were wedged together tightly. He stopped when it was an inch or so beneath the piece of heavy lumber.

"Find some flat, wide pieces of wood or sticks. I'll use them to shim under the timber to make a tight fit."

Dad and Stewart hacked off small pieces from a branch, I handed the thin strips to Jim so he could wedge them against the beam, then we studied our handiwork.

Chapter 10

I could feel the tension emanating from my fellow searchers. Now that the short column of rocks was finished we must make haste and remove Gary Shaw as quickly as possible.

"Let's get the debris off his chest so he can breathe easier," my father said.

Stewart Jenkins looked up and muttered. "Where the hell is the chopper? Should have been here by now."

That was a good question, but none of us had an answer and we couldn't simply wait around.

Jim gave a last look at the rock structure then moved closer to the trapped man. "We should get started, work our way down to his legs ... slow and steady."

With one eye on the beam I started to brush away the rubble. Dirt and rocks of various sizes had to be removed until the large timber was exposed. A short time later we could see the end of the beam that pinned the hiker's legs. Several large rocks surrounded it.

"Have to move at least three of these things," my father stated.

Jim studied the problem. "Yeah ... almost a damned if

we do and damned if we don't dilemma."

"Stew and I will take hold of his arms and be ready to pull him free. If our luck holds there will be a little time before everything falls apart."

The men nodded; thankfully Mr. Shaw didn't panic, just squeezed his eyes closed.

"Eeny, meeny, miny,moe ... catch a tiger," Jim uttered. With both hands he carefully removed a rock. The timber shifted a tiny bit and settled on the stacked stones. Dad grunted slightly as he lifted another. I tightened my grip on Gary's arm, and glanced at the obelisk about two feet away.

"I think we'll need Stew down at this end to help lift. Maris can you drag him by yourself?"

If I doubted my ability, this wasn't the time to admit any uncertainty. "Not a problem, ready when you are." My mouth was dry and I could feel the sweat run down the back of my neck as I took a deep breath.

The three men grabbed hold of the heavy beam. Dad counted to three, I pulled, and Mr. Shaw moaned in pain when I dragged him away.

Dad, Jim and Stewart rushed toward me after dropping the timber, then turned to watch as the plank rested on the rock mound. After a few moments it slipped at the top and the entire entrance of the cave crashed down.

No one said anything for quite a while, we just stared, somewhat mesmerized, and coughed due to all the dirt in the air.

"That was fun," Jim smirked.

Stewart called the Base Camp again. The chopper was on its way, should be here in a few minutes.

Our hiker was moved under the trees, I unfolded the space blanket and covered him, always amazed at the ingenuity that went into this material.

The cloth was first developed for NASA, which is why it's called a space blanket, and made of heat-reflective plastic coating that reduces the heat loss in a person's body.

Jim had elevated the fellow's legs slightly by placing his saddlebags beneath them. The injured man was breathing a little easier now and asked for some water. Jim offered a drink from his canteen and cautioned him to take it easy, only small amounts at first.

I had to admit this was a new side of Mr. Hayden; a mature adult had replaced the annoying juvenile delinquent.

We could hear the faint pulsing, whap of rotor noise. Dad and Stewart went to stay with the horses and keep them calm. The helicopter would have to land a distance away, because of the trees and foothills.

Soon medics would tend to Gary Shaw and we could be on our way back before dark. I was tired, mostly from the adrenalin-producing rescue.

"This calls for a celebration when we return to civilization." Jim announced as we watched the chopper fly away.

"All I want to do is get home, have a hot meal and go to bed," Stew replied.

"Couldn't agree with you more, I'm gettin' too old for this stuff," Dad admitted.

"Will Connelly too old ... never!" I teased. "We should make it back before the sun sets if we get a move on."

Jim returned the hunting knife to the scabbard on the outside of his saddlebags. I had noticed the beautifully tooled leather pack earlier. "You have quite the rig, don't think I've ever seen anything like that before, scabbard on one side and holster on the other."

Jim grinned. "Gift from my folks."

"Didn't get a good look at your pistol, what is it?"

"The 'gun that won the west', Colt .45, Peacemaker not an authentic one of course. What about you?"

I had to chuckle. "Seems we do have something in common, would you believe a Cimarron single action .357 Magnum, a reproduction of your 1873 Colt."

"Now that is cause for a party of some kind, great minds and all that."

"We have a distance to ride before we can pat ourselves on the back, I have a feeling by the time we reach Base Camp the only thing I want to celebrate is a hot shower and a soft bed."

I was waiting for some asinine remark, but Jim simply grinned, shrugged his shoulders and got on the horse.

The sky was streaked orange from the last rays of sunlight when we arrived at camp. We received kudos from several of the Posse members as we reported to return our equipment and give a formal statement.

There was an update on Gary Shaw, his ankle was broken in several places, but eventually the guy would be up and around, which was good news, it could have been a lot different.

I helped Dad load the horses in the trailer, he declined my offer to follow him home and unload and do all the necessary things that had to be done to care for the animals.

The moment I stepped through the door my long-suffering dogs assaulted me. They were starved for food and company; both were easily solved once they stopped leaping around.

For the next half hour, I sat on the couch with Faro on one side and Hallie on the other, we had a lovely discussion of how the day went. I was thrilled to see nothing inside was destroyed due to my long absence, in the past, that hadn't always been the case.

Hallie couldn't resist the pillows on my bed and tried to drag them through the doggie door. When that failed, she minced them on the kitchen floor, seems the memory foam forgot how to reassemble itself ... it took forever to clean up. Now the bedroom door is always closed when I leave the house.

Faro liked wood, when he was younger he gnawed off

the molding around the door. Thankfully his taste turned to firewood, carried the smaller logs around and shredded them on the patio or living room rug.

Gotta love the great beasts.

I was famished and decided a bowl of chicken noodle soup with lots of crackers would be quick, easy and satisfying. Then a hot shower ... see if anything was worth watching on television for an hour or so and go to bed.

At least that was the plan until the doorbell rang. The dogs dashed away with their usual exuberance and I peeked out the window.

Standing on my porch was Jim Hayden with what looked to be a pizza and a six-pack of beer. I guess he was bent on celebrating.

As usual Hallie grabbed an arm, Faro had a pant leg and my guest was escorted into the house. I saved the pizza from total annihilation.

"Hi guys, you're so helpful ... and huge ... and whatever ... next time I'll bring something just for you, I promise."

"Sorry about that, I usually put them outside and block the doggie door when I'm expecting visitors. For some reason guests don't like to be attacked in such a manner, I have no idea why."

Jim placed the beer on the kitchen counter then began to pet and coddle the monsters. "Hope you like peperoni pizza."

"The dogs love peperoni pizza, I have a fondness for it too. What a nice surprise, thank you."

Jim separated himself from the dogs. "I'll open the beer while you get the fine china. There must be an opener around here somewhere."

"In the top drawer next to the sink."

I took two plates out of the cabinet and set them on the counter. "You want a knife and fork?"

"Not unless I'm forced to be civilized."

89

"Perfect ... thank you again for this gourmet meal. I'll warn you now that Faro will rest his head on your knee and look pitiful until you feed him and Hallie just drools, usually on your pants."

Two slices of pizza ... I could have eaten more but didn't want to act like a glutton. It was the three beers that made me a tad light headed ... not stupid mind you, just a little swimmy.

We sat on the couch, not especially close, but close enough for me to notice the dark green of his eyes and the delightful grin. I reminded myself this guy wasn't my type, an outrageous flirt and philanderer, and one shouldn't be drawn into his web.

I learned a little more about his background. He was from northern California, Redding, and the reason he was familiar with Search and Rescue was his father worked for the Forestry Service. The Shasta-Trinity National Forest has over four hundred miles of trails for people to become lost.

His mom, believe it or not, was a schoolteacher, and he had an older brother and sister.

He preferred the weather in southern California, more sunshine and didn't have to wear a jacket in July when visiting the beach.

"I must go, have the day shift tomorrow, patrolling camp grounds around the lake."

"Sounds like an amazing way to pass the time," I chuckled.

He rose from the couch. "It's not bad in the morning, evening is another story."

"Yeah, so I've heard ... thanks again for dinner."

My canine companions and I escorted him to the door. He scratched the heads of the beasts that crowded next to his legs. "You better get some sleep," and edged around the door.

"You too, it's been a long day."

90

I turned on the porch light, put the empty beer bottles in the trash, refrigerated the last two pieces of pizza and wiped down the counter.

The evening had been nice, didn't even have to fend off any advances, which was a pleasant surprise. Maybe he wasn't a total jerk after all.

After making sure the doors were locked, turned off the lights including the front porch, took a long shower and went to bed.

Penny placed another small piece of donut in front of Nicole. "The rescue was just another day's work for the Sendero Mounted Posse, or so you claim."

The three of us were sitting at Rasmussen's Bakery. I was scarfing down a giant, fluffy, yeast donut stuffed with cheesecake and topped with caramel sauce. I planned to eat half and save the rest for dinner ... or lunch ... or not.

Penny was savoring bites of a decadent, vanilla custard filled creation, and trying to keep Nicole happy with the idea of sharing. The blond dervish wanted her own pastry, something with "sprinkles".

"If you behave, I'll get a pink sprinkle donut to take home, you can have it after your nap."

"I see you've sunk to using bribery."

"A little bribery goes a long way ... go on with your story."

"Nothing more to tell, the chopper took Mr. Shaw to the hospital in Santa Clarita, and we had a long ride back."

"So your neighbor surprised you with his ability to function like a rational human being?"

"Indeed, we even shared a pizza and a few beers."

Penny's eyebrows went up and she smirked. "Now that is exciting, tell me more."

I huffed a little. "There is nothing to tell, we talked, he went home."

"Uh-huh, from what you have reported about bimbos

91

coming and going at all hours of the night, the guy likes the girls."

"Well maybe he doesn't think of me like that, could be I'm not his type and he certainly isn't mine."

"Sure, whatever you say."

I shrugged, took a sip of coffee and glanced out the window. An interesting vehicle caught my attention; it was across the street in the parking lot of the hardware store. A white van similar to the one I had seen at the Coverdale Retreat. Couldn't hurt to take a look, the thing was just begging for me to investigate.

"Have to run across the street for a moment."

"What for?"

I quickly rose and took my phone from the purse. "I'll be right back."

The morning traffic wasn't particularly heavy so dashing across the middle of the street wasn't hazardous to my health and safety.

I walked around the van and looked through the driver's side window ... didn't see anything exciting. This probably wasn't even the same conveyance, I mean, white utility vehicles were not exactly uncommon.

Nonetheless, I took a picture of the license plate; it was a little hard to see with whatever was smeared on it.

After one more circuit around the vehicle, went back across the street to explain my actions to Penny.

"I thought you said the color was tan."

"Could have been wrong about that, saw a white van parked in the Coverdale Retreat driveway early yesterday morning."

"You going to have Scott trace the license?"

I nodded. "Yeah, thought I might do that ... kind of curious about why the plate was so difficult to read, it's not like we've had any rain to muddy the streets recently."

"We don't get much rain this time of year period, maybe a little in late August."

"Probably nothing will come of my snooping anyway ... we should go, don't forget the pink sprinkles treat for Nicole, she has been a perfect angel."

The little girl giggled. Penny picked up her daughter and kissed the top of her head. "Truly a celestial being."

Jason Tanner narrowed his eyes as he watched the blond woman dash across the street and enter the bakery. He was about to leave the hardware store from the side door when he noticed her wander around the van and take a picture.

He fought to control the sensations of fear, panic, and anger that made it difficult to breathe normally.

Who was this bitch and what was she doing snooping around? If he hurried he might be able to follow when she left the bakery, find what she was about.

Chapter 11

Scott finished his drink and set the glass on the patio table. "The vehicle is a Ford cargo van registered to a guy named Jason Tanner, he has a few priors, nothing terribly exciting. Drunk driving, shop lifting, receiving stolen property, here's the most recent driver's license picture. Recognize him?"

Scott handed me a paper with an enlarged photo and information. The fellow had close set brown eyes, thin dark hair and looked like a million other men.

"So he could be the guy that ran me off the road ... sorta-kinda?"

"Sure, but not much can be done about it."

I sighed. "Yeah ... wonder what he's doing at the Retreat, says he lives in South Gate."

My brother claimed the paper and stretched out his long legs. "I have no idea, maybe he moved here recently. Can't really say it's the same van you saw parked in the early hours of the morning anyway.

Oh, the information you gave me the other day about the young people found in hotel rooms with missing kidneys is being quietly scrutinized by the California Bureau of Investigation."

I traced a finger down the side of the glass where moisture had formed. "Didn't know we had a Bureau of Investigation, is it like the FBI?"

"Similar, CBI has special investigation teams from the criminal law division. In this matter there is a need for cross-jurisdiction coordination."

"Do they work out of an actual physical location?"

"Several regional offices across the state, the case is being handled by a team in Los Angeles."

"Why keep it quiet?"

Scott shrugged his shoulders. "Must be a good reason."

I had to agree; glad to know the gruesome crimes were on somebody's radar.

I was still pissed about being run off the road; Dana and I could have been wrapped around a telephone pole and suffered horrible injuries or even death. Whoever was driving so recklessly didn't even bother to slow down, and people at the Retreat probably lied about the van being on the property.

"Hungry, I have some sliced turkey and cheese?"

"Nah gotta get back to work, thanks for the Coke."

"Tourists keeping you busy?"

"Nothing really bad, mostly loud music late at night in the camp grounds, drinking, the motorcycle club revving their bikes at ungodly hours."

"Doesn't that group come every year for a few days?"

"Like clockwork, but for the most part, mind their own business." Scott gathered up his glass and we went inside.

I watched from the front porch as he drove away. I should probably put in a few hours at the museum. If I were fortunate someone else had finished cataloguing all those boxes of pictures, but since I wasn't terribly lucky there would be plenty left to do.

I knew the main reason I was avoiding the museum was

the painting. I guess one could think of it like the amusing art in the Harry Potter films, those figures in the portraits moved and even carried on conversations. As fun as that might be, I didn't live at Hogwarts and wasn't proficient in the use of magic.

Maybe today I could ignore it, no reason to scare the bejeebers out of myself.

The other volunteers had been busy; all of the boxes under the table were gone, leaving several cartons and a plastic crate on the tabletop.

I lugged a large container to the side desk and pulled off the tape that secured the flaps. Lots of pictures, old post cards and letters, receipts and so forth, must have been the contents of a desk. The bank passbook was from the 1920's as were the stock certificates.

Mr. Atkins would need to find relatives and return the certificates; most likely the corporations that issued them didn't exist anymore. I'd take them to his office before I left.

Of course, that would mean I'd be in the vicinity of the paintings. No problem, I wouldn't stop, simply pass by without looking.

Did I mention that people liked to be frightened ... in a controlled environment?

The cowboy in the picture was now standing in front of Diamondback Cut.

The skin on my arms prickled, my heart raced, and breathing was a little difficult.

The fellow with three fingers had a grin on his face, the hat, which had shadowed his features was now pushed back on his head.

All right! You have my full attention; what is the message, the significant point?

Once outside, I sat in the car, my head against the back of the seat, and eyes closed. Why me, I'm not psychic, perhaps a little nutty now and then like everyone else.

Obviously, I was supposed to do something ... whatever it was concerned Diamondback Cut. I'd been there and found nothing but the possibility of encountering lots of snakes. One must admit I wasn't inside the Cut very long, a few minutes at the very most.

What I needed was more backbone and force myself to walk the several hundred yards of the narrow ravine and study each side carefully ... and look for what exactly?

All this rationalizing was getting me nowhere. I required more information and the place to find information was the library, or the Internet. I chose the library; the idea of having a tangible printed page to peruse always made me happy.

Two hours later I was at my kitchen table surrounded by more than enough books to keep me busy. There were several on Murrieta, two on cattle ranches of California, a history of gold mining in the San Joaquin area, and Johnston McCulley's short stories that featured Zorro. The dashing "fox" who set about "avenging the helpless and aiding the oppressed".

Just the person I needed because I was helpless in trying to figure out what I was supposed to do for the spirits or supernatural beings that wanted to be friends.

The sketches of Murrieta featured a wild-eyed vaquero that didn't bare the slightest resemblance to Isabella Castro's cowboy. I doubted the pictures in the book were accurate; Joaquin probably didn't want to be recognized, after all, he was an outlaw.

I was particularly interested in the Castro land. It took some time but eventually found that the original land grant of twenty-two thousand acres was given to Jose Covarrubias.

His daughter, Maria, married Antonio Castro and the couple was presented one thousand acres around Sendero as a wedding gift.

Through the years the property was divided and sold off

leaving a little over a hundred acres owned by the many times great grandson, Dennis Castro. The family no longer lived in the area, preferring to be in Santa Clarita.

It must be over ten years or so since the Castro's left, my parents knew Dennis slightly.

Okay, how did this help me? I didn't even know if the cowboy in the picture at the museum was Joaquin Murrieta, I was the one speculating it might be the case.

The words from my dream about "*fortune favors the brave*" resonated very clearly when I let myself think about it. One could say that Joaquin hadn't been very fortunate; his severed head displayed in a jar of whisky was rather anticlimactic.

I sighed, rubbed my eyes and wondered where the dogs were; they usually stayed under foot, following me from room to room. I went to the screen door and saw them at the fence, alert and on duty. They did that when some animal was in the field out back.

My house sat on a slight hill that sloped down to the road below. There were houses on either side but a distance away due to the size of my property, which was one of the reasons I bought the place.

It was also time to have the weeds cut again, or the fire department would send a notice of some code violation.

The noise was jarring; it caused the dogs to go wild and me to almost have a heart attack!

I managed to stub my toe on the nightstand before rushing into the living room. The television was blaring an infomercial about some waterproof sealant, while I frantically searched for the remote.

After what seemed like forever managed to mute the sound, turn on a light and sit down.

What the hell! It was twenty minutes after two in the morning.

Faro and Hallie crowded around me on the couch. I patted heads and spoke softly to the pair in an attempt to calm them and myself, then looked carefully around the room.

The sliding glass doors were closed, the metal security bar in place. I had paid dearly for impact–resistant sliding doors that were "hurricane-proof" just in case a storm swept through due to global warming. Oh yeah, there was no such thing as global warming according to some people.

Before going to bed last night I'd secured the doggie door with the heavy-duty metal insert, which was still in place when I checked the kitchen. The dead bolt on the front door hadn't unlocked itself either. Marvelous, just fricking marvelous! Time for a cup of tea!

My parents sat at the kitchen island drinking coffee. "You're sure it wasn't some kind of power surge that caused the television to go on?" Mom asked.

"Don't think a power surge works that way," I muttered.

My dad took another sip of coffee. "A spike in the electrical current can come from a lightning strike or more likely an air conditioner or refrigerator, sometimes faulty wiring or a transformer problem."

I leaned against the counter. "I don't have an air conditioner ... so you think it was just an energy spike, doesn't something like that damage whatever it hits?"

"Depends on the nature of the voltage hike in the device or appliance."

"Everything seems to be working, no bleeping noises from the fridge, computer is fine ... so is the frenetic TV."

"I'll take a look at the breaker panel before we go," Dad stated.

My mom studied my face. "You look tired, you should take a long rest this afternoon."

"Sounds like good idea, didn't get much sleep last night due to circumstances beyond my control," and nodded toward the television.

99

After the folks left I sat on the patio and looked at the lake. The view was calming, and I could watch the puffy white clouds drift into interesting shapes.

"Hey, thought I might take a drive around the lake, want to come along?"

I looked toward the fence and could see Jim peeking through the lattice. The dogs hurried toward the voice and jumped around and barked.

My first impulse was to decline the offer, but then decided it would be nice to get out ... and away from "*ghoulies and ghosties and long-legged beasties and things that* go *bump in the night.*"

"Sure, give me a few minutes, I'll meet you out front."

There is something magical about how the light plays on the water. Once we passed the campgrounds, I suggested a different route, an area where the river surged over large rocks.

Most tourists didn't know this place existed, which suited me just fine.

We sat on a boulder overlooking the rapids. "I'm impressed, this is wonderful."

"It is rather nice but can be dangerous if a person decided to venture away from the bank."

"I might be foolish at times, but not that foolish."

"Good to know, as Shakespeare wrote. '*Lord, what fools these mortals be.*' But one should be allowed to be silly once in a while."

Jim smiled and gazed at the fast-moving water. "So what made you decide to become a teacher?"

"My folks said that being a cowboy didn't pay very well, and an industrial spy was probably not the best choice either. What about you?"

"After college didn't have any idea of what I wanted to do ... saw an advertisement about becoming a deputy sheriff and applied. It's been interesting for the most part."

"So, you didn't have this burning desire to help people and be of service?"

"Ah ... not as much as some others I guess, it's a job and I try to do the best I can."

"I have s similar philosophy, shouldn't let the occupation define who you are, there is a life away from the classroom ... go live it. Don't get me wrong I like what I do, the kids are great for the most part, it's the administration and ever-changing curriculum that's annoying."

Jim made himself comfortable against a rock and closed his eyes. The sun was warm, the sound of rushing water soothing.

There was space enough to stretch out, so that's what I did, let my mind drift and listen to the restless water, watch the light and colors halt the passage of time.

"Why aren't you married with a houseful of kids?" my companion inquired.

"Could ask the same of you."

Jim rubbed his chin. "I was engaged a couple of years ago, didn't work out."

"My short-lived marriage didn't work out either, we must be doing something wrong in the romance department."

He smirked. "A fear of commitment perhaps?"

"More like a significant other taking life so seriously that it's crippling, and a passion boarding on obsession for work."

"Sounds stifling."

"Suffocating. I guess there is something fundamentally wrong with my mental and physical makeup, so you don't have to worry that I will become mawkish."

Jim chuckled. "Mawkish ... sounds incredibly nauseating ... and I might add that you have nothing to worry about in the physical attribute department either."

The ride home was pleasant, we seemed to have the same taste in music. The Dave Matthews Band, Red Hot

Chili Peppers, the beloved music of Clapton, The Doors and Fleetwood Mac.

Found out he played the guitar, something I enjoyed doing too ... for my own pleasure since I wasn't especially talented.

I was starting to believe we might eventually be friends, which would be nice since we lived in such close proximity, better than the alternative.

He still wasn't my type!

I was extra careful when locking everything that night. In fact, I was almost on the verge of being obsessive-compulsive. I did leave the windows open several inches to circulate the air but made sure the hinged wedge locks were in place.

I had thought about keeping my pistol on the nightstand but decided it was a bit paranoid ... didn't mean I couldn't have it close by, in the drawer. Probably wouldn't be much use against a ghost anyway ... but one should be prepared.

Jason Tanner sat in the car parked on the street below the blond woman's house. She had dogs, big dogs, also discovered a cop lived next door. Breaking into her place might not be the best idea. He would have to think of another way to rid himself of the snooping bitch.

He'd keep the van parked in the garage and use the old "beater" to get around.

Jay had warned him to drive the van only for business, it wasn't his fault the "tank" had a flat tire when he needed to go to town.

Being slapped around made him mad, one of these days he wouldn't take it any more ... but Jay always apologized, he liked that about Jay, always sorry afterward.

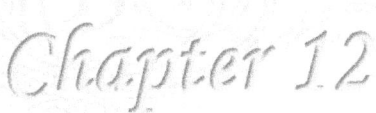

Chapter 12

Penny called the gang together for a mid-week meeting, she sounded very mysterious during the short phone conversation.

Later that afternoon I joined Adam and Sandy who were waiting at our usual spot in the cantina.

"Sounds like Penny has something important on her mind," Adam stated.

"Just what I need another enigma in my life."

Laura, our waitperson, bustled over to set my drink in front of me. "Just wanted to let you know that Fuego will be here Saturday, one performance only, at Pinky's."

Fuego was a local band that had gained popularity up and down the state. Years ago I had performed with the group and been sorta-kinda, involved with the leader, Ricardo Vega. Romance had turned to friendship over the years; Rico was also Laura's cousin.

"Rico expects you to sing a couple of songs for old times," she continued.

"He could have given me a little advanced notice, I haven't done anything like that in forever, I'll pass."

Laura frowned. "He'll be disappointed ... at least come and listen to the music."

"I'll think about it."

Penny and Christian arrived, Dana, as usual was last. Everyone was finally settled with their drinks and looked at Penny in anticipation.

"So what important occasion are we celebrating ... Tuna Tossing, Coolest Tie-Dye T- Shirt, the Toilet Seat Throw?" Adam inquired. "Better yet, Maris can be seen for one night only with Fuego on Saturday ... at Pinky's ... ain't that right?"

I groaned and flipped him off.

Penny looked rather serious. "None of those very significant events, FYI, Tuna Tossing is only held in Australia."

Adam and I were gleefully about to chime in with the usual Waa-Waa-Waa, when she continued. "I heard from my sister. Claire has been in contact with other social workers in different counties." She paused for a rather long moment.

I impatiently urged her to continue with "And ... what?"

"The other teens that Adam told us about weren't random victims, every single one of them were in the Independent Living Program. All were headed to group homes to begin a training program or schooling of some kind."

I took a deep breath then let it out slowly. "So ... that means someone had to know when and where those poor kids were traveling. Did she say how they were getting from place to place?"

Penny shook her head. "I didn't think to ask."

Adam joined in with. "It's doubtful they had a car, I would venture to say it was some form of public transportation ... probably a bus."

"So how did they get to the motels ... they were found in motels, right?" Dana offered.

"If they were on a bus, someone from the group home would be at the station to meet them," Christian said.

"What if the kid was met by the bad guy instead?" I proposed.

"Wouldn't it be suspicious if there were two people waiting for the same kid?"

"Didn't think about that. Well, I'm sure the CBI will figure it all out."

Christian looked puzzled. "The what?"

"The California Bureau of Investigation."

Christian scrunched up his nose. "You made that up."

"No ... I didn't make up anything, Scott says a special task force is working on these atrocities."

It was quiet at the table until Dana spoke. "What song are you going to sing with the band?"

I huffed. "Ain't happening, my singing days were over long ago, I'll be happy to watch and listen with the rest of the crowd."

Sandy looked a little concerned. "You people realize that Pinky's is notorious for all the wrong reasons."

I had to chuckle. "If there aren't three or four fights a night the place isn't jumping."

"And you would know this how?"

"When I wasn't sneaking in for a beer at age seventeen, I was with Fuego, the Latin salsa beat was as wild as the customers."

When I got home later that evening, I called Scott and told him about our conversation ... not the one concerning the band ... the stuff Penny had disclosed. My brother listened, asked a few questions and said he would pass the information on to the task force, he thought they probably knew the victims were in the system.

I'd done my civic duty; so let my mind wander back a few years to my short career in music. I had a decent voice, could imitate quite a few female singers, Annie Lennox, Gloria Estefan, Grace Slick and the feathery alto of Stevie Nicks.

That was the problem, one had to have a distinctive voice and style of their own to make it "big" become the overnight success that took twenty-five years to achieve.

I didn't have the single-mindedness, and ambition required ... much too lazy if the truth be known.

Faro and I had our usual altercation over who got the couch. He preferred to have it all to himself and only grudgingly allowed me to park my body in a small space at the end. Hallie plopped down on or under my feet, which made it difficult to move if and when I wanted to do so.

Time to watch a mindless adventure movie on Netflix, couldn't go wrong with the incredible, beyond belief, action hero's I enjoyed. Oh, to be so brave, so strong, and recover so quickly from such punishment the bad guys dished out. I mean how many times could a person get hit in the head and not suffer permanent brain damage. Ah ... the magic of the cinema.

Saturday morning Rico Vega called, he was insistent I sing ... for old times. We finally negotiated a duet ... "Stop Draggin' My Heart Around" a Stevie Nicks/Tom Petty number.

We talked for another fifteen minutes or so and agreed to meet before the nine o'clock performance to practice ... my idea. Lord, it had been awhile since I was on stage my stomach was already tying itself in knots.

I should dig out some of my old stuff see if anything fit.

The plastic tub was dragged out of the closet. Several items of apparel were removed ... couldn't believe I had the nerve to wear such things. The slinky, red lace see-thru number was a definite no! I doubted it would fit so didn't even try.

Perhaps the black tank top with flames outlined in rhinestones would work. I held up the skinny jeans against my body and whimpered a bit. There was time to run to the mall in Santa Clarita and get a new, slightly larger, pair.

The black, over the calf boots, with the stiletto heels looked decent enough, should wobble around in them for a while ... falling over wasn't an option.

By seven-thirty that evening I was regretting my decision. The reflection in the mirror looked terrified rather than sexy. Big hair, large hoop earrings, boobs straining to be free from the tank top, wonderful outfit ... could pass for a hooker any day of the week.

I'm sure the crowd at Pinky's wouldn't even blink. Over the years I had seen just about everything pass through the doors, from a guy in a tuxedo jacket and plaid shorts, to a four-hundred-pound woman in a fake fur mini skirt and fringe crop-top.

Oh yeah!

My friends assured me they would be there, Dana called to tell me she and Steve Mitchell wouldn't miss it for the world.

I really could use a drink ... but needed a clear head at least until I went through the doors of Pinky's.

The club was set back from the road adjacent to the icehouse. The building was large and quite attractive, in keeping with the theme and design of Sendero Village. Big Fat Benny owned the icehouse and I suspected he had something to do with Pinky's as well.

Inside wasn't bad; lots of tables and chairs were clustered against the walls, a large dance floor in the middle and a raised stage for the entertainers. The place was already busy, people leaned, or sat at the bar, and many of the tables were occupied, by nine it would be loud and hopping.

I asked if Rico Vega was around and one of the bar tenders pointed toward the back.

Nothing much had changed. Through the door, marked "EMPLOYEES ONLY" was the office and a lounge-dressing room for the talent.

I was about to knock when the door suddenly opened

and I almost crashed into Ricardo Vega. We were both a little surprised. "Maris!"

"Hi ... it's been a while."

He crushed me to his chest, then held me at arms length. "You look terrific ... what's it been . . .two years?"

"More like three ... you haven't changed much, same old charming self."

"Come in. A couple of new faces for you to meet."

Bobby, the drummer gave me a hug. Danny, keyboard, waved from the couch. He looked his usual laid-back self, a joint hanging out of his mouth.

I grinned. "See you stopped by for some fresh vegetables from Mac and Mo."

He inhaled deeply. "They have the best stuff in the whole state."

Rico moved toward a very pretty young woman with neon, red hair. "Maris, meet Yvonne, great voice."

I nodded, "Hello, glad it's you going out there to face that mob for the evening ... one song and I'm gone."

Lord, was I ever that young? Rico pointed across the room to another guy. "This is Alex, plays a mean bass. You want a drink?"

A healthy slug of whisky -- make that two -- and I was a little calmer. Rico and I went through the song quickly, it didn't take long to become familiar with the words and music again, we had performed it a hundred times.

A half hour later we set up the stage, checked the amplifiers and microphones, brought out the instruments, the keyboard and drums were already in place.

The plan was to start off with some hot, fast, numbers to get the crowds attention, then Rico and I would sing the duet and I could get the hell off stage and enjoy the rest of the show.

I leaned against the wall and looked for my friends. People were talking, laughing, drinking, and milling about. I finally spotted Steve Mitchell; one could hardly miss the gentle giant. Couldn't see anyone else, but was sure they were all in the vicinity.

The microphone hummed, Rico began to speak the familiar words of introduction, glad to be back home ... and so it began.

After three wild numbers I made my way up the steps, the drums thundered, the plaintive whine of the guitar reverberated; I took a deep breath and became Stevie Nicks.

Baby you came knockin' at my front door.
Same old line you used to use before.

Just like old times and as in the past, Rico surprised me by not stopping when the number was through. He went into the wild "Let's Get Loud" which I managed to fake my way through then literally ran off the stage and headed for the bar.

"Two shots of Tequila, line 'em up please." The gang gathered around and enthusiastically congratulated me, paid for my drinks, then escorted me to their table guarded by Steve.

Now that it was all over I could enjoy the show, which I did with great exuberance. It was fun to dance and drink however many margaritas. Adam and Sandy were the first to leave, then Penny and Christian.

Dana and Steve were deciding how to get me home when Virgil Pasco and his brother Ray-Ray stumbled over to congratulate me. Virgil wanted to dance so we merged into the crowd on the floor.

We were interrupted by some idiot who wanted to cut in, grabbed my arm and started to drag me away.

Even though I was slightly inebriated, make that, a lot inebriated, I wasn't going anywhere with the moron. I pushed him away, Virgil, who was really snockered, tried to intervene.

The next thing I knew the intruder was on the floor,

blood streaming from his nose. "Way to go Virgil."

"Don't think Virgil will be of much help, the tool passed out." Jim muttered and guided me off the dance floor, then massaged his hand.

I opened my mouth to say something profound but couldn't do anything but giggle.

I vaguely remember my neighbor driving me home in my car.

I turned over to pet Hallie, who always slept next to me, and was surprised to find her gone, then smelled the delightful aroma of coffee that wafted through the air.

I doubted the dogs were that talented, I didn't remember setting the timer on the coffee pot, in fact, I was having difficulty remembering much of anything at the moment. It would all come back to me ... eventually ... I never got that sloshed.

Looking at the face in the bathroom mirror was disturbing. The squirrels must have nested in my hair and the heavy-handed use of the smeared mascara reminded me of a raccoon. I managed to comb my hair into less of a haystack and after a wash and liberal slathering of aloe, looked a little better. Eventually made my way to the kitchen.

I could use a cup of coffee, some aspirin, and check on the dogs.

Jim Hayden leaned against the kitchen counter, a large mug in hand. "Thought you might like some coffee. I fed the monsters."

I stared at him for a moment then sighed. "Oh yeah, you drove me home last night and ... stayed?"

He grinned. "You asked very nicely."

I closed my eyes and tried to think back. "So, I asked you to hang around?"

"Yeah, something about things that go bump in the night ... and a ghost."

I took a mug from the cabinet and poured the fragrant

brew with an almost steady hand. "Must have been the booze talking," then carefully sat down at the island.

"You have a great voice, I'm impressed."

"You were there for that?"

"I was."

"Terrific ... was there a fight, seem to remember some kind of altercation with Virgil Pasco."

"Not exactly with Virgil Pasco, he just happened to be around, I think he had quite a bit to drink and fell over a few people, it wasn't much of a fight anyway."

"Un-huh." I looked down at my bare feet. "Guess you helped me to bed and took off my boots too?"

"Yep, removed the boots and covered you with a blanket ... thought about helping with the rest of your outfit, but ..."

"So thoughtful ... I do appreciate your assistance!"

He chuckled. "My pleasure."

Chapter 13

It was already warm by ten o'clock when I came outside with another cup of coffee. I was feeling better after a long, hot shower.

"I should get the pool out, it'll be hot this afternoon."

Jim smirked. "Can hardly wait to see you relaxing around the pool. Must be an imaginary one."

I sighed. "Not for me ... for the dogs, they love the water."

"Where is it?"

"On the side, in the storage shed."

"I'll get it, but refuse to blow it up, unless you have a compressor."

"It's not the inflatable kind, just a plastic wading thing."

Jim and the dogs wandered around the corner and eventually returned with the kiddie pond. "Where do you want it?"

"At the edge of the cement, they make quite a mess."

I brought the hose and washed off a small amount of dust that had accumulated, then filled it about half full.

Both dogs sniffed the rim and drank a little, Faro put in

one paw and drew it out quickly, Hallie barked and danced around.

"Don't think they're especially thrilled?"

"It takes a little time for them to get used to it."

We watched while the big oafs acted silly and finally Faro ventured in and sat down.

"So, what about this ghost of yours."

I procrastinated a bit by drinking some coffee. "As I said before, just the booze talking, you shouldn't take me seriously."

"Come on ... promise not to laugh. Sometimes I get strange premonitions about things or people. I believe a few of us have an awareness or impression of something different in our environment."

"So, what "premonitions" have you experienced?"

His expression was thoughtful, and it took a while before he answered. "I guess it's a little voice in your head warning about things, or a feeling that an unseen something is standing near or touching you."

I looked at him carefully; he seemed to have an understanding of otherworldly occurrences.

Jim sat quietly next to me drinking coffee and watching the dogs. It probably wouldn't hurt to tell him about the dreams, if he thought I was a nut-case he could stay on his side of the carport.

In due course I mentioned the painting and why I decided my "ghost" might be Joaquin Murrieta.

My guest didn't act as if I had a contagious disease and make some lame excuse for leaving. But posed the question I couldn't answer ... what did the spirit want?

Around noon he offered to cook. I probably should have something in my stomach besides coffee. My handy companion prepared scrambled eggs and toast for me and a bacon and cheese omelet for himself.

Since he had to work at three I mentioned we should get

his truck from the parking lot at Pinky's.

He informed me it wasn't necessary, his vehicle was here, Steve Mitchell had delivered it while Jim drove me home. That meant Dana would have a wonderful story to tell the gang, which over time, would become embellished beyond recognition.

Jim also wanted to visit the museum and see Isabella Castro's paintings; perhaps the cowboys would change positions in front a witness ... doubtful. Nothing had happened with Penny or when my mother examined them.

We agreed to meet on Monday morning and have a look ... couldn't hurt.

After he left I went back to bed, before dozing off decided that Jim Hayden had been considerate, one might say, even gracious last night and this morning. I should probably revise my opinion of him ... be friends ... like Adam and Christian. That would be a good thing ... he wasn't my type anyway.

Dinner at my folks is pleasant; I was frequently invited on Sunday. We caught up on the latest gossip going around town and new projects at the ranch.

Dad wandered off to watch television while Mom and I cleared the table. Eventually asked if she had any more information on works of art that were considered haunted.

She had discovered a few things and we went outside on the patio to chat.

In the 1930's Morris Kantor painted a picture of the living room in a colonial house ... it was disclosed that dark shadows or forms appeared in the picture and from time to time these shapes changed positions.

An unknown artist is said to have used his own blood as the color pallet for his composition, then committed suicide after the painting was completed. Different owners of the macabre picture reported hearing voices coming from the canvas and a shadowy figure lurking about.

There are numerous portraits where the eyes follow those who pass by, and several pictures that people proclaim a sudden gust of cold air envelopes them when standing near.

That was enough to send a small shiver down the back of my neck.

It seems that Isabella Castro's pictures were not the first or probably the last paintings to exhibit weird stuff. Thing is ... I seem to be the only one affected by her works. How lovely!

I declined dessert, kissed my parents goodbye and began the short drive home.

Even though I had sorta-kinda let go being run off the road, I occasionally went out of my way to cruise past the Coverdale Retreat, curious to see if a tan or white van was around.

I slowed at the gates and looked toward the portico ... nothing ... as usual.

The narrow road was somewhat winding through the foothills. Drivers had to be careful; at times, approaching cars were over the line when coming out of a curve.

I decelerated, checked the rear view mirror and noticed a car closing fast, my first thoughts were this person should slow down, not a road for speed racing unless you were an idiot.

Obviously this driver fit the description of an idiot. The car was getting too close for comfort, I moved over slightly so it could pass, which it did, but just enough to stay even with me.

Bastard! I grasped the wheel a little tighter; thankfully the road was straight for some distance. I was about to slow down again when the vehicle slammed into the side of my car! A shock of fear went through my body and for a moment couldn't think of what to do!

What the hell! I gripped the wheel, my seat belt tight-

115

ened instantly when I was jerked from side to side, the strap dug into my neck.

I was fighting to keep my car on the road! The crazy person dropped back, I thought maybe this madness was over but the car sped up and hit me again.

For a brief moment when we were side by side I looked over, even though the man was wearing a baseball cap I recognized him. It was the face from the enlarged photo on the driver's license that Scott had shown me ... Jason Tanner!

I was determined to stay in control of my car. The road began to curve and a good possibility that I could be forced into the side of a hill.

I let off the gas; the other vehicle surged ahead, then cranked the wheel about half way around and pulled the emergency break. As the car began to rotate, released the hand break, stepped on the pedal, straightened the wheel and headed away from the demon driver. I could hear brakes squeal as the bastard tried to stop.

The other car was an older, heaver vehicle; it would take some time to change directions. I should be able to get away, and drive to the Sheriff's Department.

My father had taught when in a scary situation while driving, if possible, never stop the car; if that can't be avoided, get out as quickly as possible and run, don't wait for the bad guy to make it to your vehicle. If being followed, drive to a police station or fire department -- never go home.

Once I pulled into the parking lot in front of the Sheriff's office was able to take a deep breath, calm down and let my hands stop shaking. After looking at the damaged car I hurried inside.

The lobby was almost empty, only one person set on the bench against the wall. A duty officer stood behind the long counter.

Sergeant Sam Mayfield looked up as I approached and smiled. "Maris Connelly, haven't seen you for quite a spell.

116

How is Will?"

"Dad is fine, just had dinner with him."

"Good to know, so what brings you here on this warm Sunday evening?"

I took a deep breath. "Want to report some fool tried to run me into the side of a rather substantial hill a few minutes ago."

Sam's eyes widened. "Are you okay?"

"A little shaken, mostly pissed off. Is my brother around?"

"Let me check," and lifted up the receiver on the phone and spoke to someone.

Scott wasn't on duty, but I was quickly buzzed through the door and told to go to the open area in the back.

There were twelve desks and workspaces in the section reserved for the deputies. Behind a glass window was the Lieutenant's office, further on down the hall was where Craig Robinson, the Sheriff, could be found during the day.

Lynn Parrish, a senior deputy, waved me over. "Sam said you have a problem."

I nodded to the other deputy, Brian Hosty, then sat in the chair near her desk. "Yeah, you could say that, I'm still a little jittery."

"What happened?"

I took a deep breath and started from the beginning ... the first encounter, the Coverdale Retreat, tracing the plates and now this latest hit and run experience. Lynn was writing as I disclosed the details. Then we went outside to look at my car.

The poor thing was a mess, large dents on the driver side and back passenger doors, scrapes and gashes, smears of a reddish paint color and the side mirror was ready to fall off.

The deputy walked around the car and made notes on her clip-board. "He got you good, can you describe the other car."

I tried to secure the side mirror, a futile gesture. "An older model, maybe late 90's Lincoln or Mercury, kind of a junker, maroon, four door sedan, a relic of the past."

"If push came to shove that "relic" could have forced you into something with no problem."

"I know, it's not like he didn't try. For whatever reason, the bastard has it out for me, so what's next?"

"We'll try and locate this guy, start with the address on the license, then attempt to trace him from there. Put out a description so our deputies can be on the lookout for the car. This Tanner fellow might not be the person who ran you off the road the first time."

"True, but I do know he's the guy who did all this damage the second go round."

Lynn traced her fingers over the side mirror. "Better get this fixed, the dents and scratches can be put off for a while. You should get checked out too."

I rubbed the back of my neck. "Don't think anything is broken, smashed or twisted. Might have a bruise where the seat belt dug into my neck. I'll take the car to Diego's Garage tomorrow, get the mirror re-attached.

The first thing I did after petting the fawning dogs was contact my brother, he wasn't too happy to hear of my latest adventure. I assured him I was fine, however, my poor car could use some TLC.

The second thing I did was pour a large glass of wine and savor it while sitting on the patio.

This summer was turning out to be a real pain in the ass. Not only was some nut-job trying to kill, maim, and generally make my life miserable, there was a ghost haunting me for whatever reason.

I guess my mantra of "*Life is a bitch and then you die*" wasn't far from wrong, at least for right now.

I should call the gang together they always added a little

humor to any situation. Might even tell about the animate pictures and ghostly dreams. I'm sure Christian would be thrilled, he didn't believe in paranormal stuff; Adam was on the fence about such things. The girls, especially Dana, were quite willing to consider a reality beyond the physical universe.

Monday was going to be busy.

The next morning Jim examined my car and rubbed his fingers along the scratches, he didn't look happy, in fact he seemed upset. "You're lucky, damn lucky not to be in the hospital or worse. Why didn't you tell me about this SOB?"

"The story is long and complicated, it's not like I kept it to myself, Scott knows and by now so does most of the Sheriff's Department."

He huffed a little more. "I'll follow you to the garage to drop off car, then we'll go to the museum and have a look at the paintings."

"Let me get my purse ... don't put too much faith in seeing something out of the ordinary in those pictures, I guess the ghost is selective in who he wants to entertain."

Jim studied the paintings, as predicted nothing exciting happened, the faces of the cowboys were vague, the three men leaned against the corral fence as always. I explained about Diamondback Cut, how it wasn't near the ranch house, Isabella Castro must have included it for a reason.

Jim thought the incorporation was significant ... it must have been important at one time.

He suggested we take a ride and check it out.

Perhaps the Cut wouldn't be so daunting with a companion along. Not that the snakes cared, they would still be around, hidden in cracks and crevasses.

I was creeping myself out just thinking about it ... not good.

We should discuss this over a milkshake; I deserved a pineapple milkshake, after the stress of last evening. After all, being on the receiving end of an attack by a demented freak was something to commemorate.

Perhaps commemorate wasn't the correct word but couldn't think of another excuse for such self-indulgence.

We sat by the fountain in the plaza with our refreshing repast and decided to ride early on Wednesday morning, Jim had the day off, we'd visit the Castro place and Diamond-back Cut.

Then did a little window-shopping for the next hour be-fore picking up my car.

All in all a pleasurable day, despite the reason we were out and about.

Later, at home, put in calls to Penny, Dana and Sandy, it was extremely important that we meet this evening. Dana asked if I were giving up teaching for a singing career, or maybe "following that hunky Rico Vega around".

My definite "NO" didn't dissuade her from making a few more snarky remarks.

I knew the evening would be entertaining, mostly at my expense.

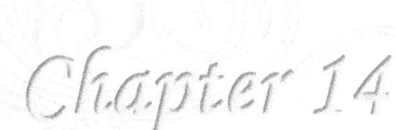

Chapter 14

"You don't look half bad, could have been on the receiving end of a fist during the fight," Christian announced.

"What fight?"

"The one you and Virgil Pasco were in on Saturday. I was impressed, not about the fight, your singing."

I rubbed my temple. "I don't remember any fight, just some guy falling over and Jim Hayden escorting me off the dance floor. He said Virgil was drunk and stumbled into someone. Besides you weren't even there."

"My source of information is unimpeachable," he smirked and looked at Dana.

"Undoubtedly, your informant is confused, which is not difficult to believe knowing the background of such a person," and smiled sweetly at my friend.

"I beg to differ with that statement. When have I ever been confused?"

"Hmm ... how shall I count the ways, what about our trip to see the Queen Mary?"

Dana looked insulted. "We made it didn't we?"

Penny and Sandy began to giggle, as I continued with

the ridiculous story.

The legendary Queen Mary built in the 1930's, served as an elegant ocean liner and then a troopship during WWII. It is now a tourist attraction, a floating hotel, moored at the Port of Long Beach.

Getting there from Santa Clarita should only take about an hour via the I-5, and 710 to Long Beach. Dana managed to end up in San Pedro, her idea of a "short-cut".

The four of us drove around in circles for about an hour, reminiscent of Einstein's definition of insanity "*doing the same thing over and over again but expecting a different result.*"

I was laughing hysterically each time we ended back on the same freeway, which didn't help the frustrated driver. Off in the distance one could see the Queen Mary nestled at her birth in the harbor. After suggesting we stop at a gas station for directions, once again continued on our endless quest for the elusive ship. It hadn't helped that Dana got into an argument with the attendant, insisting he was wrong about the route to Long Beach.

Sometime later, and a few miles closer to our objective I mentioned that if we drove through an alley, avoided the trash cans and dumpsters, then jumped the curb, we could be in the parking lot of the attraction.

Our one-hour jaunt took about three hours ... another adventure in travel, and nothing out of the ordinary for us.

"Shall we get to the reason I called this meeting? Before you hear about it in the grocery store, I'll apprise you lovely people of my fun experience last night," then swilled down a mouthful of margarita and began the narrative.

It was eerily quiet after the conclusion of my hazardous exploit. Adam scraped at the label on his bottle of beer and took a deep breath.

"Let me get this straight ... some maniac has tried to force you off the road twice!"

"Well, I don't really know if it's the same guy both times."

Adam removed his glasses and rubbed his eye. "I think there is something going on at the Retreat other than people with copious amounts of money recuperating from whatever."

Christian grunted in agreement. "So the authorities know all about this hit and run business and are looking for the SOB and the car?"

I nodded. "Scott will be all over it, so I guess there's nothing to do but wait and see what happens."

Penny raised her wine glass. "Happy you weren't hurt, and hope the cops find the rat-bastard."

We clinked glasses. I couldn't resist adding. "May we be who our dogs think we are."

Scott banged on the door and yelled. "Maris, put the dogs outside and let me in!

The request was unusual; my brother was accustomed to being mauled when entering the house.

I blocked the doggie door, then lured the beasties to the patio with a Scooby-Snack.

When I finally got the front door unlocked and open, discovered my brother wasn't alone. Standing behind him were two rather serious and official looking men.

My first thoughts were about my casual attire. Cut-off jeans, a faded T-shirt with a mastiff face on the front and no shoes. At least the shirt didn't have holes or stains, and I had combed my hair ... sort of.

If Scott was mortified about how I looked, his face didn't show it. "Maris, this is Sergeant Andrews and Detective McAllister from the California Bureau of Investigation."

The Sergeant was a stocky guy, with graying hair and

dark eyes. The other fellow was a poster boy for the Nordic Olympic Games, both winter and summer, probably a close relative of the god of thunder, Thor.

I opened the door wider and motioned for them to come inside. "Please sit down, would you like some coffee?"

The men declined the offer and perched themselves about the living room.

The place wasn't too much of a disaster, newspapers and magazines on the coffee table and a James Patterson, *Mystery Women's Club,* novel on the end table.

My brother got right to the point. "Tell them about the hit and run."

"Both times?"

"Yes, start from the beginning."

I took a deep breath and told of the night Dana and I were run off the road, how I followed the car to the Coverdale Retreat, and the second encounter on Sunday.

Sergeant Andrews asked about the color of the van, and if I was sure the vehicle went to the Retreat.

The Nordic god didn't say anything, just wrote things in his little notebook. The Sergeant asked why I had taken a picture of the white van's license plate?

I answered that I had seen a white van parked near the entrance of the Retreat when driving to the base camp for the Search and Rescue operation. It looked like the same vehicle.

Could I be wrong about the driver of the hit-and-run car? Sure, it was same man in the license photo ... after all, it was getting dark and the situation rather stressful.

I replied that my assailant was the guy in the picture ... no mistake.

Detective McAllister could actually talk. Did I know anyone that worked at the Coverdale Retreat, or ever been inside the building?

No to both questions, he asked for a description of the

car that damaged mine.

I refrained from making any obscene remarks; my father's words about telling only the facts and nothing else when being questioned by the police resonated in my brain. They weren't interested in opinions or a point of view ... keep it short and accurate ... don't ramble.

A yip from outside drew everyone's attention. Sitting nicely at the screen door were the monsters, Hallie had a red rag in her mouth, at one time it had been a stuffed toy lobster. The dogs had de-stuffed it but loved the pathetic remnant and often bestowed the mungy thing as a gift.

"You'll have to be patient a bit longer guys."

"They're Mastiffs ... right?" said Detective Nordic-god.

"Indeed, real sweethearts. I'd let them in but they have no manners."

Scott smirked. "My sister isn't a dog-whisperer. Do you have any more questions?"

Sergeant Andrews stood. "No, not at the moment. Thank you, Miss Connelly, I'll give you my card, please call if you recall anything more."

I accepted the card. "This Tanner guy, do you think he has something to do with the Retreat?"

"Don't know much of anything right now, we've just opened the investigation."

"So, you are looking into the mysterious Retreat?"

"Maris!" Scott cautioned.

Detective McAllister's eyebrows went up. "How do you mean mysterious?"

Scott sighed. "Probably not the right word. When the defunct golf club was being remodeled, people in town gossiped about it. Everything from a private men's club, conversion into small apartments, to a place to hold special events was put forth.

I couldn't resist. "Don't forget a house of ill-repute. My friends think it's a laboratory for creating zombies or hiding

125

aliens."

"Illegal aliens?" Sergeant Andrews replied with interest.

"No, that would be too mundane, aliens from outer space, you can't possibly think our tiny planet is all alone in this vast universe."

The two detectives stared at me, then looked at my brother.

My brother rolled his eyes. "Maris!"

" ... what!"

I stood on the front porch and watched the men drive away. That was interesting, why was the CBI involved with a local hit and run incident?

The Sheriff's Department was quite capable of handling the situation and should eventually find Mr. Tanner if he was still around. I would have a chat with Scott maybe find out what was going on ... and what he knew in regards to hunky Detective McAllister, couldn't hurt.

Jim and I stood at the entrance to the Cut. So far the ride had been uneventful, even pleasurable. We had stopped at the Castro place, spent some time with Old Tom and eventually arrived at our destination.

"Doesn't look different from any other gap, maybe the sides are a little steeper than most," Jim stated.

"It contains snakes, lots and lots of snakes ... a gazillion!"

"If you don't bother them, they won't bother you, probably just slither away."

"Uh-huh try telling that to the one that's waiting in the bushes or behind a rock. The place didn't get its name for nothing."

"Come on, I'll lead, what are we looking for again?"

"Don't have the slightest idea, just a hunch that Old

Joaquin wants me to investigate."

Jim chuckled. "**X** is supposed to mark the spot ... right?"

"One size doesn't fit all, we are not created equal, and **X** never marks the spot."

"I sense a distinct lack of enthusiasm in that comment."

"Lead on with your fine self, watch where you step."

I could feel my heart rate increase as we moved forward, and thought it had suddenly gone quiet and hotter, definitely hotter.

At least I could take a better look at the rugged banks if Jim were keeping his eyes open for snakes.

The sides were overgrown in some places with clusters of vegetation; a large collection of rocks of various sizes and shapes dotted the sloping surface.

The rocks were rather colorful, black and rusty red obsidian, speckled gray granite, white quartz crystal and pink feldspar littered the slopes, very different and attractive in a rugged way.

"Are you keeping an eye out for snakes?"

Jim snickered. "Both eyes are wide open, no critters of the snake variety, a few small animal tracks here and there."

"Good, remember what your folks advised when you were a kid ... stop, look, and listen."

"I believe that was something to do when crossing the street."

"Can't hurt to apply it to our situation ... oh my god ... on that flat rock to your left about six feet up!"

Both of us stood still. "Whoa ... now that is a snake!" Jim said softly. "Stay calm, turn around and walk away, he's hasn't coiled as yet, if we don't get any closer, we should be fine."

I don't think I took a breath until we were out of the Cut.

Once in the clear I smacked him on the arm. "Some

sentinel you turned out to be!"

"Ow! That hurt, didn't see the monster, he blended into the surroundings, besides I was looking at the ground not up."

"People never look up," I muttered.

"You want to venture back in?"

"No! I've had my fill of heart stopping adventure today. We should head back, Mom said she would have lunch ready."

After stuffing myself with a chicken salad sandwich and chunks of cold melon, Jim and I headed home. He had errands to run and I should devote some time to cleaning my house.

The bedspread needed to be washed; the dog hair wouldn't magically disappear on its own. Even after a wash there were still frizzies if one took a close look, but it did smell better.

It was almost dark when I took my guitar out to the patio, the evening was warm, a slight breeze rustled the leaves of the oak tree on the side yard. A perfect night to sit outside, look at the stars and softly play a few favorites.

After messing around with Bob Dylan's, *Knocking on Heaven's Door*, a voice came from the other side of the fence.

"Want some company?"

I chuckled. "What if I said I wanted to be alone?"

"Hmm ... we could be alone together."

"Is that an oxymoron?"

"Might be a contradictory statement ... something like a plastic glass? Mind if I bring my guitar and join you?"

"Why not ... are you any good?"

"Nah, not especially."

I met him at the front door. After conversing with, petting and scratching the dogs we went outside to the patio.

Jim moved one of the chairs away from the table and sat

down. "So, what shall we play, nothing too difficult please?"

"Do you know *Scarborough Fair*?"

He nodded. "What key?"

"A minor, then G major ... okay?"

"Fine."

He was a double down liar! While I strummed chords and made up for deficient playing with my voice, he was a fingerpicking, truly talented, guitarist. He also had a decent baritone too.

We finished the musical evening with Neil Young's, *Old Man*.

I mentioned that Scott had brought agents from the CBI and asked if they had set up shop at the Sheriff's Office.

Jim hadn't seen the men, but heard they were around; space had been allocated for them to work.

Of course he didn't or couldn't give me any information on what the detectives were working on, which made me even more curious.

We said good night at the front door, I put the light on and waited until he made it to his place, then went inside.

I had enjoyed the evening ... even though he wasn't exactly my type.

After crawling into bed, my thoughts drifted as to why the CBI was here, what were they investigating? I was sure it had something to do with the Coverdale Retreat; why ask if I had been inside or knew anyone who worked there?

My brother had managed a short official visit. It might be interesting to drop by and see for myself what the place looked like ... it wasn't as if it were a prison or anything.

I'd have to think about how such a thing could be accomplished.

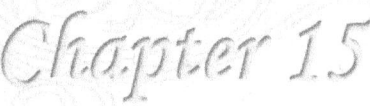

Chapter 15

"Tell me again why we're doing this ... whatever it is we're doing," Penny moaned.

"Stop whining! We need to see inside the Retreat, the guy who tried to smash me into a mountain might work here. I'm sure his van was the one I saw parked in front of the place. Plus ... why are agents from the CBI snooping around, asking questions?"

"I don't have the slightest idea . . .maybe your friend Jason is a doctor?"

"Other people work here besides doctors, the jerk could be a gardner for all I know."

"Doesn't seem to be any vehicle like you mentioned in the parking lot."

"There are buildings in the back, could be the van or old junker are in there."

Penny sighed. "I doubt if the tour will include a garage."

We were sitting in Penny's car parked at the Coverdale Retreat. I had called for an appointment on the pretext that my mother required a rest from her grueling schedule.

I was using my former married name Mrs. Anthony Warner and Penny was my sister, Mrs. Bellamy. We had a consultation with Jan Stottler, the woman in charge when Dr. Coverdale was unavailable.

"It's no big deal, a brief interview and a tour, nothing to worry about."

"You really expect to find this Tanner guy hanging around? And if he is, perhaps he will be wearing a nametag that says "HI…I'M JASON!" I never cared for the name Jason, reminds me of a machete wielding maniac."

"You want to wait in the car? I'll go in by myself."

Penny seemed to struggle with a decision. "Yes . . .No … I want to see this "health farm-rejuvenation center."

The etched glass doors slid open automatically when we approached. The lobby was elegant, somewhat Colonial Spain, atmospheric lighting, archways, exquisite décor, and soft background music.

So glad we dressed appropriately for the occasion. I did have a few nice things in my closet such as the soft pink silk blouse and maroon tailored skirt I had decided to wear.

The receptionist greeted us warmly and checked the appointment calendar. After a brief phone conversation stated that Ms. Stottler would be with us shortly.

We made ourselves comfortable on the tufted, ivory velvet armchairs … they looked expensive. "Don't think these chairs could survive at my house. Faro would gnaw on the carved legs and leave brown fur in all the tufts." I murmured softly.

Penny snickered. "Probably cost a few thousand each … check out the marble floors."

We waited about five minutes before a person came down the hall and through the archway. She was conservatively dressed in a dark grey, pencil skirt suit, and matching three-inch heels. The woman's dark hair was straight; cut perfectly to hang just below the jaw line, her makeup was flawless.

"Good morning, I'm Jan Stottler."

She shook our hands and asked us to accompany her to a small but well-appointed reception room.

We sat around a glass top table; Ms. Stottler asked if we would like some refreshment ... we didn't.

"So ... how may the Coverdale Retreat be of assistance?"

"We understand that many of your guests come here to rest ... get away from the pressures of their work."

Ms. Stottler nodded; her dark grey eyes appraised mine. "Quite a few of our lodgers find it helpful and healthful to have an intermission from their hectic life. I believe you are inquiring for a relative?"

"Yes, my sister and I feel it would benefit our mother to slow down and indulge herself for a time."

"What is her occupation?"

I had suggested, while making the plan to snoop, that our pretend mom should be in high-end real estate. Penny thought something like that would be too easy to investigate, if someone was so inclined.

She came up with a Representative of Fine Art Collector.

"An exact title is somewhat difficult, but out mother represents art collectors. She acquires fine works of art for people who have a limited knowledge of paintings but wish to collect." Penny stated with satisfaction.

I added. "She travels all over the world and we feel it's time she did something for herself."

Ms. Stottler smiled slightly. "I'm sure your mother would find our accommodations and services beneficial. A tour through the facility will give you an idea of what we have to offer."

"Thank you, we would appreciate that very much."

Our guide rose and we followed her into the hall. The

first stop was to see an example of a typical room, or so our hostess professed. It had everything a pampered, wealthy person could want. Next were the spa, terrace dining areas, fitness room and sauna. Last was the tropical pool with waterfall, where they probably filmed a Tarzan movie.

I carefully observed the male attendants; none of them were the psychotic Jason Tanner.

Guests lounged around the pool, many of them sported facial bruises from recent surgeries to either improve their appearance or hold back the ageing process.

We returned to the reception area where Ms. Stottler proceeded to the wall unit and returned to the table with several pamphlets and a notebook. "I have some brochures you can look through, they have information about what the Coverdale Retreat can provide in the way of care for guests."

I took the leaflets and tucked them inside my purse. "We appreciate your time and the information, and we'll try and persuade mother to do something nice for herself."

Ms. Stottler opened the notebook. "I'll jot down a few items as reminders. Mrs Warner and Mrs. Bellamy daughters of ... what is your mother's name?"

Penny's eyes widened, we hadn't discussed a "mom" name. "Ramona Johansson!"

I exclaimed.

"And where does Ms. Johansson reside?"

"Santa Monica."

Our hostess looked thoughtful. "I have a friend who lives in Santa Monica just off Montana Avenue."

"Mom is in the Ocean Park area." It really was time to leave before the questions became too personal. "Thank you for the tour and information, we will do our best to convince mother she should slow down."

Once outside we took a deep breath. "Where did you come up with Ramona Johansson?" Penny asked.

"One of my students was Ramona, and Johansson is

moms maiden name."

Penny unlocked the car. "Let's get out of here."

"Before the main gate slams shut and locks us out, drive up that road off to the right."

"Why?"

"Just want to see where it leads."

The road went around the side and was eventually blocked by a barrier that had a sign *Deliveries Only* with a push-button intercom ... so much for getting a look in the back.

Penny dropped me off at home. My efforts in sleuthing had been less than spectacular, but I did get to see inside the mysterious Retreat. I took the brochures out of my bag and spread them on the kitchen counter. There was actually an entry for "if a guest wanted to bring his or her own nurse".

No fees were listed, so assumed, if one had to ask they couldn't afford it.

I was still curious about the buildings in the back, maybe I'd have a look just before dark. I could park on the road and hike the short distance and check it out. Couldn't hurt and wasn't doing anything wrong, property around the Retreat was open range; cattle roamed freely regardless of land ownership so I guess a person could too.

I really must be bored to go to such lengths; there was plenty to do around here like stain the fence or gardening. The patch of greenery under the front windows could use some attention.

However, lounging on the patio with something cold to drink and a book was an even better idea ... less energy involved.

"Everyone stop chattering, I have an announcement to make!" Christian demanded.

Being obedient people, our group turned our attention in his direction.

"I have received the information on the beach house

134

rental ... and Dana you still owe three hundred dollars of your share."

"You'll have it next week ... promise. My brother said he would get it to me by Wednesday.

I snickered. "What lie did you tell this time?"

"Needed the brakes fixed on the car, it's getting more difficult to come up with plausible excuses," she sighed.

"I'm sure you'll find something novel the next time you need a loan."

Christian rapped on the table and began to read. "Three bedrooms, three and a half baths, wrap around deck, ocean front, and most important the lockbox number."

I groaned. "Not a lockbox, we don't do well with lockboxes. Why can't we meet the owners and get a key?"

Adam began to laugh. "Ah, yes ... fond memories of Hawaii, a different experience than most."

"It was different because we couldn't find the damn lockbox and Penny broke into the vacation rental."

Penny frowned slightly. "It's not my fault the property didn't have decent security, all I did was jiggle the window in the door, which allowed me to reach inside and unlock the pathetic excuse for a lock."

Sandy offered a plausible justification. "We were tired from the flight, then had to purchase groceries, and it was dark. Probably the reason everything got so mixed up,"

Christian chortled. "Yeah, that's why we maneuvered our way inside, cooked dinner, and stayed the night ... before finding out we were in the wrong place.

It was a good thing Maris's mother called on the house phone of the rental next door. Very fortunate the people staying there were fine with switching places after checking the paperwork,"

Adam continued. "If I recall we helped our neighbors locate their lockbox. The directions should have been more explicit, but it was really dark. Everything worked out nicely after transporting groceries, washing the bedding and eventually finding the right keys for both places the next morning."

I grumbled. "See, what did I tell you about lockboxes ... stupid things."

"Did you know that twenty-seven people have disappeared on Mt. Everest?" Dana said. "I have a feeling the Abominable Snowman ate them."

Penny huffed a bit. "The term is Yeti, a legend from Nepal, with no real evidence of its existence."

"The human-like creature probably lives in a yurt, somewhere in the Himalayas," I replied.

"Ooh ... it might be fun to stay in a yurt" Dana squeaked.

I glanced up and saw Big Fat Benny approaching. His two "friends" trailed several paces behind.

"Good evening Maris, I wanted to stop by and tell you how much I enjoyed your singing the other night at Pinky's. You should perform more often."

I summoned a genial facial expression. "Thank you for the kind words Mr. Edmonds, but I was doing it as a favor for a friend and have no plans to continue."

The large man smiled. "It was a pleasure anyway ... give my regards to your mother."

He nodded and left the cantina, followed by his associates.

Watching the trio leave gave me an idea. Perhaps Mr. Edmonds might be a resource to find Jason Tanner. If the jerk were hanging around, Big Fat Benny would probably know, or find out. It couldn't hurt to ask, maybe stop by the ice house and speak to our local gangster, or whatever Benny's calling happened to be.

Heard the faint sound of music coming from next door when getting out of my car. After making my way through the dogs and giving them a treat went outside on the patio.

It was a beautiful evening, warm breeze, bright moon, glittering stars and a woman's voice emanating from Jim's side of the fence. Couldn't make out the words from where I stood, perhaps if I moved closer and peeked through the lattice I might see and hear better.

I was tempted, then wondered why I was so interested in what my neighbor was doing? It shouldn't matter to me what he did or with whom he did it ... but was a little annoyed for some reason.

Really, Maris! Get a grip ... Jim Hayden wasn't important in my life, just an acquaintance, fun to be around, and nothing more. He'd soon be gone, and our paths would never cross again.

I should have a conversation with my brother, see if he knew anything about detective McAllister, the tall, blond, blue eyed, obviously able-bodied CBI guy.

I'd give Scott a call tomorrow after I went on my recon mission to check out the back part of Coverdale Retreat.

⌘

Driving the same road where the psycho had tried to force me into a mountain made me vigilant of my surroundings. I probably checked the rear-view and side mirrors every few seconds.

Once passed the Retreat, drove slowly up the hill that wound around the sanctuary, made a U-turn and parked on the side of the road. It would require a hike through the brush for a distance to get close enough to see the back buildings.

I was wearing jeans and boots, because the terrain was covered with thick clumps of chaparral shrubs, Manzanita, and rabbit brush.

There were pinion and Digger pine and quite a few valley oak trees scattered about the low hills.

Finally reached the block wall and walked around for some distance. I didn't realize the wall was so high one would need a ladder to look over the gray cement blocks.

I guess a person could gaze into the back area with binoculars up on the hill. But to actually see if vehicles were parked between or in the buildings one would have to climb over the wall.

I would give it some thought ... trespassing wasn't good, getting caught skulking about ... really bad.

The men watching from under the oak trees trained their field glasses on the woman wandering around the wall. This was unexpected, an interesting break from the monotony. Ryan McAllister focused on the face of the stealthy snooper.

Well, well, if it wasn't the attractive and quirky Maris Connelly ... interesting.

Chapter 16

Wandering around the area in back of the Retreat made me realize it wasn't possible to simply peer over the wall. The stupid thing was too tall and difficult to climb, at least for my limited cat burglar skills. I'm sure James Bond would be on the other side in seconds.

I carefully made my way back to the car, avoiding the prickly shrubs and occasional hole, mumbling about applying to spy school.

Time to enlist my friends, try to convince Penny and Dana to go along with this crazy idea. I'd keep Sandy out of it; she worked for the Sheriff's Department and getting caught wouldn't be good for her continued employment.

As for the three of us teachers, a charge of trespassing wasn't a career buster.

I drove back to town apprehensive about the visit to the ice house and talking to Big Fat Benny, I only knew him by reputation and what little my mother had told me.

Then reasoned that the company was a legitimate concern furnishing ice to Sendero and other businesses in the Mountain Communities.

The man's gambling parlor, saloon, hideaway, or whatever, was not a very well-kept secret. I had no idea when or where the illicit games of chance took place and didn't really care.

The ice house was a large building with an office in front and loading bay in the back. The usual procedure for buying a large quantity of ice for parties and such was to speak to the person inside the office, place an order, pay the bill, and drive around back where workers would load it into your vehicle.

This time was a little different; I took a deep breath and opened the glass office door. A woman seated behind the desk looked up from her task, smiled, and came to the counter.

"Good afternoon."

"Hello ... ah, would it be possible to speak to Mr. Edmonds?"

She hesitated slightly. "I'll check, sometimes he leaves out the back way. Could I have your name?"

"I'm Maris Connelly."

The secretary disappeared through a door and returned a few minutes later.

"Please come around the counter."

I followed her down a short hall; Big Fat Benny loomed in an entryway.

"Thank you, Helen ... Maris, this is a surprise!"

Helen quickly departed, as Mr. Edmonds escorted me inside his office.

I don't know what I expected, a few slot machines and a card table perhaps. The large room contained a substantial wooden desk, leather chairs, bookcase, and lovely pictures of Paris street scenes on the walls ... quite a nice workspace.

I couldn't resist taking a closer look at the paintings. "I'm a fan of quaint scenes too, I see you like Marilyn Dunlap."

Mr. Edmonds joined me in front of a picture of an old-fashioned cheese shop on a cobbled street. "I like Dunlap, David Glover, Carole Spendeu, and many more.

Please sit down."

I perched on one of the leather chairs; he eased himself behind the desk.

"Thank you for seeing me, I know you're a busy man."

Benny was tall and heavily built with piercing blue eyes and a full head of faded brown hair. He studied my face and seemed amused.

"What can I do for you ... I doubt it involves the production of ice."

I inhaled deeply. "It's rather complicated."

I tried to be as succinct as possible; Mr. Edmonds listened quietly, and occasionally tapped his beefy fingers on the desk.

I presented my phone with the picture of the license plate. He thought the mud-spattered and difficult to see numbers were done on purpose too. Then asked the reason for my visit since the authorities were involved.

I didn't want to say, psycho Jason Tanner, was such a low-life that he might spend his leisure time in unsavory environments such as Benny's establishments.

Instead, thought the delivery drivers might keep an eye out for either a white van or the old maroon junker. The ice trucks went to all the Mountain Communities on a regular basis.

Benny Edmonds wasn't stupid, I'm sure he knew what I was after ... information on Jason Tanner. Perhaps the demented driver was somewhere in the area lurking

about, bent on pursuing me for whatever reason? The second encounter was intentional, no possibility of it being an accident.

Mr. Edmonds had all the details, description of the cars and Tanner. He wrote down the number of the van, the man would probably have the driver's license picture in a few hours. I'm sure he "knew people."

I was assured that his crew would look out for the two vehicles. Before I left, as usual, he inquired after my mother.

As I drove away, thought how much of an impression my mom had made on this man. Her act of kindness was never forgotten, how terribly sad that Mr. Edmonds had experienced such awful treatment from other kids.

When school started again, I'd try to make sure no child was treated in such a manner and enlist the help of my fellow teachers.

I parked in the carport with no problem; Jim's truck was gone. The condition of my poor car triggered a flash of anger ... it had to be repaired, and I wasn't going to waste time driving all over the place, especially to Santa Clarita.

Diego's would be just fine, no matter where I went I'd still have to pay a two-hundred-and-fifty-dollar deductible. What a damn nuisance, not to mention the added expense ... I could use that money to do something fun!

"You want to do what!" Penny exclaimed.

"It won't be a problem, it's not like we'd be stealing anything."

"It's still trespassing on private property or breaking and entering."

"I didn't see any sign about trespassing, and we're not breaking into anything, just climbing over a wall and looking."

"What if there are guard dogs ... ever think of that?"

"Didn't see anything about dogs, if that were the case it has to be posted."

I relaxed on the couch and put my feet on Faro's back, he grunted and closed his eyes again.

I had already called Dana about my plan to climb the wall at the Retreat. She thought it would be a great adventure especially if she could dress for the occasion.

Penny wasn't so enthusiastic. "What do you hope to find anyway?"

"The car or van that has caused me problems and pissed me off."

"If we find something ... then what?"

"Tell the authorities, they could get a warrant to search, hit and run is a crime."

"So is trespassing."

"Only if we're caught, which won't happen. All I want to do is look at the back part of the property, see if a vehicle could be hidden there."

"You're like a dog with a bone, can't let it go."

"The experience was terrifying, I still check the mirrors every few seconds when driving, expecting a car to sneak up behind me."

She huffed. "What am I supposed to tell Christian? See you later dear, I'm off to wander around in the dark, climb a block wall and look for a mysterious maroon car?"

I laughed. "Why not, he wouldn't believe it anyway. Okay, say we're having a girl's night out, going to Santa Clarita for dinner and a movie, simple as pie."

Penny grumbled a little more. "What does one wear to something like this?"

"Dark colored old clothes, we have to walk a ways through prickly bushes with the ladder, a rope and flashlight."

"You don't think it will look kind of funny leaving the house with a ladder?"

"I have everything we need. This is what you do, drop off your night prowling clothes during the day, then meet at my place later, change, and we're off."

"Yeah, we're off all right, stark raving mad."

It was difficult not to laugh when Dana arrived the next evening; she was dressed head to toe in camouflage.

"Where did you get that ... outfit?"

143

"Santa Clarita Military Surplus Store. The place is amazing, I'm thinking of going back and buy a gas mask."

I snickered. "What would you use a gas mask for, doubt we'll encounter any bio-hazard stuff anywhere."

Dana parked herself on one of the kitchen chairs. "Just something to have ... a great conversation piece, or use at Halloween, might also come in handy for cooking disasters."

"Well you look just ... great, love the American flag embroidered on the baseball cap."

"Yeah, I really like it. I brought another flashlight too."

The dogs were outside I had blocked the doggie-door, so the girls could come in without being assaulted. The pooches were hanging around the screen door looking piti-ful. I'd give them a treat before we left.

Penny arrived, once inside, stared at Dana, and shook her head, probably in disbelief. "Maybe we should discuss this escapade a little more."

"We might talk ourselves out of it." I stated.

"Stop thinking and get changed, I didn't get all dressed up in a cool commando outfit just to chicken out," Dana de-clared.

Penny sighed. "Where's my stuff?"

"In the second bedroom."

One had to admit the three of us looked ridiculous. Da-na in camouflage, Penny in black with a knitted beanie, and me in dark blue cargo pants, olive drab MASH 4077th T-shirt and boonie hat.

I thought about taking a picture but decided it might be a reminder of an adventure gone wrong, maybe even disas-trous.

My five-foot stepladder was already in the car; the front passenger seat could fold flat, so there wasn't a problem stowing it away.

I unblocked the doggie-door before leaving, so the crit-ters could come and go as they pleased.

After driving slowly up the street in back of the Retreat without any lights, I parked on the side of the road. The dome light was switched off so nothing inside the car would be visible.

Now all we had to do was carry the ladder to the wall, climb over, and hope nothing awful happened.

Agents McAllister and Andrews had made themselves comfortable under the oak trees up the hill ... as comfortable as night surveillance could be. The Coverdale Retreat was "iffy" but since they had nothing else at the moment, keeping it under close observation was the best they could do.

The CBI had issued a BOLO to the counties where the victims with missing kidneys had been found ... be on the lookout for a tan Ford van.

After months of nothing, a motel clerk mentioned he had seen a light-colored van driving fast out of the parking area. No plate numbers, but maybe it was a Ford.

The Sheriff' Department in Sendero reported the incidents involving a van, which might be a connection ... granted it was microscopic, but at this point, the only thing they had.

The CBI came to Sendero where two vans, two hit-and-run occurrences seemed to be centered around the Coverdale Retreat. They had a name, Jason Tanner. He was a person of interest, registered owner of a Ford van, driver of another vehicle that tried to damage Ms. Connelly. Slim pickin's to say the least.

From victim's statements, a man with longish dark hair, sunglasses and a baseball cap, and a blond woman met them at the bus station and escorted them to a car.

Once inside the vehicle, everything went black ... until the young people woke up mutilated in a motel room.

Bill Andrews didn't like the quiet of the countryside. He was a city guy use to traffic noise and teeming humanity. McAllister would rather be somewhere a little cooler and not sitting in the dark under a tree. He could use a chilled glass of wine and tried not to think of creepy-crawly things that wanted his blood or to burrow under his skin.

Bill Andrews whispered. "We have company, take a look over there," and handed Ryan the night vision binoculars.

McAllister watched the figures, and softly started to narrate. "The Three Musketeers carrying a ladder ... make that ... The Three Stooges, Curly, Larry and Moe. The one wearing camouflage just stepped in a hole and fell down . . .oops, the flashlight went out too.

You probably won't believe this, but our not so stealthy intruders are women. I can see our old pal Maris Connelly and friends quite clearly. They've put the ladder and rope down to help Camouflage Curly find her flashlight ... that's right, shake the thing a few times to make it work.

The one with the beanie thing on her head must have pressed the wrong button on the flashlight; it's started to strobe. Strobe-Larry seems panicked; Maris/Moe grabs it and frantically tries to make it stop pulsating.

All is well, Camouflage-Curly is out of the hole, her flashlight seems to be working ... nope, went off again. Guess they can manage with one.

The girls have positioned the ladder next to the wall, but seem to be having a little trouble getting it to fold out. Damn! That must have hurt; Strobe-Larry pinched her finger or broke a nail and is flapping her hand in pain.

Camouflage-Curly to the rescue, she strikes the hinge on the ladder several blows to make it straighten out. Maris/Moe pulls on her side and after a brief struggle the pesky thing is ready to climb ... almost.

Rock it back and forth several times to balance it, now step on the first rung ... too wobbly, adjust it again after kicking away some dirt.

Strobe-Larry on one side, Camouflage-Curly on the

146

other and up goes Maris/Moe ... and back down again, forgot the flashlight.

Okay, up the steps ... long pause to figure the best way to get off the ladder and onto the wall carrying the flashlight, throws a leg over the top, decides to lay down ... and gracefully rolls off the other side."

All through the blow-by-blow account Bill Andrews is choking with silent laughter. Ryan placed the field glasses on the ground, buried his face in the crook of his arm to keep from chortling out loud. Each time he tries to make a comment it turns into   uncontrolled mirth.

"I hope she's okay, didn't hear any screaming," he finally managed to gasp, then began to cackle again.

Bill picked up the binoculars. "I wonder how she plans to get back over the wall, fly?"

Ryan made himself take several deep breaths. "What's happening now?"

"The two on this side are trying to uncoil the rope, I guess the plan is to climb back over using the rope. Maris/Moe has the only working flashlight that's now on the other side of the wall."

"I'm tempted to help, but not enough to actually make our presence known. No telling what they might do if they saw us venture their direction in the dark."

Bill chuckled. "Wouldn't want to be responsible for a medical emergency, we'll stay put and watch."

Chapter 17

I lay in the bushes for quite a while trying to decide if I was mortally wounded. My uncontrolled heartbeat could indicate I'd croak any second.

Okay, I was breathing, able to move my arms and legs, and could feel the spiky stalks of whatever shrub I landed upon stab into my back.

With all the grace of a newborn foal I managed to extricate my body from the trampled foliage and locate the flashlight.

I could see Penny peeking over the wall. "Are you all right?" she said in a low voice.

"Yeah, just scratched up a bit. I'm going to have a look around, be back shortly, dangle the rope so I can find you."

Eventually, I wriggled my way through the bushes and headed toward the buildings. These two structures were tucked out of the way and separated from the pool area by a driveway, wrought iron fence, and a massive amount of bougainvillea.

Bougainvillea plants can inflict severe damage with their large, tough thorns. I've encountered a few and came away with deep, painful, lacerations, a shrub to avoid.

The buildings were small; one looked like it could be a garage, due to the roll up door, which was securely locked.

The other was about the same size, no windows and a metal entry door that had a rather formidable reinforced latch.

The night reconnaissance hadn't resulted in much of anything. A car or van could be parked in the garage ... or the place was just for storage. The other building was probably used for supplies and stuff ... so much for a spectacular discovery, my inquisitiveness hadn't been satisfied at all.

I sighed and turned around, crossed the flat area, then scrambled up a short incline, went through the bushes near the wall and found the rope.

Called softly to the girls that I was going to toss the flashlight over and be ready to pull me up. A few moments later grabbed the rope with both hands, pushed with the sides of my boots on the cement blocks and pulled with my arms until I could put one leg over the wall.

The agents watched, as Maris crawled over the fence and climbed down the ladder, quite surprised nothing awful happened. It didn't take very long for the girls to fold the ladder, coil the rope, and make their way out of the field without mishap.

No alarms had sounded so whatever Maris was doing hadn't been detected.

McAllister was more than a little curious to find the reason for a nighttime sortie. Might be worthwhile getting to know the lady a little better.

The three of us sat around the kitchen table. Bagels and cream cheese with a sparking rosé seemed like an excellent idea.

"This whole scheme was for nothing!" Penny muttered.

"I wouldn't say it was for nothing, I found two locked buildings and no suspicious vehicles."

Dana sliced a bagel in half and tore off bits to feed the dogs that drooled on her camouflage pants. "You monsters are almost as persistent as my cat."

"I wouldn't call Evenrude a cat, more like a forty-pound, tac-trained killer, she-devil."

Penny slathered more cream cheese on her bread. "Where did you come up with a name like Evenrude?"

"Because she has the loudest purr ever, sounds like an outboard motor. Just because she hates everyone except me is no reason to say mean things about her. Rudy even nips me when she's had enough attention. I also think that Tanner guy is probably long gone, so now you can forget about it."

"Yeah, guess so, but I still have to fix my car, which is a pain."

"Think nice thoughts, in a few weeks we'll be at the beach, nothing to do but veg-out, play in the ocean and relax. Maybe my sweetie, Steve, can spend a day it's not that far to Oxnard."

One had to agree with Dana; it would be a fun week, only an hour drive and lots of things to do along the coast.

⌘

It was like some magnetic force pulled me back to the museum even after all the boxes in the basement had been sorted.

Perhaps things were back to normal, I hadn't felt anything weird for a while, no soft voice speaking Spanish in the night, or an impression of something moving about the bedroom.

A few people had stopped to look at the three pictures, and Castro memorabilia, then went on to other exhibits. I watched from a distance pretending to study the beautiful Native American baskets inside a glass case.

Nothing had changed in the pictures from what I could tell, but that didn't mean when I approached things would be ... customary.

I took my time walking around the displays, then stood in front of the paintings. The Diamondback Cut seemed to shimmer, and the face of the cowboy was quite distinct, dark eyes and a big grin ... his arm and hand stretched toward me.

My skin prickled, I blinked several times and tried make my heart stop fluttering.

I wasn't going to panic and hurry away ... this time I'd stay.

In a breathless whisper I murmured. "There must be something in the Cut you want me to find. I'll try again but have no idea what to look for ... a sign of some kind would be helpful."

A few seconds later the painting had returned to its usual, undisturbed self.

Well, that was interesting, chilling, but interesting. No thunder, lighting or earthquake occurred as I slowly walked to my car. Maybe I should go at this from a different angle. Isabella Castro ... what happened to her?

I'd call mom when I got home see if she knew something ... were there more paintings, if so, what was the subject matter?

"Don't have the slightest idea about Isabella, aside from the three pictures in the museum."

I was on the phone sitting outside watching the dogs chase around the yard. "Nothing at all!"

"Maris, the girl wasn't famous, she was a local artist ... and a woman. During the time Isabella was painting, females were not supposed to do anything but marry, have children and tend to her domestic duties. A few women artists painted using a man's name."

"I guess I could look into the historical documents. The California State Archives for birth and death records is online."

"I think that might be the place to start."

We continued to chat about the usual things ... dad, horses, the grandkids that visited over the weekend and so forth.

The call ended when the doorbell rang. Since the dogs were distracted I could answer without them bothering whomever. I peeked through the little window and found two CBI agents standing on the porch.

As I unlocked and opened the door, wondered why they had returned. "Good afternoon."

"Good afternoon Ms. Connelly, may we come in?"

I stood aside to let them enter.

We sat in the living room. "Would you like something to drink, ice tea, soda?"

"Nothing, thank you," said Sergeant Andrews.

"A few more questions just to clear up some things," McAllister stated.

I nodded and maneuvered my bare feet under the chair. The gorgeous man probably thought I didn't have any shoes, since I was always barefoot when we chatted. I also noticed he studied my shirt and wondered if he "got" the quip. *My two favorite plays by Shakespeare are Romeo and Juliet.*

"Why were you and your friends scaling the wall at the Coverdale Retreat?"

What a great way to open the conversation, direct and to the point! It probably wouldn't be good if I denied everything, nothing wrong in telling the truth since I couldn't think of anything better.

"To see what was on the other side," I replied and hoped my voice wasn't as shaky as my hands, which I kept folded in my lap.

The Detective took a deep breath. "And what did you find on the other side?"

"Bougainvillea."

"Bougainvillea?"

"Those things can inflict a lot of damage, I mean like ... they're lethal!"

McAllister narrowed his eyes a little. "What else?"

"Two small buildings."

"Ms. Connelly, what did you hope to find?" Sergeant Andrews asked.

I pushed back the strands of hair that had come out of my ponytail. "I was looking for the van or maroon car. I know you think I'm loony, but I know what I saw ... two vans or possibly one vehicle that has been painted. A beige van almost sent me into a telephone pole and disappeared behind the gates of that place, and the same model white van was parked in front later.

When my brother questioned people at the Retreat, he was told it had to be a mistake; no van had passed through their entryway. From what I have seen of those gates, some-one must grant access before a vehicle can enter.

As far as I know the very substantial iron portals are never left open, at least not when I have driven by."

Detective McAllister continued. "So, you thought it would be a good idea to have a look."

"It couldn't do any harm, why not check those buildings in the back, they might be hiding something. There must be a connection between Jason Tanner, the Retreat, and him try-ing to run me into the side of a rather substantial hill. He is the registered owner of a van and the driver of the maroon car."

Sergeant Andrews was very blunt. "You cannot contin-ue to involve yourself in this matter, no more climbing over fences, I would suggest you keep away from the Retreat."

I was about to make a scintillating reply when the dogs erupted through the doggie-door. Faro was chasing Hallie, probably because she had the mangy red rag in her mouth. They halted for a fraction of a second to decide that the visitors weren't a threat, and then proceeded with their standard greeting.

Hallie would really like to be a lap dog so advanced on Detective McAllister, while Faro jumped on the couch between the two men and grabbed onto Sergeant Andrews sleeve.

I dashed to take hold of collars and drag the hulking beast off the startled policemen.

It took a bit of doing but finally had the animals under control ... sorta-kinda.

"I'm so sorry, they can be rambunctious when meeting new people."

Detective McAllister gingerly removed the red, soggy, rag from his lap. "I gather they flunked out of obedience school."

"Yeah, we were asked to leave when Faro tried to carry a Cocker Spaniel around by his head. Don't get me wrong, he wasn't attacking, just really liked the little guy."

Sergeant Andrews got to his feet and was checking his jacket sleeve for any rips, tears, or lacerations ... all was fine just a bit moist. "We'll call ahead the next time we visit."

Faro stood on his hind legs and put his front paws on the somewhat apprehensive man's shoulders. They were eyeball to eyeball.

"Faro, get down ... he must like you, doesn't do that to just anyone," I announced and tried to control my gasps of laughter.

The Nordic-god Detective gave Hallie a scratch behind the ears, which encouraged the animal to rub her slobbery jowls on his pant leg. "Ms. Connelly please leave the sleuthing to us, we don't want anything to happen to you or your friends."

I took a deep breath and sighed. "Fine, but I wouldn't be surprised if something wonky was going on at that high-class joint."

Andrews and McAllister made their way through town to the Sheriff's Department.

"Maris Connelly, her friends, and those dogs are a disaster waiting to happen," Bill muttered.

Ryan chuckled. "You have to admit they have a certain entertainment value. Don't tell me you were intimidated by the dogs, Faro was being friendly."

"That monster could have eaten off my face if he wanted to!"

"Obviously he didn't want to, or you'd be missing a nose."

Bill grunted. "Thanks to 'The Three Stooges' we know a little something about the two buildings in back, but no reason to barge in and have a look around. It would be really nice to locate Jason Tanner; he might have something interesting to say."

Ryan nodded; his thoughts were a long way from the reckless and egregious Mr. Tanner. He was wondering how to move the relationship with Maris to something a little more personal. That might be a little tricky, kind of a gray area; she was a victim as well as a witness in a case.

In reality the hit-and-run involved the Sendero Sheriff's Department not the CBI. His actual meeting with her was about an entirely different matter ... the van. So, to his way of thinking she wasn't technically involved in his case ... not really, not very much, maybe.

He would give this matter some more thought.

⌘

"Next summer we should go back to England. I've thought up a new quest for us to pursue," I announced when the gang was assembled at the cantina.

Adam adjusted his glasses." I've been thinking about

155

that, time for another odyssey. What do you have in mind?"

"What's left, we've hunted for and found Atlantis, King Arthur and Merlin, the Loch Ness Monster, and the Seven Ancient Wonders of the World," Dana declared.

As usual, Penny had to clear up matters. "Technically, we might have some difficulty with a few things."

I rolled my eyes. "Oh, come on, what things!"

"I mean we can't say for sure that the Greek Island of Santorini was Atlantis, even though it was partially destroyed by a volcanic eruption in the 16th century B.C."

"We visited the ruins of Akrotiri, saw for ourselves the town was advanced for a Minoan Bronze-Age Settlement. Three storied buildings, indoor plumbing, and no human skeletal remains, which meant the population had time to get away to Crete or wherever." I replied.

"We found Merlin's cave in Wales, unfortunately the old boy was gone, "Christian added. "King Arthur's supposed birthplace at Tintagel, in southern England was fun."

Dana moaned. "Must have been a gazillion stairs, Merlin could have magicked an escalator for god's sake."

Sandy brought up that even after spending part of a day sailing around Scotland's Loch Ness we failed to catch sight of "Nessie". But that didn't mean the creature wasn't there.

The Ancient Seven Wonders have been somewhat daunting, but we persevered. The Great Pyramid at Giza is still around; the other six wonders are ruins.

We stood where the Statue of Zeus was located in Olympia, Greece. Surveyed fragments of the Temple of Artemis at Ephesus, Turkey, and contemplated the stones that remain of the Mausoleum at Halicarnassus.

In the harbor at Rhodes we wandered about where the Colossus was said to have been, same with the Lighthouse of Alexandria, Egypt.

There is a slight problem with the Hanging Gardens of Babylon ... the remains of the ancient city of Babylon are in

Iraq. So, we decided that artifacts, such as clay tablets, jewelry, amulets, and so forth from Babylonia, in the British Museum, would have to do.

"I think we should follow the Viking invasions, start with Lindisfarne, in northern England, then on to York, Dublin, Paris and end up in Iceland."

"FYI the Vikings didn't ravage and pillage Dublin, they expanded the tiny settlement that was already there," Penny stated, then frowned slightly. "I thought we were going to Hogwarts, do a Harry Potter trek through England?"

"I think we should vote, I've wanted to matriculate to Hogwarts for years," Dana stated.

Christian snorted. "You do realize Hogwarts School of Witchcraft and Wizardry isn't real, besides you're too old, gotta be between the ages of eleven and eighteen to attend."

"What do think a magic wand is for ... I could be sixteen again. Wouldn't go for a whole year, maybe take a summer class in Potions or Flying."

The discussion became heated over which courses were the best ... Defense Against the Dark Arts, Care of Magical Creatures, Charms, History of Magic ... I favored Transfiguration. What wonderful new form would suit me?

Chapter 18

The Los Angeles County historical documents archives started around 1907. I didn't think I'd have much luck in finding anything on the Castro family in the 1850's.

At that time the ranch was rather isolated, not especially close to the few small settlements nestled in the mountains, even the tiny village of Los Angeles was fifty miles or so away.

But all was not lost; it was customary for the family bible to be a place to record births, deaths, and marriages. Could be the Castro family had such a text.

Old Tom, the caretaker, was sure to have contact information for Dennis Castro.

I'd go riding later; have a little conversation with the caretaker.

Perhaps my mother would like to come along if I could manage an invitation to their place in Santa Clarita. Leslie Connelly had the right credentials, a professor, artist, interested in Isabella Castro and her work, as well as knowing the family. In fact, it would be better to have her initiate the communication.

It must be Jim's day off; he had moved his truck and was in the process of vacuuming the inside. The fellow was religious about keeping his vehicle clean, a trait I was sadly lacking. Every once in a while, I maneuvered my car through the "minute wash" at the gas station.

I stood at the window and stared, couldn't help but admire his fine self; as usual, attired in board shorts, his tanned body powerful and well-toned. He looked up, saw me and waved, then motioned to come outside.

"When are you going to have your car repaired?"

I sighed. "I don't know, soon, I guess."

"You might want to take a few scrapings of the maroon paint, just to have some evidence in case the old beater is ever found."

I looked back at my sad little car. "If I recall, the deputy did that when taking my statement, but it couldn't hurt to have another sample as a backup."

"If you get a plastic baggie I'll do it for you."

I hurried inside and returned with a small sandwich size bag and watched as Jim carefully scrapped shavings of dark paint into the packet and sealed the top.

"Keep it tucked away somewhere," and handed me the small sample.

"Thanks. Haven't seen you around much."

"Busy, taken a few extra shifts, covering for some of the guys wanting a few days off. What's new with you?"

"Not a blessed thing, doing a little research on the Castro's."

Jim leaned against my car. "Haven't experienced any more weird stuff?"

I traced my toe over a small crack in the cement driveway. "There was something with the paintings in the museum, gave me the willies, probably need to make another trip to Diamond Back Cut."

"Don't go alone, wouldn't want anything to happen to

you. The Cut is a different kind of place ... and there are the snakes."

I gave a slight shudder. "Yeah ... snakes. The next time I have a burning desire to visit, I'll let you know."

Jim stepped a little closer, his dark green eyes locked with mine, he reached out and brushed back a strand of hair that dangled around my face. "Something to be said for burning desire." Then backed away and returned to his chore.

I hustled into the house clutching the baggie. Okay, what should I make of that little incident? I mean, he didn't do much of anything other than push back my hair. But he stood so close, with no shirt, and green eyes ... and stuff.

Get a grip Maris, Jim Hayden was being Jim Hayden; he liked women ... a lot ... and wasn't my type.

⌘

The Castro house in Santa Clarita was in an upscale neighborhood, not a mansion, but very nice. Mom had made the phone call and Mrs. Castro invited us to visit, she remembered my mother and father before the family moved away.

Valerie Castro was a heavyset woman, with thick salt and pepper hair and friendly bright brown eyes. She cheerfully greeted us at the door and escorted us into a well-appointed living room.

"Lesley Connelly, it's been quite a few years since I've seen you."

Mom smiled. "At least ten or so, this is my daughter Maris."

"Maris, I remember you as a tom-boy on a horse."

"Guess I haven't changed much, still love to ride horses."

160

"Would you like something cold to drink?"

"Nothing thanks. We really appreciate you seeing us," my mother replied.

Mrs. Castro rubbed her hands together. "After your phone call I brought out the old bible and a few drawings that I'm sure were done by Isabella. They're in the other room." She gestured for us to follow.

The book and three sketches had been placed on a soft towel spread over the dining table.

"The bible is old and written in Spanish, the first date is from 1790," Valerie said almost reverently.

Mom gently touched the creased and worn leather cover. It was dark brown with scrolls of a faded gold color. The title in large script read *La Biblia Los Sacros Libros* .

Valerie carefully turned to the page where the family names were neatly written. Some of the entries were faded and one had to look closely in order to read the script.

The first line was for Ygnacio del Valle and Ana Alvarado and the date married.

The list continued with marriages, births and deaths of relatives. About half way down the page we located Jose Covarrubias, then his daughter Maria. She was the girl who had married Antonio Castro.

The Castro family was large, four boys and two girls, Reina and Isabella. Reina married a Del La Torre, and in 1854, Isabella wed Juan Moreno. Unfortunately, she died two years later.

So, Isabella was only twenty when she died, right after giving birth to a son who also perished. The child's name was Joaquin. How sad, I envisioned her living a long happy life.

I sighed and turned my attention to the sketches, the first depicted a galloping palomino horse, another gave prominence to a beautiful tree by a lake,

and the third was of a handsome young man.

161

I inhaled deeply and studied the familiar face of the cowboy from the museum pictures. The same person, who changed positions, grinned and beckoned.

Mother looked at me carefully, aware that I was a little disturbed. I continued to gaze at the sketch until she nudged my arm. "We want to thank you for letting us see these lovely family heirlooms, Isabella Castro was a talented young woman. As I mentioned in our phone conversation I've been curious to know if she created more works of art."

Mrs. Castro smiled. "At least we have a few pictures to remind us of her, and a little peek at what it was like in this area a hundred and sixty years ago."

I finally found my voice. "Do you know who the young man in the sketch might be?"

"I have no idea, could be anyone, or a person she imagined."

We said our goodbyes, mother invited our hostess to come visit sometime, and we left.

Before Mom started the car she asked. "You looked like you were in shock, what happened?"

"The guy in the sketch is the same person that magically moves around in the paintings at the museum!"

She took a deep breath and started the car, we drove a few blocks then merged onto the freeway before speaking. "Are you sure?"

"Very sure!"

"You mentioned that the fellow in the painting could be Joaquin Murrieta. Isabella married someone called Juan Moreno in 1854, I think Murrieta was killed in 1853."

I adjusted the vent so the air conditioner wasn't blowing on me. "It's said that Murrieta wasn't the person who was killed, could be the stories are true. Think about it, if the outlaw was presumed dead, then no one was looking for him anymore.

Isabella's husband had the same initials, JM, and the

baby who died was called Joaquin. Could be our local bandit changed his name and lived on at the Castro ranch."

Mom shrugged. "Well, we won't ever know what actually happened those many years ago."

"True, but why am I on the receiving end of this ghostly attention?"

"That is an excellent question, all we can do is hope everything will settle down soon."

I couldn't agree more; at least whatever was going on didn't seem evil, just weird and a little unnerving. Legends ... always some trouble when it came to legends.

The next morning I decided to take my car to Diego's for repair, I had stalled long enough. It would be necessary to engage a rental, which was a pain and costly.

Diego Estrada had been in the auto repair business for years. He and his two boys, Bobby and Jesse, were well known and respected for their excellent work and honesty.

I parked near the open garage doors and went looking for Diego. I found him in the small office. "Hi ... see you're hard at work."

He stopped writing and looked up. "Maris, good morning ... finally decided to have the body work done? Might take a week or so."

I frowned. "Yeah, figured as much, can one of the boys give me a ride home?"

"Bobby is out back tinkering with his latest project, should be able to give you a lift."

We walked around the corner and into a smaller garage where I could see someone hunched over the front end of a car. It wasn't just any old car it was a 1957 Chevy Bel-Air, a real classic.

"Bobby! Come out of there, Maris needs a ride home?"

The fellow straightened up, wiped his hands on a cloth, massaged his back, and turned around.

I had gone to school with Bobby; he was a couple of

163

years older. I'd been an after school tutor and helped him with English, putting stuff down on paper wasn't his strong suit. Mechanics was another story.

"Wow, what a great ride! You gonna race it?"

Bobby grinned. "Hey, Maris ... nah, not this one, fix it up and sell it for a nice profit."

"What do you have engine wise?"

"383 ... a killer street machine, goes like a bat. Still a lot of work to be done it's a mess."

I peeked at the engine then looked inside, the interior was a shamble. The back seat was missing, the front bench area was torn, a towel covered the driver's side, and the headliner was sagging.

"Got a ways to go in there."

"Yeah, a complete gut job inside. Understand some jerk banged up your car?"

I nodded. "Better the car than me, but still have to repair the damage, and rent a car until you lovely people get mine fixed."

Bobby closed the hood and made sure it was latched securely. "Tell ya what, if you don't mind driving a wreck, you can use this one, purrs like a kitten. It will just sit here for a while, waiting for stuff to be upholstered, found some bucket seats for the front."

I grinned and rubbed my hand over the mostly primer exterior. "You sure about this? I have a tendency to put my foot down a little too hard when driving a "go-fast" and this is definitely a "go-fast".

Bobby chuckled. "Try to keep it under seventy-five or eighty. I've had it up around a hundred thirty at the track. Don't think too many cars can get passed it on the street. Keys are in it."

I climbed behind the wheel and started the wicked machine. Just like Bobby said, the engine purred and the wonderful, unique deep rumble of an aggressive modified muffler made me laugh.

"Straight through glasspack?

"Flowmaster 50 series, be nice and keep it on the mild side ... not a flat out 'wake the neighbors' roar."

"I'll be sure to drive like the proverbial "little old lady" no stop-light tag. Thank you, I'll take good care of it ... promise."

Driving this thing on the freeway was appealing, but I didn't want to risk attracting the attention of the Highway Patrol. One could always count on those guys lurking around somewhere. Instead, I knew a section of country road that would be perfect to let this monster run.

My father taught us kids to drive on this particular road. It was mostly straight, no traffic, and doubtful any law enforcement would be loitering about.

I cranked the machine up to eighty-five, wasn't brave enough to go faster. What a rush!

Eventually headed back to town couldn't spend the day racing around like a mad woman, though it was tempting.

When I pulled under the carport couldn't resist making it growl just for a few seconds. Long enough for Jim to appear at his door, then walk around his truck and stare.

"Where did you find that? I doubt the rental car place just happened to have this thing on hand."

I rolled up the window and got out. "My friend loaned it until mine is fixed. Gotta love it!"

"Sounds like it has some muscle."

"Oh yeah, couldn't resist trying it out just a tad, might get away from you if a person isn't careful."

"Something you should consider, wouldn't want to see you in a ditch or worse."

"Not working today?"

Jim stretched, then ran his fingers through his hair. "Working nights for the rest of the week, just about to take a nap when you showed up."

I patted his arm. "Promise not to make any loud noises, get some rest, see you later."

A white compact drove slowly past the two people talking in the driveway.

They glanced at the vehicle and continued their conversation. The occupant of the car made sure he couldn't be identified. The guy was wearing sunglasses and the longish hair was hidden under a baseball cap.

Jason Tanner couldn't seem to keep away from the blond bitch. She was the cause of his difficulties, Jay was pissed and said they had to lay low, not make any more deliveries for a while. No shipment! No money!

He needed money ... he owed people ... people who didn't like it when he couldn't pay.

Jay had smacked him around after learning about the hit and run with the old junker, now both vehicles were not to be driven and parked out of sight.

Jay wouldn't trust him to use that flashy gas-guzzler so he had to borrow Ashley's pathetic car. His girlfriend wasn't too thrilled about it either.

He would have to be patient, something difficult for him. However, thinking of ways to make the blond bitch pay occupied a lot of his time.

He followed her around, knew where she went. She spent a lot of time at the museum, visited the house where the woman with the little kid lived, and the place near the school where the short blond resided.

He had tailed her to the farm outside of town twice. But didn't like being on a country road, not enough traffic to hide what he was doing, thought it would look suspicious to park on the side of the road for hours.

It was only a matter of time before she would be in a situation favorable to him and the snooping bitch would no longer be a problem.

Chapter 19

I answered the call on my cell phone and immediately recognized Big Fat Benny's distinctive voice. "Good afternoon Maris, I have information about the individual you seek. This person has been seen in Lavelle, at the Frenchman's Tavern."

The tiny village of Lavelle was across the interstate, near the much larger town of San Emideo. Lavelle had a bar, mom and pop market-gas station, minuscule post office, and an interesting antique place that was open three days a week.

There were also cabins scattered up the road in the pine tree forest, many permanent residences, others were rentals.

I inhaled deeply. "Thank you so much Mr. Edmonds, I'll make sure my brother has this tip, I know the Sheriff's Department will check it out."

"Always a pleasure to help, if you require anything else, let me know."

I wondered what kind of help he was talking about; glad the man was sort of my friend and not the other way around. Wouldn't want to get on the wrong side of Mr. Edmonds.

So, the rat-bastard was hanging around Lavelle,

couldn't hurt to take a look, Tanner might be renting a cabin in the area. It was a wonderful excuse to drive the 57, maybe stop in at the Frenchman's Tavern and have a beer.

After that little jaunt, I'd give Scott a call; he'd probably have someone from the Sheriff's Department stop by the bar.

Penny and Dana were unavailable, but Adam wanted to get out of the house, his boys would be occupied with their summer activities for several hours.

"Gonna let me drive?"

I grinned. "Reckon so, if you promise not to hurt it. Bobby Estrada was nice enough to loan it for a few days.

Adam closed his eyes and sighed. "This reminds me of Linda Jo back in Oklahoma, she had a 57, not a cop car in town could catch her. Jo drove the booze her family made at their place around Bluedog Slick."

"She was a "shine runner?"

Adam nodded. "Jo knew every road in Osage County, and at what speed she could take a curve in all weather conditions."

"So, the Revenuers never got her?" I chuckled

"Nope, could shoot the gap at Tallchief Cove and scream by Collinsville with someone on her tail, and flat run away."

"Forgot you were an Okie," I teased. "We'll cross the overpass to San Emidio and have a beer in Lavelle."

"What's in Lavelle?"

"Just want to have a look around, take the 57 up into the hills."

Adam narrowed his eyes. "Un-huh ... don't confuse me with Dana, she might believe your cock and bull story."

We sat in the car; I pressed on the gas ever so slightly. "Ah ... just listen to that sound and feel the power of the engine."

"Don't change the subject."

"Could be that psycho, Jason Tanner, is around the area ... maybe."

"Could be ... we might run into some trouble."

"Like you never saw trouble in Afghanistan."

Adam sighed. "That was when I was young and stupid, long ago and far away."

"We'll chalk it up that now you're just stupid like me."

"Why do I let you talk me into the crazy stuff we do?"

"Because deep down you know there is a wild side that's demanding to be free."

Adam rubbed his hands together. "Lead on Sherlock, remember, I drive back."

Frenchman's had just opened when we arrived, no one inside but the tavern keeper. We sat at the bar, ordered a beer and chatted with the talkative fellow. I asked if the tourists kept him busy during the summer and added that we were from Sendero. As a reasonable excuse for our visit, mentioned we had heard that new parcels of land were for sale somewhere in this area.

He didn't know of anything around Lavelle, more likely in San Emidio.

I returned to the subject of tourists, the more disruptive kind, and disclosed that some of the drinking establishments got a little wild on the other side of the highway.

The bartender alluded that Pinky's could qualify as wild and laughed, said the Frenchman wasn't in the same league.

I couldn't think of how to inquire about Tanner, especially if the authorities would be doing the same thing. My brother might be pissed if he knew I was snooping in police business. Adam and I left a short while later.

The road up the mountain was narrow and winding. We could see cabins nestled back in the pines, some were grand log homes, others, small A-frames, and a few partially hidden in the trees.

Sometimes we could find a car parked in a driveway or

near the house, but mostly didn't find any vehicles at all.

I pulled over and we changed drivers. Adam enjoyed every minute behind the wheel; he punched it going from Lavelle to the overpass. I promised we would take it out on the country road, where he could really fly.

Jason Tanner fought down the fear that made his stomach queasy. He had peeked through the curtains when he heard the rumble of pipes cruising past the cabin and recognized the bitch's new car. Even though few vehicles traveled the road, he always checked to see who drove by.

What the hell was she doing around here? No way she could know the old beater was tucked away in the garage out back. He hadn't driven it since trying to run her into a mountain.

Only went to the local bar, which was walking distance and used his girlfriend's car when he followed the nosy biddy around Sendero. It was time to put a stop to her meddling!

Exactly how to do that was making his head pound, he wasn't too good at working things out. Jay always made nasty comments when he tried to offer his opinion about stuff. So he kept his mouth shut and did as he was told to avoid a smash to the face and hurtful remarks.

A while back Jay had screamed and ranted that the hit-and-run would involve cops then threw a bottle at him. He had to hide at Ashley's place for several days.

He'd figure something out on his own, not tell Jay anything until it was over. It was the blond bitch's fault the business had to shut down.

To his way of thinking, if he could get the woman out of the way, everything would be like before. Business would pick up and he could make some badly needed money ... but most of all Jay would be happy again.

⌘

Scott was silent for a moment not especially thrilled at the phone conversation. "Where did you get the information that Tanner might be found in Lavelle?"

"Does it matter? Can't really remember who told me, everyone in town knows about the hit-and-run anyway," I replied, evading the question.

"I'll stop by and check it out, you wouldn't be prying into police business, would you?"

"Oh please, I have no interest in that sort of thing, just thought you might find Mr. Scumbag."

"As I said, I'll stop by, have a chat with whomever. Quite a few rental places around there; too many to even consider checking on.

"Yeah, cabins in the pines and in San Emidio too."

"I also heard that McAllister, the detective from CBI, has been asking about you, have any guess as to why that might be?"

To my way of thinking this revelation could be good or bad. Good that he was interested and also bad that he was interested. Lord, I hoped the man didn't blab about my climbing walls and so forth.

"Asking what about me? Can't say we run in the same social circles, I hardly know the guy."

"Does your social circle include brawling at Pinky's with the Pasco's?"

I figured the family would hear about that ... Sendero is a very small town. "I wasn't brawling, I sang a couple of songs and danced ... end of story."

Scott drew in a long breath. "Riiiight ... I'll run over to Lavelle, see what's going on."

A few hours later Scott had conversed with the bartender at the Frenchmen's Tavern and showed the picture from

171

Tanner's driver's license. The fellow thought it might be the same guy, except now the hair was longer and the face thinner. What he remembered most was the copious amount of booze the man put away and went on about a relative who worked at some doctor's office or something of the sort.

Never saw what kind of car he drove and would be sure to notify the Sheriff's Department if the fellow came in again.

Scott took the road into the mountains, found nothing out of the ordinary, just lots of cabins and places for a person to hide away.

He'd have this area patrolled a little more frequently for a while, not much more he could do right now. It would take a lot of man-hours to check on who owned each property and if the premises were rented out.

His sister could be a handful at times ... should have Dad talk to her about letting the police attend to things.

⌘

"What's the latest crime report?" I asked Sandy that evening at the cantina.

She shook her head and smirked. "Where to begin ... it's been quite a week.

Our local loose cannons were at it again. The De Looney and Kingsley kids blew up the old shed in the De Luna's back yard, they have a penchant for illegal fireworks.

Mrs. Pettigo was rescued from the large tree in her front lawn. Evidently she was trying to make a nest for the birds with lint from her dryer and became marooned when the ladder fell down."

Penny had to add that most birds don't construct a nest in the middle of summer, except for the Goldfinches who are late nesters. To that tidbit of information, we offer our standard reply of Waa Waa Waa.

Sandy continued. "Gene Woods was taken to the clinic ... he was gored by a dead deer."

Everyone at the table was mystified and morbidly tickled at that statement. I managed to gasp out. "How does one get gored by a dead deer?"

Sandy sipped a little more wine. "A group of kids were playing hide and seek, and Gene dashed under a bed, which unfortunately, was already occupied by a set of antlers. Made quite a gash down the kid's leg.

Lastly, Mrs. Abernathy was livid because a drunken tourist found his way on to her property and was sleeping amongst the yard gnomes and flamingoes. Several of the great pink birds were crushed."

Christian was trying to talk without cackling. "Oh no, Mrs. Abernathy's pride and joy ... that awful, too cute yard, full of woodland creatures has been desecrated?"

Sandy nodded and tried to look properly shocked and sad. "Yeah, some of the gnomes were dislodged from their hobbit houses too. The deputies had to forcibly pry the broom out of her hands and save the inebriated guy from being pulverized.

Of course there was the usual squabbling, drinking, and carousing around the camp grounds."

Dana gleefully waved at Steve Mitchell and Jim Hayden who had entered the cantina. We slid over to make room and in a matter of seconds Laura arrived to take their order.

Jim grinned and oozed charm. "Hey Laura."

"Hey Jim, same as usual?"

Same as usual? The guy was here so often to have "same as usual" why didn't that surprise me? But it did, and I was annoyed for some reason. This was my hangout why was he loitering about and being so cozy with Laura?

Maris, Maris you're pathetic, really pathetic! The guy could go where he pleased and with whomever ... not your

173

concern or business.

It was also not my business that I noticed Detective McAllister sitting at the far end of the bar absorbed in a soccer game on television.

The group went their separate ways around seven that evening, Dana left with Steve and Jim said his goodbyes to everyone and moved to lounge at the bar.

I'd probably hear him driving in much later and hoped he could navigate the small space on his side of the carport. Only cared because I didn't want any scrapes or dings on the 57.

Couldn't resist a last look at Detective McAllister who continued to be engrossed in the game. Goodness, he was lovely to look at and imagined that "goodness" had nothing to do with his fine self. Oh my!

⌘

Jason Tanner slouched down in the seat and watched as the blond bitch unlocked the door and wrestled with the huge dogs.

The man was parked across, and a little way down the street in the white car. He would wait for a while before checking out the windows and front door of her place. The sliding glass doors in back would have been much easier to gain entrance but the dogs were in and out all the time.

He couldn't even get close to the fence without the two monsters lurking about the other side.

The cop's truck was gone so he wouldn't have to worry about him for the moment. Just wanted to see what kind of locks he had to deal with, it was amazing how people considered themselves safe, secure and out of harms way, with most of their silly protection devices. He could only hope the woman was the same.

The side gate to the back yard was padlocked; he wouldn't venture that way because of the dogs. The bedroom window was open about three inches; it wouldn't take much to cut the screen and raise the window, something to check out later.

The door was quite substantial, not easy to assault, better move on to the large living room windows. The one in the middle was solid; the two smaller ones on either side might be easy enough, they were also open a few inches.

From his position he could see into the living room and some of the kitchen and hear bits and pieces of a conversation. At first, Jason thought there was another person in the house, but soon realized the bitch was speaking to the dogs.

Peeking through windows was kind of a hobby; Jason couldn't remember why he was so drawn to this activity, he had been creeping about and spying since he was thirteen or fourteen years old.

He loved to observe people at night, the secret watching was exciting, even thrilling for some reason.

This time was strictly a way of gathering more information to add to what he already knew about the blond.

Getting rid of her was the number one thing on his mind; everything would go back to the way it had been before her. He would have money, which was a good thing, but most of all Jay would be happy ... yes ... to see Jay happy was the best thing in the world.

Chapter 20

"I have to go to San Diego in the morning, will you feed Evenrude for a couple of days?"

Dana was never one for telephone niceties like saying "hello or "good morning". "What's in San Diego other than your weird brother?"

"Family duty is calling, my niece 's birthday."

If the care and feeding of Evenrude was involved I needed assurances. "Is your homeowners insurance paid up?

"Of course it is, why do you care?"

"I care a lot, just in case your forty pound killer cat attacks me and inflicts wounds that require a trip to the clinic."

Dana sighed. "Rudy isn't that bad, and all you have to do is check the dry food, give her a half can of Soulistic Aromatic Chicken Dinner, and make sure the water dish is full."

"You're kidding, Soulistic what?"

"The chicken dinner is her favorite right now and keeping to the morning and afternoon schedule is important."

"Schedule? Like a certain time?"

"Yeah, seven in the morning and five in the afternoon."

I was beginning to feel a little apprehensive. "So what happens if I'm a little late, seven-thirtyish or whatever?"

There was a long pause before Dana replied. "I think it would be smart just to keep to the schedule ... one should never press their luck when it comes to meal time."

I wandered out of the kitchen into the living room and sat on the couch, which I had all to myself since Faro and Hallie dashed outside for some reason.

"You could have given me a little more notice, and why didn't you say anything about it before we left the cantina?"

"Must have slipped my mind and then there was Steve and everything."

I huffed a little then agreed; yes, I had a key to her place ... somewhere, and would feed the cat tomorrow evening and the next two days at seven and five. We talked a bit longer about her wonderful boyfriend, and after again promising to be nice to the cat, ended the call.

Jason crouched outside the front window and listened to the one-sided phone conversation. When the dogs bounded into the room he carefully crept away and scuttled back to his car, then headed toward Lavelle.

He hadn't thought much about the bits of conversation he had heard but eventually realized the woman would be somewhere away from her place at a specified time. All he had to do was follow her to wherever she was headed all by herself and ... a big problem would disappear ... simple as that.

Jim Hayden chatted with Laura when possible, and with her sister Angelina, who was tending bar with one of their brothers. In between lulls in the conversation and the soccer game, he looked toward the end of the bar at Ryan McAllister.

From the gossip around the Sherriff's Department he knew the fellow was asking about Maris.

The deputy had to admit the man possessed model good

177

looks and was a member of the elite California Bureau of Investigation. The guys at the station had their own version of the acronym CBI ... Celebrated But Inept.

The members of this group seemed to swoop into an inquiry, monopolize, and often took credit for the hard work of other law enforcement agencies.

Now, this McAllister guy was checking out Maris Connelly. Why? How did she figure in whatever was going on in his investigation? Jim wasn't thrilled about such an interest, especially now that he seemed to be making a little progress with his neighbor.

As much as he wanted another beer, he knew when to stop drinking ... most of the time ... he had to drive home, and a third drink might have repercussions. Especially if he marched himself down to the end of the bar and damaged the pretty face of that tool, Ryan McAllister.

There would probably be another time and place to have a conversation.

One good thing he had going was that he lived next door to the effervescent and irreverent Maris. They had many things in common, which included horses, music, and dogs. He doubted if one lacked an affinity for canines, chances of a successful relationship weren't good.

He should ask her out on a real date, try some fine dining, maybe in Santa Clarita. He knew a place that served great food and featured a rather good jazz group.

On the drive home Jim made the decision to ask the crucial question and try to be prepared for a negative reply.

He sat in the truck for a while and checked his watch to see if it was too late to ring her doorbell. Why was this so difficult? He'd never had a problem like this before, women usually enjoyed his company and were pleased to accompany him wherever, dinner, a movie ... to bed.

One more glance at the time and made the decision it would be stupid to knock on her door at a quarter to ten.

Tomorrow was better; he'd casually wander over and ask her out, right after work ... just a walk in the park.

⌘

I made sure that I arrived at Dana's place a little before five o'clock the next afternoon. Haven forbid being late to feed the persnickety cat.

Once inside the door stopped and called. "Evenrude? Where are you hiding you evil monster?"

Dana had spent something like a hundred and fifty bucks for a super deluxe cat mansion tree thing with posts, platforms and cave like sleeping areas that the cat often skulked upon.

Then there were the drapes and couch the vile thing hid behind, and sometimes on top of the refrigerator where she might conceal herself and lie in wait for a person to walk by.

I really didn't expect an answer to my question, but maybe she wouldn't slip up behind me and attack my ankle as she had done many times before.

I cautiously went into the kitchen and looked around. No cat! Perhaps she was outside. Wonderful, I could check everything, dry food, water, find and open the gourmet chicken whatever, and get away without incident.

I guess the whirr of the can opener was magical. I heard the soft whish of the cat-door in the laundry room and watched the stealthy feline approach. Evenrude was a huge Siamese, elegant and vocal, with cream-colored coat, black mask, and almond shaped, tanzanite, blue eyes.

She jumped onto the counter and stared at me, her tail slowly swished back and forth. "What a nice kitty, I'll scratch your head if you promise not to bite me." I reached out with a tentative hand and gently rubbed her fur. "That wasn't so bad, was it?"

179

Evenrude sniffed the small bowl used for her food and burbled loudly. "Hang on Rudy, I'll have your chicken junk ready in a second."

She sat back on her haunches and watched my every move with narrowed eyes as I scraped half a can of food into the dish. The cat loudly vocalized one more time then attacked the flaky mounds of chicken, and swiftly emptied the bowl.

"That was fast, you must really like this stuff, your human said one half a can ... so you'll get the rest in the morning. There's plenty of dry food, and the water is full, I'll return tomorrow."

Evenrude sniffed the dish, her tongue flicked around her mouth and nose and before I could move away, in a lightning flash, scratched my hand and jumped off the counter.

"Damn you ... you rotten beast, if I could catch you I'd wring your neck!" I examined my hand that was bleeding slightly, then quickly washed the area with soap and water. When I returned home would put some antiseptic salve on the wound.

Tomorrow morning I'd know better than to stand so close when the monster was eating.

What was I thinking, Evenrude didn't need an excuse to attack, an assault could come at any time. Once in a while a person managed to get away without damage to their appendages, especially if Dana put the devil's spawn in her bedroom and closed the door.

On the rare occasion that happened, the pissed-off feline would announce her displeasure with loud human like screams.

Jim took a deep breath and rang the doorbell. He could hear the mad scramble of dogs and Maris trying to make them quiet down. She opened the small glass window, then the door. As usual the dogs burst out to welcome the visitor with great enthusiasm.

180

"Hi guys, I'll pet you once I'm inside."

"Faro! Hallie! Come, let the nice man in the door."

Jim coddled the dogs with pats and compliments of how beautiful and wonderful they were until the animals were satisfied with the attention and calmed down.

"Just get off work?"

"Yeah, daylights for the next few days."

"Would you like a beer?"

"A beer would be perfect, thanks."

Jim sat on one of the chairs around the kitchen island and I fetched the beverage from the fridge. "So what's new and exciting in law enforcement?"

Jim took a long pull from the bottle. "Nothing catastrophic, same as usual at the camp grounds. Scott added more patrols around Lavelle, mentioned that the jerk who side swiped you might be in that area."

"I assume there hasn't been a sighting of the old maroon car."

"Nope."

I shrugged and sat next to him with my diet Coke.

"I know a wonderful place to have dinner and listen to a decent Jazz ensemble in Santa Clarita, would you like to go with me some evening?"

I furrowed my brow just a little. "Would this be something like a date?"

Jim took another drink and carefully set the bottle on the counter. "I guess you could call it that if you're so inclined."

"Is this a special occasion, a celebration of some kind?"

"Nothing like that, just thought you might enjoy the music, and a change of scenery."

I inhaled deeply and thought about what to say. It wasn't as if the guy wanted to take me away for the weekend or anything like that, just a casual dinner. But, this was Jim Hayden, the chick magnet, if he had expectations the guy

181

was sadly mistaken. "Sounds like fun ... when?"

"How about tomorrow evening?"

"Fine."

Jim grinned, then saw my hand. "What happened?"

"Dana's tactical trained killer cat scratched me. The hateful thing is a menace, with no tolerance for people, even though I was nice enough to go out of my way to feed her while Dana is away."

"You washed with soap didn't you, sometimes scratches get infected."

"Did everything I was supposed to do, soap, water, antiseptic ointment, shouldn't be a problem."

Jim touched my fingers gently. "Wouldn't want anything to interfere with your ability to play the guitar."

"Probably wouldn't hinder my pathetic musical talent, the aptitude to strum a few chords doesn't take much skill."

His deep green eyes studied my face, which made me a little nervous. "Just the same, take care ... I'll see you tomorrow."

Jason Tanner drove past the residence where the bitch had unlocked the door and disappeared for a few minutes. He'd been watching her place since early morning to make sure he could follow her to wherever she was going.

The man realized she was headed to the short blonde's house for some reason. The woman didn't stay long, maybe ten minutes. Jason planned to return before five to see if she came back.

He'd have to investigate in the wee hours of the morning, check out the back doors. It might be possible to get inside and be waiting when she arrived.

It was cool at three thirty in the morning. The neighborhood was dark and quiet as Jason slipped around the side of the garage and reached over the top of the gate. He chuckled softly when he found a simple slide latch.

He couldn't believe his luck and hoped the rest was as

easy ... it was. The back door was a traditional kind with the glass and screen in the top half. The window was open about five inches. Near the bottom he noticed a pet door, large enough for a small dog or cat.

After slicing the screen, he reached inside and turned the lever of the deadbolt, then twisted the lock inside the doorknob. The whole thing hadn't taken more than a minute or so.

Once inside he stood quietly and listened, then waited anxiously to see if a dog came to investigate. Nothing to indicate any yapping mutt was guarding the place. He adjusted the flashlight to see the surroundings.

Washing machine and dryer, storage cabinet ... the laundry area, then ventured into the kitchen.

Not much to the room, somewhat small, but had all the usual stuff. At the end of cabinet area on the floor were a dish with dry pet food and a plastic bowl of water. Since no dog charged at him, Jason decided the blonde was probably taking care of a cat while her friend was away. He might as well make himself comfortable for a few hours.

The attack came from above! Evenrude leaped from the top of the refrigerator onto the intruder's back and shoulders with pinpoint accuracy. She clung to him, biting with razor-sharp teeth, sinking her claws and mauling his neck and face. The frantic man was spinning around in circles trying to dislodge the snarling feline.

The victim was terrified, in shock, and unable to defend against the wild thing that was gouging and ripping his flesh.

Jason tried to reach around and grasp the crazed harridan, but couldn't dislodge it off his neck. He cried out in pain when the creature tore at his ear, the only thing he wanted to do was get away, maybe if he jammed his back into the wall the monster would let go.

He staggered to the wall, flailed his arms and dropped the flashlight. He thrashed wildly at his back, shrieked, cussed, and scattered the bowls of pet food and water over the floor. Awarding one last bite to his face the cat sprang away and silently disappeared.

Jason hunched over, moaned, and with a shaky hand felt the side of his neck and face. He could feel blood oozing down his back, there seemed to be a ragged tear on his earlobe, and his face was bleeding profusely from several deep bites.

The pain was intense from a multitude of scratches, torn flesh and puncture wounds. He had to leave, someone might have heard his screams and he must find what damage the crazed animal had inflicted ... my god what if the thing had rabies!

He thought the beast was a cat but really hadn't seen the creature; anything could have crawled through that pet door ... a rabid skunk or raccoon, he could be infected with a horrible disease and go mad!

Chapter 21

My pale lilac summer dress seemed to mesmerize Jim. He puffed out his cheeks and let out a low whistle. "You look wonderful, so, ah ... different."

"Don't tell me this jazz place is a hot-dog stand on a corner? Should I change to something more casual?"

"No, no! Don't even think of doing that ... I wasn't expecting anything so ... so shapeful."

I ran my fingers over the fine gold chain necklace with a lighting slash; it matched the zigzag dangle earrings. "I don't think shapeful is a real word. I'm serious, do you want me to find something different?"

He continued to gaze at me. "You're lovely."

I chuckled softly. "You're lovely too, an upgrade from a uniform or board shorts."

He was wearing dark blue slacks, white dress shirt, and sports jacket in hues of blue. No tie, the ensemble didn't need one.

"Wait here, I'll back the truck out so you can get in easier, I should have done that earlier."

I stayed on the walkway while he eased the truck from

under the carport. He then dashed around to the passenger door and helped me inside. I was impressed; the guy had manners when he wanted.

Our meal was excellent, as was the smooth jazz music. Conversation flowed easily; it wasn't until we were standing outside our respective houses that I became a little apprehensive as to what I should do. Invite him for a drink, shake his hand and dash inside, or see how he was going to handle the situation.

Jim waited until my door was unlocked, when I turned to face him, he encircled me in his arms. "The evening was perfect, perhaps we can do it again soon." Then kissed my cheek. "Good night."

I really didn't expect anything like that, not from Jim Hayden; I envisioned something a little more lecherous, a fight to preserve whatever I should preserve.

After petting the dogs and assuring them it was thrilling to be home I went to the bedroom, kicked off my shoes and undressed.

Even though I didn't want any romantic entanglement with my next-door neighbor I was irritated, I mean ... he didn't even kiss me, other than a peck on the cheek, which I didn't consider a real kiss.

I guess I sort of liked being held close, the subtle whisper of warm earthy amber and sandalwood scent he wore produced a slight fluttering inside.

What a dumb ass! Isn't that what I wanted Jim to be, a friend like Adam and Christian? Good grief woman make up your mind!

He probably wasn't all that great in the kissing department anyway, so I've been saved from that experience ... no pathetic kiss, no disappointment.

Jim removed his jacket and threw it over the chair, then got a cold beer and slouched in the overstuffed chair.

He thought he'd handled the evening well enough. That

glancing buss on her cheek was difficult. What he wanted to do was pin her against the door and create a fire so hot they would be reduced to ashes.

Maris Connelly was what he wanted, and it was going to be a challenge to convince her that she wanted him too. So he would apply the three C's ... be cool, casual and copacetic.

⌘

It was a good thing this was the last day in the care and feeding of Evenrude. Dana would owe me big time for this endeavor.

As usual, when entering the house called out. "It's just me, your dear friend and provider of food and drink you monster!"

I kept my back to the wall just in case she decided to jump from the cat-climbing thing. When I entered the kitchen saw the mess on the floor, spilled water and cat food.

The she-devil must have thrown a tantrum; I wasn't optimistic about her mood for breakfast. I started toward the refrigerator when I saw the flashlight on the floor and noticed the wall had rust colored smears. Okay, this was odd and a little alarming.

I stood very still and let my eyes wander over the room, then walked a few steps closer to the laundry area.

The back door was wide open and Evenrude was perched on the washing machine. A chill went down my back and I fought the instinct to run.

Somehow, I doubted the cat had developed magical powers and the ability to open locked doors. I slowly approached the statue like animal. "Good morning Evenrude, looks like you've had an adventure of some kind." I wanted to check the door that should have been closed and locked.

Upon closer inspection saw the screen had been cut, and quickly backed away, dashed through the house, out the front door, and called my brother.

Scott and Deputy Frank Velez surveyed the kitchen. "Did you touch anything?"

"Not hardly, didn't even feed the cat, probably why she's sulking outside."

"Looks like a forced entry, but nothing seems to be missing, all the electronics are still here, no drawers dumped out," Frank muttered. "Wonder what happened, the intruder left a flashlight and what looks like blood on the wall?"

I grinned. "Evenrude happened, some poor schmuck broke in, and was attacked by Dana's wild thing."

My brother frowned. "You can't be serious!"

I was chortling. "You haven't had the pleasure of meeting Evenrude, she's a terror, and can inflict a huge amount of damage in seconds.

Since something was left behind rather than stolen, the cat must have attacked the thief and scared the crap out of him. Believe me when I say that a surprise assault can do quite a bit of damage, a huge beast like Evenrude can make someone believe they've encountered a cougar."

"We'll try and lift fingerprints from the flashlight, wall area, and back door, doubt if anything will turn up, not many thieves operate without gloves."

"Is it okay if I wait around until you guys are finished, then I can clean up, feed the cat and call Christian to come and put in a new screen?"

Scott nodded his approval.

I sat in the car with the door open and made several calls. First to Dana, who seemed to take the news rather well, and used the break-in as an excuse to come back sooner than later.

Christian said he would stop by in an hour or so after getting supplies at the hardware store.

Penny and Adam thought we should meet up later to celebrate the event.

Dana arrived at the cantina around five thirty. She had driven back earlier and I had joined her at the house. After wandering through her place and making sure nothing was missing we discussed what might have happened.

The only thing that made sense was that Evenrude had done her job and scared the bad guy away before anything was stolen.

I told her that Scott said the window in the back door should be kept closed and the old dead bolt replaced with a new double-cylinder lock that requires a key to operate the door from either side. She immediately called the hardware store and made an appointment with the locksmith.

She thanked Christian for the new screen, and in classic Christian panache, he grinned and said he would send the bill later.

Dana had something more to contribute to the conversation, by asking if she could have an engagement party in Penny and Christian's back yard.

Seems her sister-in-law's, sister, Beverly, was getting married in a few months. She and her fiancé lived in an apartment and didn't have any room for a gathering.

Beverly, and her significant other, Harley, resided in Fillmore, just a hop, skip, and a jump from Sendero and asked if Dana could host a small party, mostly for family.

"Wait, wait, wait ... how did you get selected for this honor?"

Dana wrinkled her nose and sighed. "I don't know, I guess it's because I live close to the happy couple."

"Do you even know these people?"

"Of course I know them ... Bev mostly, Harley, not so much, but he was very nice at the birthday party in San Diego. So can we use your lovely, large back yard? I promise you won't have to lift a finger, my brother and sister-in-law

189

will provide the refreshments and my friends will help clean up."

Adam smirked. "What friends are you talking about?"

"Why you guys of course."

I slurped a large quantity of margarita though the straw. "So you want to enlist this motley crew to be the wait-staff, you gotta be joking?"

"Ah come on, it'll be fun, it's not like we haven't done stuff like that before. Penny hosted the anniversary party for her old family friend a couple of years ago, and we helped with everything.

Sandy started to laugh. "And look how that turned out, Maris was removed from serving coffee for being drunk and disorderly."

"I take umbrage to that remark. Just because people didn't have coffee cups was no reason to get uppity."

"Carrying around a pot and pouring hot coffee into plastic glasses or beverage cans was probably "off putting", Adam reasoned. "The strolling waitress with coffee occurred after her turn in the serving line."

"If I remember right I took a tiny sip of wine when correctly guessing if a person wanted beef or chicken."

Christian had to add. "More like a gulp rather than a sip then doubled up if they wanted both."

"Oh yeah, that was fun."

Dana looked so pathetic that Penny sighed and reluctantly consented to have the party. We discussed it a little more and decided what could go wrong ... just family and a few friends.

Sandy got my attention. "Look who walked in ... Detective McAllister from the C-B-I."

I watched the Nordic-god saunter toward the bar. "Why do you say CBI like Hannibal Lector, eating someone's liver with a glass of Chianti?"

"Because those two agents temporarily taking up space

in our office think they're something special, much better than our guys."

Penny studied McAllister. "He looks like the actor in the movie *Thor*. Very nice, very nice indeed."

Christian groaned loudly. "Probably just a pretty face and little else," Adam grunted in agreement.

With drink in hand, Ryan McAllister walked to our table. "Very nice to see you again Maris, I was wondering if we could talk."

A conversation in front of this bunch could be disastrous. "Sure ... ah why don't we move to another table, somewhere a little more private."

Christian smiled wickedly. "No, no ... please join the group, we were just saying how you resemble an acquaintance who moved away."

Adam continued. "Yes, a long time ago to a galaxy far far away."

Sandy clutched Adam's arm and batted her eyelashes. "Help me Obi-Wan Kenobi! You're my only hope!"

I quickly got out of the chair. "My friends have had a little too much to drink, you'll be much safer ... ah, I mean better off, away from their mindless babbling."

McAllister looked rather puzzled but followed me to another table. To make the evening a smashing success, Jim Hayden and Steve Mitchell entered the place.

They headed for the gang, paused, talked, Steve sat down by Dana and Jim looked around the room until his gaze rested on me.

From where I was sitting, he seemed to square his shoulders and take a deep breath, then casually strolled to our table.

"Maris."

'Jim."

He stared at my companion with narrowed eyes. "Detective."

191

"Deputy."

"You know each other?" I said brightly.

Jim nodded. "We've been introduced at the station. Ron McCauley if I remember correctly."

The detective managed a fake smile. "Ryan McAllister, forgive me but I don't remember your name at all."

Christian rubbed his hands together. "Think Jim can take him?"

Adam adjusted his glasses. "Thor has him in height and weight."

Christian smirked. "I'll put ten on Hayden, he's probably quicker."

Steve jumped into the conversation. "Yeah, I'll risk my money on Jim, I've seen him take down some mean drunks. But ... he's suffered a few blows to the head several times too. Could be a little off his game tonight, he's had a couple of drinks."

"You don't really think there'll be a fight do you?" Penny said softly and looked a little alarmed.

"Probably not much of one if Thor does a number on his body, I'll put my ten on the hunky blonde." Dana replied.

"Traitor!" Steve wheezed.

"Didn't you just say he's had a few? Puts him at a disadvantage ... right?"

This was fricking great, the male ego at work, competitive masculinity at its best.

"Let me refresh your memory, Jim Hayden, meet Ryan McAllister. Thank you for saying hello Jim, the gang mentioned they hadn't seen you recently."

Hayden looked at me for a few moments, then took a step back. "I'll have to stop by and pay my respects. Take care Maris ... Detective McGonagall."

He turned and strolled back to the motley crew and sat where he could watch our table.

"You and the deputy seeing each other?"

"I wouldn't say we are actually "seeing" one another. He lives next door, and on occasion we get together."

"So there won't be any problems if I ask you out?"

I smiled. "Not as far as I'm concerned, no problem at all."

'Good, how about tomorrow evening?"

"Tomorrow is perfect."

I tried to concentrate on the conversation, which started out with the weather and kept away from politics and religion. He preferred a cooler climate if given a choice.

When asked the inevitable question as to why I wanted to teach school, refrained from saying things like ... one works long hours, but the pay is really rotten, and that I simply loved the intriguing choices of mystery meat in the cafeteria, or the old standard of holidays and summers off.

Ryan seemed to be quite knowledgeable about wine. I could appreciate his enthusiasm since I always keep a bottle of wine in the fridge for special occasions ... you know like Mondays and Wednesdays.

Decided not to mention that I add grape Kool-Aid to make the ten-buck a gallon jug of Mountain Red taste better ... or that Jim Hayden was having a roaring good time with my friends. Bastard!

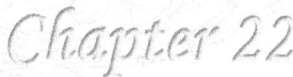

Chapter 22

Diego, from the garage, called to say they would be keeping my car a little longer. There was a problem with the driver's side window, something electrical. I didn't mind at all, the 57 was great fun to drive.

My dinner date with Ryan had gone well, he was an interesting man, who liked to ski and enjoyed hockey.

He hardly flinched when drinking the wine I provided later that evening. I successfully coaxed the dogs outside so we humans could sit together on the couch.

We said our goodbyes around eleven, after a kiss of some duration at the door. I waited for a tingly sensation that didn't quite materialize, probably a little too soon for that to happen.

A relationship with the Detective might be engaging even though our interests were not really the same. The old adage of opposites attract could be applied in this situation.

At least the fellow didn't act like an adolescent making a difficult transition into adulthood like someone else I knew. I was still pissed about Jim's behavior at the cantina.

I was on my second cup of morning coffee when there was loud knocking and the doorbell rang with persistence. "Maris open the damn door!" my brother yelled.

The dogs were in the very back of the yard, so I could open the door without the usual display of jumping and barking.

Standing outside were Scott and Jim; they almost burst into the house. From the serious looks on their faces something was wrong.

My brother huffed a few times and ran his fingers through his hair before speaking. "We got the results of the fingerprints from the break-in at Dana's house."

"I thought you said there wouldn't be any prints ... bad guys wear gloves."

"They probably don't when putting batteries in flashlights."

I took a deep breath. "Okay."

Jim swept past me and stood by the screen door and watched the dogs chase each other and muttered. "They belong to Jason Tanner."

Scott sat down at the kitchen island. "Quite a coincidence, don't you think?"

My stomach did flip-flops. "I think we all need a cup of coffee," and went to find two more mugs.

Scott wasn't jumping to conclusions when declaring that Tanner must be stalking me for some reason. There was no other way he could know where Dana lived unless he followed me. Therefore, Jim would be in an ideal situation to be my watchdog, a logical move since he lived next door; his new assignment was ensuring my safety.

I wasn't going to be stupid and protest, it was chilling to learn that someone was skulking about and watching my movements.

"Do you think he broke into Dana's home to wait for me?"

"Yeah, I do, you were vulnerable. Think about it ... the large dogs, and a cop living next door isn't very convenient. An empty place is much better."

195

"Does this mean I'm confined to the house?"

"No, it means that Jim is your constant companion ... inside and out. There will be patrol cars driving by day and night looking for anything out of the ordinary. You could move to the ranch, that might be for the best."

"I could, but I won't put mom and dad in any danger, they would probably stick to me like glue, which would be upsetting for everybody."

"I'm going home and change clothes, pack a few things," Jim announced. He hurried away and Scott fixed another pot of coffee.

"Tell me about Jason Tanner, I'm sure you've dug up more information."

"From what I could find out, he's a drinker, been arrested for drunk driving, shop lifting, receiving stolen property as an adult. The juvie stuff is for voyeurism, at age sixteen was placed on probation and required to have a psychological evaluation for lurking and peeping about the neighborhood.

I shivered a little. "That's creepy, no history of stalking?"

"Not that I could find, but it doesn't mean he hasn't become obsessed with someone in the past."

"He's obviously fixated on me and doesn't intend to send flowers and candy."

Scott shrugged. "Could be you resemble a person that rejected him or reminds him of his nutty mother ... who knows what drives this psycho."

Jim returned, sans uniform, dressed in jeans and t-shirt and carried a small carryall bag. His eyes perused the phrase on my shirt, *Why Have A Knight in Shining Armor When You Can Have a Viking in Bloody Chainmail* and smirked.

After pouring another cup of coffee went out on the patio and waited for the dogs to assault his person.

Scott left after checking the windows in both bedrooms,

the bathroom, and the lock on the back door.

I sat on the couch and thought about my situation. There was nothing like living under a dark cloud and waiting for something god-awful to happen.

There were pros and cons to have Jim Hayden in my house, the added layer of protection was good, but it would put a crimp in the budding relationship with Ryan McAllister ... terrific!

⌘

Jason Tanner hurt all over, the side of his face and neck was red and swollen. The deep lacerations on his back made him wince every time he moved, his head throbbed, and the torn ear had to have stitches.

It was a good thing that Jay knew what to do and sent him to a clinic in the San Fernando Valley. He was given a tetanus shot, the wounds cleaned and treated with some ointment and a prescription for antibiotics.

He doubted that Jay believed his story of being attacked in the woods by a wild animal.

The more he thought about what had happened, the easier it was to place the blame on that bitch. In his mind everything was her fault and had an obsession to make her pay for his suffering.

Right now he wanted to rest, take a lot of colorful pills from the stash he kept hidden inside the couch cushion, and wash the tablets down with a few glasses of Jim Beam. Everything would be fine after some sleep; his mind would be clear; he'd be able to focus on what needed to be done.

⌘

"We're not going to sit around the house all day and

look at each other, are we?"

Jim lounged on the leather chair. "You have something else in mind?"

"Yeah, exercise Matchless and the dogs."

"Sounds like a good idea, doubt your crazy admirer will follow you around the back country, probably can't ride a horse anyway.

"I figure that between my Magnum and your Colt.45 we should have enough fire power to discourage any mad stalker."

Jim positioned his elbows on the padded arm of the chair and steepled his fingers. "Right ... you'd really fire your weapon with intent?"

"In a life or death situation, damn right I would."

"Let's hope we, or rather you, are never placed in that predicament." He rose from the chair. "I'll get my boots and saddle bag and be right back."

Ryan McAllister wasn't especially thrilled about the latest news. But Maris would have protection even if it were Deputy Hayden who provided it.

Upon learning that Jason Tanner, the owner of a Ford Van, suspect in a hit-and-run, and now a perpetrator in a break-in, increased his resolve to take this jerk's life apart.

He'd concentrate on finding family, friends, enemies; every place the guy lived from birth to the present. Ryan would know what this psycho ate for breakfast every morning when finished.

The Coverdale Retreat had been thoroughly vetted. The flamboyant Dr. Julian Coverdale was interviewed several times, background checked, his picture shown to the victims of the forced kidney donors with no results.

Nothing out of the ordinary was found on the Physician's Assistant, Jan Stottler. Nurses and other staff members were relatively clean; their backgrounds didn't set off any alarms.

The one bit of information they knew for certain was that Jason Tanner owned a Ford van. Ryan and Bill Andrews would start from there, run down any other vehicle Mr. Tanner ever purchased, track traffic tickets and violations since he acquired a license.

"So you guys are living together now?" Christian said with a smirk. "I mean what will the neighbors think?"

I smiled sweetly. "Truly, a match made in heaven, and you have an evil mind."

Christian laughed and wiggled his eyebrows suggestively.

Jim leaned close and asked softly. "Are there any boundaries with this gang?"

I shook my head. "None ... only that if you dish it out, you're able to take whatever is returned."

"Fine ... hey, Christian, you're an ass!"

Christian grinned. "Screw you Deputy Dawg!"

And we were off and running, ensconced in our usual place, with the usual unconventional group of friends. The conversation turned to starting a band as soon as we learned to play the required instruments. Adam's resounding rendition of chopsticks on the piano, and the several guitar chords I knew, probably didn't a band make.

"I've sent out the invitations to the engagement party for Beverly and Harley. After speaking with the, groom to be, found some interesting things in regards to his family," Dana announced.

Penny groaned a little. "What, they all belong to the Hells Angels?"

"No, nothing like that, it's just that some of them are a little ... how shall I put this ... a little socially backward."

Christian perked up. "You mean they're Okies?" Then looked at Adam. "No offense!"

Adam saluted with his beer. "None taken."

"Define 'socially backward'" Penny persisted. "Like ...

Redneck, crass and boorish?"

Dana hesitated for several moments. "More like ... *Deliverance*!"

"You mean hillbillys from the backwoods, as in the classic movie *Deliverance*?" I chortled.

"Let's hope they bring the dueling banjos for entertainment!" Adam said gleefully.

⌘

Jim insisted that sleeping on the couch was better than in the second bedroom, he could monitor all the doors.

Sharing a bathroom was another story. I guess the man couldn't help himself when he offered to wash my back or hold the towel after I showered. I refused to laugh at his suggestions it would only encourage him.

It wasn't too bad having him around, he was handy in the kitchen, and we liked the same, stupid action movies on television.

There was a bit of tension when Ryan came to visit, even though Jim stayed on the patio with the dogs most of the time.

I'm sure he was aware that Ryan kissed me goodbye when leaving. Jim didn't seem to miss much, even though he was playing tug and fetch with the dogs, which created a lot of excited growling and barking outside.

Not conducive to conversation inside.

"So what did McClusky want?"

"You know his name isn't McClusky ... he was just checking on me, how I'm coping."

Jim grunted. "I think we're dealing effectively with everything don't you?"

I moved closer. "Yes, and I should have thanked you a long time ago, you didn't have to be my keeper ... I'm glad you're here."

He grasped my hand and pulled me to his chest, the green eyes had become dark pools. "Glad to be here too," his lips were inches from mine when he drew away.

"We should have one last outing in the 57 before you return it."

I stepped back and took a deep breath. "Yeah, Diego said my car would be ready in the morning. We could drive around the lake, then to the white water part of the river and watch it roil over the rocks."

⌘

Jason was feeling much better after two days of rest; tonight he would make sure to stop by the blond bitch's house.

It was always comforting to prowl and hide ... concealed in the dark, the sensation of power was exciting, like he was in control for once.

He wasn't thrilled to crouch and crawl up hill through the low shrubs that surrounded the bitch's house. He'd left the car one street over in front of a place that had no lights showing.

Jason knew the dogs were usually inside after dark, so he could make his way up the side without the creatures barking at the fence.

The front windows were slightly open most of the time with the shades partially drawn. Tonight was no different, the living room lights were low and he could hear the television and every once in a while catch snatches of conversation ... the blond had company.

The discussion was something about a place called Diamond Cut ... where the hell was Diamond Cut? His brain short-circuited on the word ... *diamond*, could there actually be a place where diamonds might be found?

More talk about rocks that glittered, the only thing Jason could think of that glittered was gold and diamonds. He'd heard stories about people looking for treasure in this area.

Her visitor suggested they have another look around. Look for what exactly ... diamonds?

Rocks that glinted flashed before Jason's eyes; he should leave, go home and think. It was said that during the gold rush men had found nuggets glinting in the water, all one had to do was reach down and pick them up.

He wiped the moisture from the back of his neck and grunted in pain, his back hurt, so shifted his position slightly because of a leg cramp.

Wild barking erupted from inside the house. Time to go! Jason wasn't about to stay a second longer, he darted out of the shrubbery and began to run.

Moments later the door opened, and a man came out on the porch. The dogs rushed past, stopped for a few seconds then began to chase the figure running down the slope after the guy yelled, "Get 'em!"

Even though Jason was fast the hounds were faster. The huge animal was gaining, close enough to tear at his leg and come away with some fabric and the flesh underneath.

Jason shrieked in pain and terror! It was the shrill whistle that stopped the monsters from bringing down their prey.

The dogs continued to whine and bark as the terrified man raced madly towards the road below, falling, crawling, then gaining his feet and running.

Chapter 23

I whistled again for the dogs. It wasn't long before Hallie came panting back and Faro presented me with his prize. A scrap of denim covered in bloodstains.

"Why did you call them back, they could have held him until I got there?" Jim huffed.

"What if he had a knife, or gun, I didn't want you or the dogs hurt. Anyway, it might not have been Tanner," I reasoned.

Jim petted the dogs while I examined the segment of cloth. "Looks like Faro got a piece of him."

"You should have let them go," he grumbled.

"Think what might have happened if they had mauled whomever, could be considered an unprovoked attack and my animals might suffer the consequences. No thank you!"

Jim shrugged "Yeah, I see your point, but we both know who was prowling about."

"Well, perhaps he won't be inclined to return, might even decide to go away and leave me alone."

I had my doubts about that last statement and from the expression on Jim's face, he didn't believe it either.

My guardian didn't hesitate to put in a call to Scott, and report the incident. My brother said he'd have the area scoured and be over shortly.

It was unlikely they'd find anything; the crazy idiot would be long gone. But I had the satisfaction knowing the psycho was given a little reminder of this evenings encounter.

Scott arrived within ten minutes of speaking to Jim. He listened to what had happened, asked for a plastic bag to preserve the scrap of material, then checked everything again before leaving. He didn't look very happy.

After all the excitement it was difficult to settle my mind. Lolling on the couch lasted only a few minutes, every so often I went into each bedroom and looked around, then checked all the doors.

Jim watched in silence until I wandered into the kitchen for the umpteenth time.

He moved to one of the chairs at the island. "Tomorrow we'll purchase motion detector lights for the front and back areas, should have done that a long time ago."

I nodded. "Good idea, I was also thinking of removing the shrubs under the front window and planting something different."

"What did you have in mind?"

"Bougainvillea! Those things will kill ya. Also some pea-gravel in the flower beds, makes a nice crunching sound when walked over."

I was feeling a little better after a couple of beers, could even concentrate on a television program about island hunting. I guess if I could spare two or three million dollars I'd think about purchasing an island retreat ... or not.

My bedroom seemed stuffy even with the door open and the fan running, which made the curtains slightly sway, not conducive for sleep. I could imagine that rat-bastard slithering through the window so turned on the nightstand light for the second time. The dogs studied my actions carefully not quite sure what was going on.

I gasped when Jim appeared in the doorway.

"Are you all right?"

I struggled out of bed, moved to the door, and leaned against the frame. "Don't know what I am right now. Tired, mad, scared ... cringe when the curtains move or hear a slight noise outside."

"If you want I can camp on the chair in your room, it looks comfortable enough."

I looked at the wing back chair in the corner; it didn't look comfortable at all. "No, that's a stupid idea, and I feel idiotic for being such a wimp."

"Don't take this the wrong way, but we can share the bed, might be a bit crowded with the four of us," Jim stated with a slight grin.

I looked at him for a moment then narrowed my eyes. "I'll sick the dogs on you if you become amorous," I threatened.

He started to chuckle, probably not much of a threat since the beasts loved him.

Thankfully, I had a king size bed, Faro found his usual spot at the foot; Hallie seemed content to snuggle between the two of us.

"If you snore I won't hesitate to smack you," I muttered.

"Same goes for you."

"I don't snore, but the dogs make whiffling sounds at times, so don't be impetuous."

Jim sighed. "I don't have an impetuous fiber in my body ... go to sleep."

I reached out and grasped his hand, then closed my eyes.

I startled awake in the early hours of the morning. Jim whispered. "It's okay."

205

Hallie must have gotten a little too warm and changed position to the foot of the bed. I turned on my side and put my hand on Jim's chest. "Thank You."

"My pleasure. Go back to sleep."

I mumbled something about it raining and thought he said it didn't rain in Southern California.

The dogs were gone when I opened my eyes, so was Jim. I looked at the clock it was almost eight. After a trip to the bathroom, found everyone outside on the patio.

"I made coffee," he said.

I inhaled the clean morning air, yawned, gave the dogs a pat and went inside.

"Would you like some toast?" I called.

"Sure, the sourdough please."

"Since the dogs aren't giving me evil looks you must have fed them."

Jim came through the open sliding glass doors. "They're not shy in demanding something to eat, poor things."

I snorted. "Poor things indeed, more like spoiled brats!"

He opened the fridge and removed a jar of apricot jam. "We have a busy morning, places to go and people to see."

"Yeah, pick up my car, hardware store, garden supply. We should get started, when we get back have to dig out the plants under the window."

Jim groaned. "Not looking forward to that little chore, where do you want to relocate the greenery?"

"Probably along the fence in the back."

My cell rang; I couldn't remember where I had left it last night.

Jim gestured toward the living room. "On the coffee table."

"Thanks," and hurried away.

After a short conversation with Ryan, I returned to the kitchen.

206

"Everything okay with your boyfriend?"

"Lovely ... he just heard about all the fun we had last night and wanted to know how I was doing. He's not my boyfriend, we've had dinner once."

Jim smirked. "I bet he's thrilled I'm staying here."

I put a slice of bread in the toaster. "Things will return to normal soon, for which I'll be eternally grateful."

"Uh-huh, I'm sure McNutt is eternally grateful for all that snogging the other night."

"Snogging! You've suddenly become British?"

"One can learn a lot from reading Harry Potter books, words like parselmouth, muggle, quidditch ... snogging is such a descriptive word for kissing

"I've kissed a lot of men, doesn't mean anything."

"You haven't kissed me … yet!"

⌘

Jason Tanner had run despite the terror and horrible pain in his lower calf. He didn't stop until he scrambled into the car, slammed the door, then quickly drove away. Once the panic subsided he could feel the blood trickle down his leg and seep into the sock.

Back in the safety of his cabin, sat on the bed, rolled up his pants and gaped at the arched pattern of punctures and lacerations that still oozed blood.

What to do now? If he went to see Jay he'd have to admit his activities to receive such a bite; another story about a wild animal attack wasn't believable.

Jay had said to stay put, wait, and do nothing.

He must calm down and think there was antibiotic ointment and tablets, so he could treat the wound himself. Wash his leg with soap and water and put on the salve, maybe wrap a dishtowel around it.

Didn't need anyone to help, even though his whole body ached, face, ear, neck, back and now his leg.

The stash in the couch cushion would make it all good, allow him to sleep; everything would look different in the morning.

After a long hot shower, two tablets of antibiotics, a variety of other pills, he applied ointment to the bites and scratches, then rested his head on the pillows stacked against the headboard.

A large glass of booze, his second, waited on the nightstand, he was feeling a little better. The one good thing about tonight was the diamonds, this Diamond Cut place must be close by, he'd ask around in San Emidio. Since the blond bitch had driven by the cabin he was staying away from the bar and store in Lavelle.

Jason checked his phone; ignoring the many calls from his girlfriend. He already knew what she wanted ... her car.

He took several more healthy slugs of whiskey and closed his eyes and envisioned the glint of diamonds. He'd be rich, have everything a man could want, Jay would be proud of him ... Jason would like that.

Another thing he would like was a gun. He knew a guy that knew a guy, in South Gate who could hook him up with something.

He wasn't all that good with guns, what was the big deal, just point and shoot. Make sure the meddling woman paid for everything wrong in his life.

⌘

It had been an uneventful two days, last night we had dinner with my parents at the ranch. The offer to stay with them was discussed and refused with thanks. Jim did his best to convince them it was only a matter of time before the bad guy was caught.

My mom seemed relieved; Dad wasn't impressed, but kept his mouth shut. He and Jim took a walk to the barn and had a private conversation. Not much of a surprise to learn that Dad patrolled my neighborhood several times a day and sometimes at night.

I had a slight headache so went off to bed while Jim watched television. Faro came with me, Hallie stayed in the living room with her friend. Jim was such a pushover for the huge mutt, couldn't resist her adoring eyes and doggie-tooth smile.

When this mess was over those two would be sad to part company, but that was how most things in life went, the good times and the not so good times.

Come to think about it, I might be a little sorry to see the fellow go back to his place. It was kind of nice having him around. We seemed to get along, he fixed dinner most of the time, wasn't underfoot like I thought he'd be, practiced his guitar in the back bedroom ... did I mention he could cook?

Couldn't believe I was thinking such thoughts, must be the stress of the situation and that Jim was in close proximity all the time. So close I could reach out and touch him if I wanted, or for that matter satisfy my curiosity about his ability to kiss.

That was important wasn't it?

My extra, extra-large sleep T-shirt and cut off sweat pants wasn't the most stylish outfit a person could wear. The shirt was clean and only partly unraveled at the hem. It advertised one of my favorite sayings. *I'm Still Kind Of Mad They Never Actually Told Us How To Get To Sesame Street.*

Jim was dozing with Hallie sprawled next to him on the couch. He squinted up at me and studied the aphorism written on the shirt.

"Your taste in casual attire never ceases to amaze me."

209

"Let's get this done once and for all?"

"What?"

He sat up a little straighter; I made Hallie get off the couch so I could sit down.

"I think you should kiss me."

Jim inhaled deeply, quickly deciding not to engage in whatever Maris was advocating. He had to maintain his nonchalance attitude if he wanted to attract this woman.

"Is this some kind of joke?"

'No, I'm asking you to kiss me."

He had an amused look on his face. "I don't kiss strange women, and never on demand."

I could feel my face turn pink, to save further embarrassment, scrambled off the couch and stormed to my bedroom and slammed the door.

That went really well, made a complete ass of myself. The man was insufferable; I'd be thrilled when he returned to his side of the carport.

The next morning I was up before five, fed the dogs and tried to keep out of Jim's way. Took my time cleaning the bedrooms and bathroom. Even started on the bookshelf, pulling the volumes off the shelf, dusting each one, polishing the wood surface and stacking them back.

The infuriating man asked if I wanted breakfast, which I refused, he shrugged and proceeded to devour a bacon and egg sandwich.

Jim cleaned up the breakfast dishes, went outside, got the hose and began to wash off the back patio.

Now that he was busy, away from me, I half-heartedly flicked the dust cloth over the rest of the books and finished really fast.

An idea had popped into my head while trying to occupy the time and ignore Jim. I grabbed the phone.

"Moneypenny?"

After a few seconds came the reply. "Bond?"

"I have a mission if you choose to accept."

Penny sighed. "You have your characters confused, Bond and Moneypenny have assignments for MI6 ... *Impossible Mission Force* agents accept impractical commissions."

"Whatever ... have an idea that might locate Jason Tanner."

"I'm not going to sleazy bars looking for Freak-boy."

"I huffed loudly. "Nothing like that, you don't even have to leave the house."

"I'm listening."

"Maybe Freak-boy is renting a place around here, well not necessarily in Sendero, but perhaps in one of the Mountain Communities."

Penny inhaled deeply. "That is a lot of real estate."

"I know, so we divide it up, look at the vacation rentals advertised on the Internet. Most of the places show pictures and give an address."

"You do realize that not all rentals are listed that way, many are private, or handled by a management company. No responsible owner will give out the name of a renter unless it's an emergency or for law enforcement."

"I'm sure you can access all the rentals in your property management files, and even the names. It's worth a try, maybe we'll luck out, I would imagine Freak-boy's place is small and cheap. That should narrow the possibilities down some."

"You're grasping at straws, Miss Bond."

'Better than sitting around waiting, Miss Moneypenny."

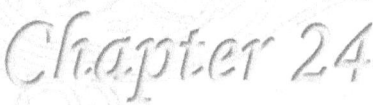

Chapter 24

I had a list of thirty some rentals gleaned from the Internet that might be possible locations Jason Tanner could hide ... wishful thinking on my part.

Penny emailed that her search of properties she and Christian managed resulted in a big fat zero.

Jim looked over my shoulder a time or two curious about what I was doing. We were actually communicating somewhat.

I found holding a grudge was difficult, especially when the reason was so stupid. I mean, a person has the right to snog or not ... anyway what was the big deal he wasn't my type.

When I told him my idea, he said it was a worthwhile project, but added that a rental might be taken in another person's name.

I'd thought about that possibility. Still, it wouldn't make any difference who rented the place if we could find one of the vehicles parked in a driveway or carport.

Couldn't hurt to cruise around and take a look, might get lucky and catch Freak-boy out watering the lawn.

Jim scratched his head, smiled sweetly, thought the plan was marvelous, said he'd drive while I navigated.

Liar ... I knew it was a ridiculous idea but needed to get out of the house, and an excellent excuse to drop by the soda fountain and have a milkshake afterward.

Milkshake in hand we stopped at the pharmacy and talked with Rosa for a moment, my sister-in-law graciously invited me to stay with them. I declined the offer, Jim made the statement that everything would be over soon; he had faith my stalker would be apprehended in the next couple of days. Yeah, right!

Ryan McAllister called not long after we came home, which lifted my spirits, and probably irritated my warden. I was invited to go wine tasting the following evening.

Jim insinuated that McFudd might be an excellent wine connoisseur, but otherwise incompetent as a bodyguard, and offered to tag along.

The Pulchella Winery Tasting Room was in Old Town Newhall. Even though I had lived most of my life twenty or so minutes away, had never been there. According to Ryan, the place was a little gem; he was impressed with their selection of interesting reds.

I was impressed with the lovely dragonfly cut glass challis that also contained Chardonnay; the white wine had a kind of tropical fruit taste, which probably could be improved with a dash of 7-Up.

The cut-glass container brought back memories of a trip to Germany and the lovely etched goblets that were used to serve beer. The small brewery declined our offer to purchase a few of the unusual mugs.

I have no idea how several of the glasses ended up in our backpacks. However, we left a sizable tip.

I learned that Ryan was from the Boston area, home to Harvard and MIT, and a hundred other colleges and universities. Seems the Bruins, ice hockey team, won a Stanley

Cup a few years back.

He preferred large cities rather than the country with its huge vistas, which seemed rather lonely to his way of thinking.

I wondered what he was doing here, the Los Angeles area sprawls between several mountain ranges and the ocean. It contains about ninety incorporated cities, has a benign climate, laid-back informality, and a passionate love affair with cars. The skyline is horizontal rather than vertical and features a long magnificent coastline, very different from his east coast roots.

I ingested at least five different colorful wines, white, red and pink, then we went across the street and had something to eat and more wine.

A little after midnight we parked in front of my house. The situation wasn't conducive to a romantic interlude due to motion sensor lights, a sheriff's car that drove slowly by and Jim standing at the window peeking through the drapes.

Ryan walked me to the door, gently brushed his lips against mine, said he enjoyed the evening and would be out of town for several days.

After the kiss I prepared for the thrill of uncontrolled lasciviousness ... didn't happen. It occurred to me that I hadn't felt any vital "tingling sensation" that's supposed to ignite one's inner being.

I waited until he was halfway to his car before opening the door, didn't want the dogs to knock him down. It was bad enough the excited beasts mauled me as I fought my way into the house.

Jim greeted me from the living room. "Did you have a good time?"

"It was very nice, a little wine ... make that a considerable amount of wine, good company and intelligent conversation."

"McGurgle doesn't seem the conversational type, well

maybe, if the subject is about a relationship with himself."

I collapsed onto the armchair and kicked off my shoes; high heels always hurt my feet. "I don't feel like discussing Ryan McAllister, or our relationship."

Jim sighed. "Just as well, I had a delightful chat with Penny, she wants you to call her tomorrow. Something about the engagement party for Dana's sister's husband's cousin."

"What?"

"I'll remind you in the morning, shall I help you to your room? Unzip your dress?

Find the T-shirt that says *The Fact That I'm Legally An Adult Is Hysterical*. It's so you."

I thought about throwing one of my shoes at the smirking twit. "Your cooking is only passable, and you speak something vaguely resembling English."

"Thank you for those kind words ... as for relationships, I'm far too immature for a relationship."

"Don't be talking about relationships, could get a girl all excited."

He nonchalantly rose from the couch and offered his hand to help me out of the chair. "Come on it's late, I promise not to make any more caustic remarks about your friend."

I regarded his face carefully then accepted his hand. "Truce ... for now."

He hauled me out of the chair into his arms and gently kissed me. The physical response was immediate, a sensation of hot and cold at the same time ... primal, more than pleasing.

He whispered softly. "Your skin always has the veiled scent of citrus," then kissed me again, this time it was fierce and hungry. I was on fire!

He drew away a fraction and muttered. "I shouldn't have taken advantage, you've had a little too much wine."

"Don't blame the wine, this is far better than I imagined, and I can imagine quite a lot."

Jim held me securely in his arms. "I think we should take this new familiarity slowly, knowing how we both feel about commitment."

I had to agree with his reasoning, and I shouldn't let the feelings I was experiencing overrule common sense. "Okay, but, I don't think we can go back to the way it was only a few minutes ago ... everything has suddenly changed and can't be ignored."

"I don't plan on ignoring anything, but it would be a mistake to rush, don't you agree?"

I took a deep breath. Jim was right; a few kisses didn't mean all that much in the grand scheme of things. I probably wasn't in complete control of whatever I needed to be in control of; nevertheless, there was a fire inside that couldn't be denied.

"Escort me to my bedroom where we'll say goodnight. No hanky-panky, just the same as usual."

The man was wicked ... I knew that grin. "Well, maybe not as usual, one shouldn't rule out a goodnight kiss."

"Only if you don't cross the threshold into my room."

"Threshold! Only an English teacher would say something like that?"

"I'll change the word to entryway, wouldn't want any confusion."

It was a parade down the hall; Faro and Hallie pushed past us and made themselves comfortable on the bed. Jim and I stood outside.

He maneuvered me against the wall and pinned me with his hands on either side.

"Remember, no rush." He proceeded to say good night without words.

One kiss led to several more, his hands moved over my body stoking the slow burn into a wildfire.

It wouldn't take much for both of us to forget our recently agreed upon course of action. "Jim!"

216

"What?"

"You know what!"

He reluctantly stepped back and I tried to control my breathing. "If I promise not to snore, we could share the bed ... like before."

"You don't believe that any more than I do ... remember, nice and slow."

"I'm really good at nice and slow," he said with a sly smile.

"Go away, think about what you're going to fix for breakfast."

"I thought you said my cooking was only passable."

"I lied!"

We sat on the patio after breakfast drinking coffee and gazing at the dark blue lake in the distance. Couldn't ask for a more beautiful morning.

Jim reminded me to call Penny.

"What did you want to tell me regarding the engagement party?"

"I don't know if I should be overly concerned about the phone calls I've been getting."

"What about them?"

"Some relative of Harley has called practically every day, seems really thrilled about the party and that he was invited."

"Did he leave a name?"

"Yeah, Uncle John."

"So call Dana, ask her to find out if he's a nut job."

"I did, but there was another strange call from an additional relative wanting directions to my house. She said she was driving around looking and evidently got lost.

I stated the party wasn't until the weekend, which seemed to concern "Norma June", I had to convince her not to drop by and visit."

"I'm so glad you and Uncle John and Norma June are

on a first name basis. Did you contact Dana again?"

"Sure did, seems Uncle John stays in a constant state of inebriation. Norma June is primarily homeless, lives in her car most of the time when not camping on her sister's sofa."

I couldn't contain the burst of laughter, which was contagious, soon Penny was giggling too.

"I have an idea this party will be memorable, we should have Jim and Steve at the bar to serve and protect the booze."

"Good idea, Christian can patrol the pool, make sure no one falls in, and the rest of us will circulate."

"Yeah, try to keep Norma June from putting a tent in the back yard."

Penny groaned. "Oh Lord, I didn't think about that."

"I'm kidding, relax, nothing horrible is going to happen, we'll get through this just fine."

"I'll kill Dana if things go south," she muttered. "We need to have a meeting at the cantina ... strategize."

It took a while for me to stop laughing after getting off the phone. I explained the situation to Jim, the *Deliverance* type relatives, and how he and Steve would be tending bar and keeping a close eye on things.

Christian and Penny had a lovely back yard, with a pool, outside kitchen and built in bar area, a perfect place to entertain.

My confederate said he was looking forward to the event, wouldn't miss it for the world.

Dana would "*suffer the slings and arrows of outrageous fortune*" if this party
was a disaster.

⌘

Jason examined his various lacerations, he thought the swelling was less puffy on the side of his face, but the deep scratches still hurt on his neck and back. The bite on his leg ached and caused him to limp a little.

He should probably take a few more pills and get some rest before trying to locate the diamond place.

Earlier that morning he'd found a little shop in San Emidio that sold maps to where one could find old gold mines. He casually asked about the Diamond Cut, heard it was really interesting.

The clerk pointed out the location, said it was on private property, maybe a quarter mile off the road.

After he rested a little more and traveled back to South Gate he would feel up to trekking off the beaten path, right now walking was painful.

God, he hated this place, just wanted to go home, hang out with his friends at the bar like before. Things were so different since Jay got the job in Sendero.

The plan was only for a few months, they'd go home with more money than those rich people who lived in Beverley Hills.

But things took longer than expected and he didn't have much luck at cards, his "kickers, fluff and Xannies" ran about eighty to a hundred bucks a cap, so whatever cash he got seemed to slip through his fingers.

His mind returned to the hunt for the rich stuff. He reasoned he'd probably have to dig for the diamonds, if people could find them just lying about there would be hordes fighting over the little sparklers. Guess he'd have to buy a shovel.

The diamonds must be a well-kept secret; the clerk in the shop didn't seem to be excited about it. Maybe the fellow didn't realize anything of value was waiting for the right person to come along.

So, there was no rush. Time to feel better, drive to South Gate, see his friend about a weapon and soon everything would return to the way it should.

⌘

Ryan McAllister and Bill Andrews sat in a small cubical that contained a battered table and several chairs in the Los Angeles CBI office. They were scouring the information that had come through on Jason Tanner.

Their suspect was born in South Gate, California, a mostly blue-collar community. He was raised in a single parent home by his mother, Louise, had one sister, Martha Janelle Tanner.

Jason had problems in school, dropped out after his sophomore year, hung around with a raunchy group of wannabe tough guys, in and out of trouble most of his adult life.

Probation reported the guy didn't have much going for him in the brain department, as his probation officer put it, "the blockhead could screw up a one car funeral procession."

As much as Tanner wanted to be included with the idiots he ran around with, seemed to be on the fringe, more of a "go-fer" than a real member. Easily led, often
mocked and ridiculed by his so-called friends.
Basically ... a real loser.

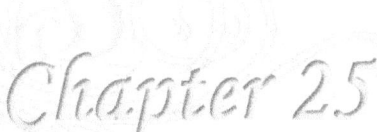

Chapter 25

I asked Jim if he needed a break from baby-sitting duties. I could go to my parent's house for a day or so. His reply was a resounding "NO" make that "HELL NO!"

He reasoned that relaxing in a comfortable place with slobbering dogs, and a good view of the lake wasn't all that difficult. Oh yeah, there was a contrary female he was rather fond of too.

It wasn't as if we were confined to the house twenty-four hours a day. There was grocery shopping, riding horses, wandering around the plaza, and a visit to the museum ... a certain curiosity.

There hadn't been any unusual happenings, no dreams, or Spanish-speaking visitors whispering to me in the night. Perhaps things were back to normal, just three pictures hanging on a museum wall.

We stood in front of the paintings; I looked closely at the cowboys leaning on the corral fence. "Well, I guess Joaquin is in a happy place once again."

"You don't really know the fellow was Murrieta."

"True, just an educated guess, one never knows what

actually happened a hundred and sixty some years ago."

"You think this haunting or whatever, started because of the earthquake?"

I nodded. "A coincidence, maybe, maybe not. All I know is right after the quake, the picture was different."

"We should head over to Penny's and help with the party stuff. You mentioned something about stringing twinkly lights all over the place," Jim muttered.

"Don't sound so huffy, we wrap a few tree trunks, string lights over the bushes in the planter and swaddle the deck posts, nothing too elaborate."

"Seems like we're going to a lot of trouble for people the gang doesn't know."

"You have to look at this endeavor as an adventure. Kind of like travel, never know what is going to happen, believe me, plenty has happened to the crew over the years."

It took about three hours to get the yard all beautiful. Dana's brother and sister-in-law had sent more than enough money to provide for the party.

The cuisine included deli sandwiches, macaroni and green salads, bowls of fruit, large veggie tray and a beautiful cake.

The bar area would feature a keg of beer, several ice filled tubs for wine, soda, and water, all presided over by Jim and Steve.

The supplies were to be picked up tomorrow afternoon, things should be ready to go by six o'clock, I was not alone in thinking it might be quite a party.

I wasn't wrong!

The young couple, Beverly and Harley, arrived a little early the evening of the happy event. After thanking everyone again for hosting the special occasion, changed into their party clothes.

Beverly re-appeared in a filmy, chiffony gown with lovely gossamer wings attached to the back.

Harley was an Elvis Presley look alike, sideburns, bell-bottom, turquoise and white jumpsuit, with a few rhinestones down the front.

Dana's brother, Trevor, looked as if he might have a heart attack, his wife, Joan hurried to the bar and brought back wine and made him sit down before he fell over.

As for the rest of us, we recovered quickly, mentioned how innovative and original the couple looked and took their picture. Then traipsed to the bar and tried not to become hysterical in front of Tinkerbelle and Elvis.

Jim and Steve looked kind of awe-struck. Christian gleefully asked if this was a masquerade party and offered to change into his Superman T-Shirt and Sponge Bob boxer shorts.

And so it began.

Uncle John turned up, managed to find the bar in short order. Spent the rest of the evening in close proximity ... sampling any and all alcoholic beverages.

The bartenders were impressed with many of his thoughts on various subjects.

The informal boozer asked if they believed in unicorns ... he had seen a few over the years.

Raisin and chocolate chip cookies look alike, which caused him to have trust issues, and what would peanut butter be called other than peanut butter.

At one point Penny found two women going through her house room by room, they gave the excuse of looking for the bathroom, then quickly made their way out to the patio. Penny thought they were casing the joint and told Adam to keep any eye on them.

Other than that, the guests were relatively well behaved until Dana, the queen of understatement, announced "they" were opening the presents.

I asked what was so unusual about that; it was about time for Tinkerbelle and Elvis to get started.

Come to find out some of the guests were joyfully un-wrapping several items.

Sandy eventually cajoled the four-slice toaster away from "Cousin It." A name we gave to this interesting looking person of unknown gender, lots of hair, not many teeth.

Penny and I rushed the happy couple to the gift table so they could open their own stuff.

Dana's brother, Trevor, remained at the table, immo-bile, and kinda-sorta in a trance. I think he was suffering some emotional stress, so made sure his wine glass was al-ways full and checked that he was breathing on a regular basis.

Uncle John consumed copious amounts of liquid re-freshment, no one fell in the pool, or pitched a tent in the yard, and the gifts were displayed and mooned over.

A few people were starting to leave; some ladies asked if they could take a plate of food home for relatives that couldn't attend.

No problem with that, we often encouraged guests to do so, less stuff to clean up and store.

The queen of understatement mentioned that people were taking food, and maybe we should stop them. Penny said we knew about it, several guests wanted a little some-thing to carry home.

Dana took a deep breath, ran her fingers through her hair, and insisted we might want to take stock of the kitchen, then went to check on her brother.

Penny and I looked at each other, finished our wine, then strolled around the patio and into the kitchen. Dana was more than accurate about the food.

The extra foot-long sandwiches, a large tub of macaroni salad, and bags of fruit had disappeared. Not only party re-freshments were missing, other things from the fridge and freezer such frozen hamburger, packages of chicken thighs, and a carton of eggs were gone too ... son-of-a bitch!

I think we were both in a mild state of shock, this was a first in all the years we had hosted celebrations. Not much could be done about it now; whatever was left on the buffet table outside would have to suffice.

This called for a drink ... and after some reflection, another great story to add to our collection of misadventures.

For the most part things had gone smoothly except for Dana's religious, fundamentalist, brother, being in a mild catatonic state, Elvis's off-key rendition of *Love Me Tender*, Cousin It's fascination with shiny objects and twinkling lights, and the theft of a quantity of food.

Dana said she would replace the hamburger, chicken and eggs tomorrow. Penny agreed to cancel the hit-man ... instead, called for pizza to be delivered so we would have something to munch on after sorting out the back yard.

All in all, a truly unconventional event.

I was studying the calendar the next morning; my summer was rapidly coming to an end. Just a few more days until the beach vacation, after that, not long before school started.

Couldn't say I had accomplished much of anything besides being stalked by a psycho and a ghost who wanted to be friends.

It was also lovely to have someone special in my life. However, he had a decision to make, whether or not to apply for the deputy position that would soon be available when Ron Walker retired in September.

Jim came inside after standing in the front yard and looking up and down the street.

I set the calendar aside." Doubt Jason Tanner will wander by."

"Just checking."

"You check front and back every hour."

"No, I don't, more like morning, noon, and many times during the night."

"Have you decided on what you're going to do about the transfer?" hoping I didn't sound too needy.

He refilled his coffee mug and sat next to me. "There's no guarantee I'd be hired even if I applied."

"True, but you have an advantage, working here all summer. Sergeant Connelly must think enough of you to entrust his gorgeous, talented and beloved sister into your care."

Jim looked thoughtful. "Yeah, about that ... I hope you realize the reason I'm here has nothing to do with you. It's the dogs I'm interested in, the gorgeous, talented and beloved sister just happens to live here too."

I took a deep breath. "Well, so glad you told me, I won't have to stop seeing Ryan McAllister, or come up with a way to tell the devastatingly handsome fellow I'm interested in someone else."

"The dogs don't like him, reason enough to say a fond farewell to McDoofus."

"You know this fact ... how?"

"Faro and Hallie mentioned it some time ago."

I was trying not to laugh; it would only encourage Jim to invent more outlandish names, when the house began to shake.

The dishes rattled in the cupboard, the framed picture of my parents that sat on the hall table fell over, and the dogs dashed out the open screen door to the patio.

Jim grabbed my arm and began to pull me outside when the tremors stopped.

I took a deep breath. "That was maybe a 4'0, should be an aftershock in a few minutes."

"I think we should wait outside for the next one, don't want to be inside when the ground shifts again."

We carried patio chairs to the lawn and sat for a while, felt a small temblor a few minutes later.

Eventually we went inside, checked the ceiling and

226

walls for cracks and stood the picture back in its place.

"Nothing looks damaged, I'm going to call Mom see how things are at the ranch."

Jim leaned against the kitchen counter. "I don't like earthquakes, hurricanes, floods or tornadoes.

Maybe we should move to New Hampshire, I've herd it's the safest state in the Union, low crime rate, and not prone to natural disasters, might think about it."

I shrugged and placed my arms around his neck. "New Hampshire has long, cold, snowy, winters and humid summers, and Franklin Pierce, the 14th President called the place home."

Jim nuzzled my neck. "You have something against Franklin Pierce?"

"From what I can remember, historians rank him as one of the worst and least memorable of the U.S. Presidents."

Jim looked suitably impressed. "Okay then, we'll cross New Hampshire off the list, but just for curiosities sake let's make a quick trip to the museum ... you know, coincidences ... pictures, ghosts, snakes ... oh my!"

The paintings were unchanged, but that was to be expected since I had a companion by my side.

Jim leaned in for a closer inspection. "Doesn't seem to be any different."

"They won't be, not when anyone is around. I told you it only happens when I'm by myself."

I glanced away from the three pictures to look at the glass-enclosed exhibit beneath the paintings. One of the spurs hanging from a peg turned slightly. I grasped Jim's arm. "Did you see that?"

"See what?"

"The large Spanish spur, the rowel ... moved," I said softly.

Jim bent over the display of artifacts in the Castro collection. "Are you sure?"

227

My heart fluttered a little as I studied the spur. "I'm not sure of anything that happens in this part of the museum any more. Why don't you leave, go look at something else, I'll hang around and see if Joaquin wants to play."

I watched Jim wander toward the stuffed animals exhibit, then turned my attention back to the spurs. Once again the rowel slowly turned, which made the hair on my arms prickle.

When I looked at the painting, there were only two cowboys leaning on the fence, the third one was inside Diamondback Cut.

I made myself breathe. "I'll go back, but don't know what to look for," I whispered.

The spur fell off the peg and landed with a soft clink, which startled me. I jerked away from the case, then looked at the painting ... all three cowboys were back in their usual place.

Jim hurried to my side and grasped my hand. "What happened?"

"I think we should go, but take a look at the display."

The rowel turned slightly, which caused Jim to exclaim. "Damn! We should get out of here! Did the picture do anything strange?"

"Yeah, Joaquin took a stroll to the Cut."

"Come on, I think we could use a drink, something a little stronger than a milkshake," Jim muttered and guided me toward the door.

It was early, the elder Cordova, Hector, father to Laura, Angelina, Hector Jr. and Jose, was on duty at El Picaro.

Jim and I had a brief conversation with the owner of the cantina, then ordered two beers and two tequilas and moved to a table.

Jim's knowledge of good tequila was impressive. Instead of tequila in a shot glass, he wanted *Don Julio Reposado* poured into low-ball glasses over ice.

Don Julio was for savoring not belting back and banging a shot-glass on the bar.

I sipped the distinctive, woody, flavored liquor. "What do you think we should do?"

Jim set his glass carefully on the table and rotated it slowly. "Go to the Cut again, Joaquin is very persistent."

"Yeah ... I really hate snakes, they slither and hiss ... but ghosts ... ghosts can be persuasive, at least this one is."

Chapter 26

Bill Andrews sighed and studied the latest stack of papers in the wire basket on his desk. He thought about the hours spent looking into small details that eventually helped solve almost every case he'd worked on.

Television and films always made it look so easy and instantaneous. Truth be known, tracking tid-bits of information from a variety of sources was mind numbing, and time consuming.

McAllister rubbed his eyes, then took a drink of tepid coffee. "I've been through every person employed at the Coverdale Retreat looking at car registrations, another dead end."

Bill yawned, pulled out several items of correspondence from the basket, a few minutes later asked. "What was the name of Tanner's mother?"

"Lois ... no, Louise," Ryan replied.

"Seems a 1997, maroon, Mercury Grand Marquis is registered to a Louise Tanner, who lives in South Gate."

"Only one problem, Louise Tanner died two years ago."

"When we went to the house looking for our boy, Jason,

no one was home, neighbors hadn't seen him around for a while."

Ryan fiddled with his pen. "Looks like we talk to the neighbors again, this time ask about the car, and the sister too."

Bill hunted for a file buried under several other folders and began to shuffle through the pages. "Martha Tanner, the sister, is proving difficult to locate, just sort of dropped out of sight."

"All right we go back to South Gate, check the house once more, ask about the car and the sister, someone might know what happened to her."

Bill closed the file and glanced across the desk at his partner. "I'm only going to mention this once, I know you're interested in the Connelly woman, but might want to keep your distance, she is a victim and a witness in this ever-expanding case."

Ryan gave the pen a toss; it landed between the stapler and container of paper clips. "Yeah, that's a problem, can't have some defense lawyer making a big deal about it, if and when, this case goes that far."

"Wouldn't take much to get it pitched, could be argued that Tanner was only a suspect because he did something to a cop's girlfriend."

"You don't have to go into detail, I get it."

⌘

Dana and Steve came for dinner; the guys were outside talking and grilling chicken. I'd prepared mac and cheese, and garlic bread, comfort food. Dana went all out and emptied the package of mixed leafy greens into a bowl, along with some cherry tomatoes and buttered croutons. She wasn't into culinary stuff.

231

We talked about the beach vacation. Steve would come on his day off; Jim had mentioned he would go back on his regular schedule since I would be in a different location and around quite a few people.

I wondered why he decided not to accompany me to the beach?

Could be he was rethinking this relationship thing; after all, we were in an unusual situation, careful not to let our emotions run wild ... difficult at times.

Jim Hayden was interested in the ladies, and women were quite taken with him too, what I didn't know, was where I fit.

We needed to have an in-depth discussion, but now wasn't the time, things were unsettled in so many ways. Hopefully, whack-job Tanner would be caught soon.

Let's not forget my persistent ghost who wanted god knows what. Today at the museum had been a little unnerving with the spur and all.

I could understand why Jim might have second thoughts about us; I had second thoughts about everything.

After our guests departed, Jim cleaned the grill, checked the gate, then walked the perimeter along the back fence with the dogs. I finished in the kitchen and set the dishwasher.

When he returned from patrol duties we relaxed on the couch for a little while, it was late and not the proper time to have a heart-to-heart discussion. Jim looked sleepy and I was tired ... after a lingering kiss we said good night.

I headed off to take a shower; he collected bedding from the guest bedroom and prepared his place on the sofa.

The dogs growled, Hallie whined softly, the noise disturbed my strange dream; I distinctly remember a soft metallic clink, and the whisper in Spanish. "*Solo a primera luz, habra un segundo.*"

In an instant my eyes opened. I gasped for breath,

looked around, and let out a squeak at the dark shape that stood in the doorway. The dogs bounded off the bed and slowly approached the shadowy figure.

The light came on; Jim scanned the room, then swiftly moved past the ecstatic and somewhat confused canines. He sat on the bed and enveloped me in his arms.

"What happened? I heard the dogs."

I was trying to breathe normally and stop shaking. "My ghostly friend was here, he left a message."

Jim gently brushed back the hair from around my face. "What did he have to say?"

"I'm trying to remember the Spanish words exactly."

I closed my eyes, rested my head on Jim's chest and thought. I recalled the jingling, it was a familiar sound ... spurs.

The rowel is the revolving disc on the end of a spur. Some riders add small metal "Pajados" or "Jingo Bobs" to the wheel to create a jingling sound when walking.

"Joaquin must like the jingle of spurs."

"Okay ... he wears spurs, what did he say?"

"Only at first light will there be a second," I said softly.

Jim inhaled deeply. "So, the guy likes fancy spurs and cryptic messages."

"I'm sure he wants me to find or do something important, so let's figure it out."

Jim rose from the bed. "I doubt we'll get much sleep after this little episode, I'll put the coffee on."

We settled on the couch with our steaming mugs. I recited all the messages my ghost had uttered. *Palomino girl, Fortune favors the brave, and Only at first light will there be a second.*

Hallie's huge head was resting on Jim's leg, he was absently scratching around her ears. "Let's assume Joaquin knows you like Palomino horses. If he is hanging around Diamondback Cut he has seen you ride by on Matchless."

233

I nodded. "Okay, I'll agree with that. What about the fortune bit?"

"I would think if one is audacious enough to mess around in the Cut, might find something of value among the pretty rocks and snakes."

I sipped more coffee. "You mean nuggets of gold? A little hard to believe there's a fortune in gold laying around after all these years, snakes or no snakes."

"Yeah, kind of an absurd idea. Let's move on to the statement about first light."

Jim brushed his bare foot against mine; our feet rested on the sturdy copper topped coffee table. "The connotation of "first light" that comes to mind is sunrise, unless, you have a different idea."

I was trying to think of another way to interpret "first light." The only thing that made sense was the rise of the sun above the horizon. Prime of the morning, in religious terms, The First Hour.

"So he's telling me to seek "whatever" at the break of day? Then what? The sun shines twice?"

Jim chuckled. "Maybe he's a Bob Dylan fan."

"What are you talking about?"

Jim had an impish look on his face, then started to croon softly. "*Until the break of day, let me see ya'make him smile. I long to see you in the morning light, I long to reach for you in the night.*"

I joined in the chorus. "*Lay lady lay, lay across my big brass bed.*"

I also couldn't resist adding. "Bob wasn't grammatically correct, the words should have been "*Lie Lady Lie*"

Jim smiled indulgently. "Then the lyrics wouldn't rhyme with the next verse of '*stay lady stay*' would they. So I guess Eric Clapton's *Lay Down Sally* isn't accurate either."

I replied sweetly. "You'll have to contact Bob and Eric and have them fix their mistakes. Shall we return to the sub-

234

ject of '*will there be a second*' ... a second what?"

Jim smirked. "Only way to find out is to be in Diamondback Cut when the sun rises."

"Lovely, absolutely frickin' lovely," I moaned.

⌘

McAllister and Andrews were occupied in consuming the delicious, but messy pastrami sandwiches at the small deli across from their office. They had spent the morning talking to the entire block of neighbors in South Gate.

The Tanner family was quiet and kept to themselves, the lady next door said Louise Tanner worked nights as a desk clerk at some hotel. As for the girl, Martha, she was older than Jason and had left home right after graduating high school.

Jason lived with his mom off and on for several years, moved in on a permanent basis after her death.

Yes, he drove the Mercury and sometimes a beige van was parked in the driveway.

There had also been a white van, but the neighbor hadn't seen any cars around for quite a while.

So Maris Connelly had been correct, there had been two different vehicles, or maybe just one that had been painted.

When the men got back to the office they would try and trace Martha Tanner, the woman had to be around somewhere. Could be that Jason was keeping out of sight with help from his sister.

Building a profile of a subject amounted to looking into all aspects of their life. Credit reports, banking information, social security, social media presence, any and all public records ... court, civil, criminal, divorce, bankruptcy, military and prison.

It took hours, even days of hunting and searching,

sometimes with little or no results, especially if a person didn't want to be found.

As busy as Ryan was, his thoughts turned to Maris. He should be up front, and hopefully she would understand, having family members in law enforcement. Right now he couldn't think of a way to say what was necessary, but it had to be done relatively soon.

⌘

"What should we take with us in the morning?" I asked.

"Our backpacks, with the usual stuff, I have a foldable shovel, in case we have to do some digging. I don't plan on sticking my hand in any burrows, gaps or pits."

I made a face and shivered a little. "Probably should add thick bushes and rock crevices to the places to stay away from. You do know that our slithery friends come out at night to hunt during the hot summer months."

"Just keep your ears tuned and eyes open to your surroundings."

I muttered. "After we do all that, be sure to concentrate on searching for some elusive "whatever" a ghost wants us to find. Should be really fun!"

Jim laughed. "Where is your sense of adventure? This may be a once in a lifetime experience!"

"Yeah ... after being attacked by a zillion snakes, your life is over."

The plan was to hike the quarter mile from my folk's place, didn't want to mind any horses. We'd be in the Cut when the sun appeared to see what might take place. I had my doubts anything would occur other than a rosy glow of morning.

My sleep was troubled; I woke several times to check the clock, and finally got up around three.

Even though I tried to be quiet, Jim was awake; he passed my door on his way to the bathroom. I took my boots and socks into the living room set them beside the couch and went to make coffee and prepare some oatmeal and toast.

I had looked up the exact time the sun would rise, a little after six we should be in the Cut waiting to bask in the light of day.

Dad was standing on the porch as we drove up. We unloaded the backpacks; my father joined us by the truck. "All I have to say is be careful, watch where you step. Your mother said you're doing this because of a dream?"

I was glad Mom hadn't brought in the ghost stuff; Dad wasn't one for such nonsense.

"You can never tell about dreams, the Greeks believed that sensations passing through one's mind while sleeping were predictions. It might be the brain examining scraps of interesting information, or a primal response to fulfill a wish."

My father just raised his eyebrows and glanced at Jim. "Try and keep her out of trouble."

Jim chuckled softly. "I'll do my best."

We turned on our flashlights and walked toward the back pasture, found the trail and trudged toward Diamondback Cut.

The morning was crisp, the terrain uneven, but it was quite peaceful. Time to clear the mind, connect with the natural world, and become a little excited about what we might unexpectedly encounter.

The unexpected wasn't new. Traveling with the gang often led to unforeseen experiences like bats chasing us down stairs. Of course we weren't supposed to be in the area marked "private" and climb the narrow, dark, passage to a mysterious locked room in the ancient castle either.

The gently rising ground wasn't too difficult; the beam from the flashlights lit the shrubs and grass on either side of

237

the trail. The hike shouldn't take more than twenty-five minutes at the most.

The loud persistent chirping of crickets was a constant companion, which was significantly better than the rattle of a snake, warning us we were disturbing their nocturnal prowl for food.

"Gosh, this is so fun." I said sarcastically.

"Don't be petulant, if one wants answers to nagging questions there are sacrifices to be made."

"Who said I required answers, I just want Joaquin to find someone else to haunt."

"Stop whining, pick up the pace, we need to be in place when the sun comes up."

I thought about throwing something at the smart-ass but needed the flashlight. Maybe I could get away with hitting the back of his head with a rock. But that would mean searching for one near the bushes, something I was reluctant to do for obvious reasons.

"You don't know where "being in place" is any more than I do."

"I guess if we stand half-way inside the arroyo we should have a decent view of the sun coming up."

I concentrated on the trail and tried not to stumble over anything. The words of the long dead bandit's spirit cycled through my head. *Fortune favors the brave ... Only at first light will there be a second.* Okay, Joaquin or whoever you are, I'll try to be brave for a little while.

See what trouble legends lead us mortals to confront!

Chapter 27

Jason parked on the side of the road where the car could be partially hidden by a couple of trees. It was still dark; he estimated the sun would be up in about half an hour. He wasn't about to go traipsing around in thick bushes in the dark, might be attacked by wolves or mountain lions. That's why he brought the gun, in case a wild animal was lurking about.

All he had to do was follow the route marked out on the map, shouldn't take him long to find the Diamond Cut place.

If he was lucky, all his problems would fade away, he could leave this awful place, buy a big house in Beverley Hills, and drive a fancy sports car instead of his mother's old clunker.

He didn't even own the van; Jay had bought it for the business and registered it in his name for some reason. After today all would be different, things were about to change.

He would rest for a little while; take a couple of pain pills. His leg ached, the dog bite was red and swollen, maybe he'd go back to the clinic in San Fernando and have it looked at this afternoon.

⌘

Jim tugged me by the hand. "Won't be able to see anything when the sun comes up if we don't actually go into the Cut."

We were standing at the entrance to the rift, the more I studied the gap the less sure I felt about this escapade.

Jim's fingers tightened on mine. "Come on."

We walked slowly, followed the beam of our flashlights. I could hear rustling sounds of small animals seeking shelter from the light. No snakes ... maybe, maybe not!

"This should be far enough, we'll turn everything off and wait," Jim said softly.

"Wonderful, wait for a snake to slither up my leg."

"Stop imagining things that won't happen, be quiet and let our eyes adjust."

Jim looked at his watch; it gave off a soft blue glow. "Forgot to mention how much I enjoy your shirts, where do you discover such witticisms?"

I knew he was trying to take my mind off the surroundings by conversing about trivia. "Believe me, it's not easy to find amusing, non-offensive, epigrams. One might say it's a hobby.

When I see, read, or hear something good I write it down and every so often order a shirt from places that will put whatever you want on the front. Customizing ain't cheap, my friend, it can run around fifty bucks or more, plus shipping."

The reason I was wearing this particular one was because of the long sleeves, I knew the morning would be chilly. The phrase across the front was fun ... *If History Repeats Itself, Then I'm So Getting A Dragon.* Many people didn't get it, but others found it humorous.

There was a soft change in the darkness; the sky had

240

become a lighter shade of purple, then dark blue, eventually various colors of grey.

Both ends of the Cut were open, but the steep sides would block the sun for a few moments. I took a deep breath and looked toward the horizon, as the sun became a glow, then a radiant fire.

A flash of dazzling light hit a large cluster of quartz rocks on our left. An incandescent beam reflected off the rocks to a spot across the arroyo for a few seconds then faded away.

We stood in shocked silence. *"And there will be a second"* I muttered.

Jim rushed to the place where the beam of light had manifested, about five feet off the ground on the side of the ravine.

The spot was nothing spectacular, just dirt and small rocks, it looked like the rest of the terrain, no huge **X** that screamed for us to *dig here.*

But we did anyway ... not with bare hands, used the small shovel Jim had brought. After cutting through about two feet of rubble the spade hit something solid.

Jim cleared debris around a quantity of stones, and carefully removed the rocks that concealed a small chamber. It was difficult to glimpse inside, so he used the flashlight to get a better look.

I was bouncing impatiently from foot to foot. "What do you see!"

"A metal box. You want me to bring it out or leave it for posterity?"

That remark deserved a smack to the back of his head, which I swiftly delivered.

"Ow! That hurt, might result in a concussion and memory loss."

"Stop screwing around and schlepp out the damn box!"

The container was less than a foot in length and seven

or eight inches tall, it had a hasp that could be locked, but wasn't. Jim placed the chest on the ground; we knelt on either side, then looked at each other.

"Go ahead, Joaquin is your ghost, he wanted you to have whatever is inside."

I swept away the small amount of dirt from the lid and opened the coffer.

A pale, linen fabric with letters in blue thread was folded on top.

I brushed my fingers over the beautiful work. "This is an alphabet sampler," and carefully handed it to Jim.

There were three pouches; two of leather the other of yellowish linen material and lace, I opened the delicate lace bag. It contained locks of hair; the first was a loosely braided, mahogany auburn color, the other a wispy dark brown tuft, both tied with white ribbon.

Jim took a closer look. "Hair? A person's hair has been preserved for all these years?"

"It was a popular custom to save the hair of loved ones, kind of a cherished symbol of eternal life, a remembrance."

I replaced the lace keepsake and untied the rawhide thong on the next pouch and tilted it slightly. A piece of jewelry slid into my hand and glittered in the morning sun. A necklace of gold, with nuggets embedded about an inch apart, each one fastened with fine gold wire. It was beautiful, very much out of the ordinary and absolutely stunning.

All I could manage was a rather breathless "Oh!"

Jim's reaction was similar. "Wow, make that double Wow!"

I carefully returned the necklace to the small bag and opened the last sac. Gold coins spilled out of the purse and overflowed my palm. Jim caught several and we examined the pristine pieces of metal.

There were twelve coins with a Liberty Head emblem and the date 1850 on one side, and an eagle with the words

United States of America Twenty D on the back.

Jim whistled softly. "No wear and tear on any of these pieces ... might be uncirculated."

I continued to examine the bright objects. "Wonder why Joaquin wanted these things to be found? They were obviously important and deeply personal."

"I guess we'll never know the why of it, but we should get going.

I'll reshuffle my backpack, stash a few things in yours, and make room for the box."

After a brief reorganization of several items, we started to make our way back. I was concentrating where to place my feet when Jim grabbed my arm. "We've got company," he muttered softly.

Entering the arroyo was a man, he hadn't seen us yet, much too busy looking at the different colored rocks on the side of the Cut. We stopped and watched quietly as the fellow picked up small colorful pebbles and examined them closely.

I squinted my eyes in order to make out a face, then stifled a gasp.

Son-of-a-bitch, that rat-bastard, Jason Tanner, was right in front of us! What the hell was he doing here!

My brain went completely blank for a few seconds. I made myself breathe. "It's Tanner!" I whispered.

Jim moved in front of me, aware of the potentially dangerous situation. I could see the muscles in his neck tense, and his hands clench into fists.

Tanner tossed the pebble aside, hobbled a little closer and finally noticed us about twenty or so feet away.

To say "Freak-boy" was surprised could be an understatement. He looked a little panicked, not sure of what to do, then fumbled under his shirt at the waistband of his jeans and drew out a gun.

He pointed it in our direction and started to sway from

243

side to side and yelled. "You! You bitch, you're the cause of everything!"

"Think about it Tanner, do you really want to fire that weapon? Murder is a horrible thing to live with, it will eat away inside your brain!" Jim said emphatically.

The agitated man rubbed a hand through his hair; the gun seemed to quiver slightly as he limped a few steps closer. "Things were fine until you stuck your nose into my business, I had money, lots of money and Jay was happy ... it's all your fault!" he rambled.

Tanner took a deep breath, aimed the gun, put his hand on a rock outcrop to steady the nervous twitching and was hit by the lightening-fast strike of a snake.

Not just one rattler, but two vipers lay on the shelf that jutted outward.

The terrified man screamed in pain and panic, flailing his snake bitten arm, slashing wildly around with the gun ... which fired.

We ran to the screaming, sobbing, idiot, who was groveling on the ground, holding his hand against his chest, the gun lay forgotten in the dirt.

Jim kicked the weapon away and tried to examine the area where the bullet entered the guy's tennis shoe.

Jim shook his head and our eyes met. "I think Mr. Tanner shot himself in the foot."

Even though the situation was kinda-sorta horrible, I couldn't suppress the laughter that bubbled forth. Jim managed a little better but had to tightly clamp his lips together and look away.

The moron was snake bit twice and had maimed himself in a matter of seconds. There were long scratches on his face and neck ... had to be from Evenrude

It was rather hysterical to reflect that Evenrude had mauled him and Faro took a hunk out of his hide. If I had known the guy was such an imbecile I wouldn't have been so unnerved.

It's funny how the mind works in a stressful situation. I must have deep psychological problems to think of such stupid things. Jason Tanner had the same qualities as seen in a third-rate horror film, really bad luck, and poor decision making skills. Such as "lets hide in the basement" from the monster, or the totally dense female admitting, "I know who you really are ... an axe murderer!" to her menacing ex-boyfriend.

Poor old Jason was not much of a threat. The pathetic man sat on the ground, rocking back and forth with his eyes closed, and moaning softly.

The bite marks were in two different places, one on his hand, the other just above the wrist. Blood oozed from the toe of his shoe.

"We need to get some help, I'll call the Sheriff's Department," Jim exclaimed, then unfastened a compartment of his backpack and brought out the SatPhone.

After explaining the situation and our location we managed to get Tanner out of the Cut and settled under some trees. We had to keep him quiet and immobile as possible, not difficult because he was rather catatonic.

I mentioned that I hadn't heard the telltale warning, Jim said that sometimes snakes don't rattle, even when startled.

A Polaris Ranger ATV, modified as an ambulance was on its way, it would be faster than calling the chopper out of Santa Clarita.

I wouldn't be surprised if my brother showed up too; the department had several All-Terrain Vehicles for situations like this.

Well, this had been a different kind of morning, and here I thought my summer was going to be dull and boring, plus there was a really great story to tell the gang.

Didn't know what to think about the "treasure" we had to get Freak-boy some medical care and arrested. Then I'd discuss, and present the valuables to my parents, after all Diamondback Cut was on their property.

⌘

McAllister and Andrews were in the process of obtaining search warrants for The Coverdale Retreat. It had taken some digging but a name had surfaced and a new line of inquiry was being pursued.

Martha Janelle Tanner, the sister of Jason, had reinvented herself. Martha married a guy named Stottler, the couple didn't remain in the state of wedded bliss very long, but Martha still went by her married name. Except now she was known as Janelle Stottler ... Jan Stottler, the Physician's Assistant and second in command at the Coverdale Retreat.

The woman had lied about knowing anyone named Jason Tanner, and probably a lot more.

It had also been established that Dr. Julian Coverdale was on the medical board that had dealings with The Independent Living Programs for this part of the State. He would have information about the young people transitioning to new situations when they were no longer in foster care. Not difficult to locate healthy, young, and vulnerable kids with no relatives to wonder why they were missing.

Now they could get a look inside the two outbuildings, as well as medical files on any of the victims who had been kidnapped and mutilated.

Bill Andrews doubted they would find documents just sitting around in cabinet drawers, but there might be data stored on electronic devices, either at the retreat or on private computers of Jan Stottler or Dr. Julian Coverdale.

Andrews and McAllister were on the road when the call came in from the Sendro Sheriff's Department that they had Jason Tanner in custody. He was at the clinic being treated for snakebite and a gunshot wound to his foot. Two deputies were assigned to make sure Mr. Tanner stayed put.

Things were starting to heat up in this body parts case; they just had to put all the pieces of the puzzle together.

⌘

Sure enough Scott had come along with the ambulance. Jim told him about the gun still in the Cut it should be bagged up.

My brother huffed a little, not thrilled I was involved, and Jim should have better sense, and so on and so forth. He calmed down when we explained what had happened.

Eventually we arrived back at the ranch and into the tender care of my parents.

We were sitting at the dining table after scarfing down sandwiches, pasta salad and chocolate cake. My mom's chocolate cake is heavenly, but I only had a tiny sliver ... maybe a little bigger than a sliver.

After the table was cleared I asked Jim to get the box from his backpack.

My father stared at the contents displayed in front of him. "I'll be damned!"

Not the most eloquent spiel ever uttered, but kind of summed up what we were thinking.

"What shall we do with these wonderful things?" I exclaimed. "They were found on your property, so I guess they rightfully belong to you."

My father ran his fingers over the necklace. "So you believe the ghost of Joaquin Murrieta told you to find this stuff?" he said with skepticism.

"I don't know that it was Murrieta, but it could have been."

Mom gently touched the locks of hair. "It's possible

247

these mementos belonged to Isabella Castro and her child. The smaller bundle is fine like baby's hair."

"Does it really matter how I was able to discover these wonderful things? A spirit, or dream, maybe even indigestion pointed me in the direction, and this trove of beautiful items is real. What do you want to do?"

"As far as I'm concerned, they belong to you ... do what you want with them. I'd be interested to know the value of the coins and necklace," my father declared.

Mom nodded in agreement, Jim smirked and jostled a coin from hand to hand.

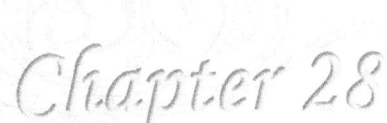

Chapter 28

For the present time the metal box and all its contents would be secured in my parent's safe at the ranch. The small vault had been the idea of several times great grandparents who didn't have much faith in banks. It was hidden under the floor of the window seat in the study.

Dad said he would do some checking for reputable dealers and try to find the value of the 1850 coins.

Jim and I didn't have much to say on the drive home, we had a lot to think about.

Now that I wasn't being stalked there was no need for him to be my constant companion. He could move back to his place and return to his regular duties, and things would go back to normal ... sort of.

The tinkly sound of his cell broke the silence. Jim looked at the caller's information then clicked ignore.

He had done that a few times in the past, it wasn't any of my business who was trying to get in touch with him, but he always seemed a little restless after the calls.

"You can get a decent night's rest now that the creep has been caught. No more sleeping on the couch."

"It wasn't so bad. In fact, the entire experience was kind of enjoyable."

I pushed some tendrils of hair away from my face. "You know we're leaving for the beach tomorrow, it would be fun if you could join us."

"Depends on the duty schedule, as you go off to frolic in the surf and sand, I return to work."

"Maybe you can finagle something and come along with Steve."

Jim nodded. "I'll see what I can do. How about going to dinner tonight, do something special.

"Excellent idea, we have reason to celebrate, the lovely box of trinkets and the psycho no longer creeping about."

"Do you think Joaquin is gone too?"

I looked out the window and sighed. "I would imagine so, but can't resist a visit to the museum and linger around the pictures."

Jim chuckled. "Kind of tempting fate, aren't you?"

"Perhaps ... perhaps not."

The plan was to move Jim's stuff back to his place, then he wanted to drop by the Sheriff's Office and check out the duty schedule. When he returned we could decide where to have dinner.

After he left I made a quick trip to The Blurry Grape Wine Shop. They carried my favorite almond champagne; one couldn't celebrate without a couple of bottles of the bubbly.

Jim's truck was in the carport when I got back, his little jaunt hadn't taken him very long. I gathered my purse and sack of wine from the car and got as far as the front steps when a very nice BMW pulled up and parked. I lingered to see who was driving.

Some moments later a woman exited the vehicle and walked toward me.

She was beautiful, long dark hair that probably took

hours to style in the "casual" look. Her short, above the knee shirt, was tight and didn't leave anything to imagine, as did the figure-hugging, décolleté, silk blouse.

The woman removed oversized sunglasses and approached. Her eyes were a deep blue and the lashes couldn't be real, I mean no one had fringe like that, except for a giraffe I saw once upon a time.

"Hi, I'm looking for Jim Hayden. I wasn't sure if this was the right place until I saw his truck. All I had to go on was the street name."

The bottles clinked together when I switched the bag to my other arm. "Ah ... yeah, he lives next door," and nodded to the left.

"Thank you."

She turned to go just as Jim opened his door and stepped out. "I heard voices and ... Sherry!"

The look on his face was one of shock; he quickly gazed at me, then back to the provocative woman. "What are you doing here?"

Sherry rushed to his side and kissed his cheek. "I tried to call, but ... never mind, Jimmy we really need to talk."

She grasped his arm and turned him toward his place.

"You go inside, I'll be right in."

Sherry reluctantly dropped his arm and walked away. "Maris, I have to deal with this, it shouldn't take long," he said softly.

I was finding it difficult to breathe. "Yeah ... it's fine ... things happen, I'll see you later."

He nodded and hurried to where the lovely Sherry waited. It took a deal of effort not to run to my door, so made myself casually stroll away and not look back.

The dogs frolicked around like I'd been gone for hours, so gave them a Scooby Snack after setting the champagne on the counter. Who the hell was Sherry!

They were definitely more than casual acquaintances ...

great!

Okay ... time to do something productive make myself useful. Wash clothes, haul out a duffle bag and start packing, nothing like a trip to the ocean to forget your troubles.

Might as well put the champagne in the fridge, something to look forward to later, when the sun went down, and whatever . . .

The phone interrupted my dark thoughts and the robotic voice announced Ryan McAllister wished to speak with me.

"Hello?"

"Maris, nice to hear your voice again."

"Thank you ... so what is new and exciting in your life?"

"It's gotten a lot more exciting now that we have Jason Tanner in custody."

"I'm happy about that too, good to feel safe again."

There was a long pause before Ryan spoke. "Yeah, about that ... Tanner's arrest creates a problem ..."

I knew what was coming next, so saved the man from trying to explain. "You don't need to go into detail, I quite understand. There should be no fraternizing between the two of us for obvious reasons."

I could hear the intake of breath and a long sigh. "That's the way of it. I enjoyed our brief time together ... ah maybe ..."

"Yeah, it was fun. Take care Ryan, be safe and keep well."

This must be a record of some kind, dumped twice in a matter of a few minutes. I guess Jim didn't exactly dump me but the wonderful "Sherry" would win hands down. The woman was stunning; she hadn't tracked him to Sendero just to say "Hi!"

I liked Ryan but wasn't particularly disturbed about not seeing him again. Jim was a different story.

I was upset ... no, more like shaken, pissed off ... hurt. I

252

rubbed my temples and blinked away tears. Why was I act-ing so pathetic? I mean the guy was an immature flirt, a Lo-thario, with commitment problems, and wasn't even my type.

I stood by the living room window gazing at the im-pressive metallic black "Beemer" outside.

Probably hot as hell and difficult to keep clean, she must spend a fortune at the carwash, couldn't see "Sherry" doing it herself.

Enough! I had things to do.

The mid-size duffle would be fine; it wasn't like we were going to England. T-shirts, shorts, couple of bathing suits, a pair of jeans, sweatshirt and sleeping attire should get me through the week.

I'd throw in three or four books; sitting on the deck overlooking the Pacific with nothing to do but read was per-fect.

Jim's guitar was still in the guest room, I brushed my fingers over the strings, then carefully moved it over and placed the duffle on the bed.

I should start the wash, didn't want dirty clothes sitting around molding for a week. Probably wouldn't actually mold, not in this dry climate. Then dig out the travel kit for my personal amenities in the bottom drawer of the bathroom cabinet.

I was making progress; mind and body were occupied doing needful things. The dogs followed me from room to room, I think they knew I was going somewhere when they saw the duffel come out of the closet.

I conversed with them while stuffing clothes in the washer. "I'm not going away for long, you guys will hardly know I'm gone. Just think how much fun you'll have at the ranch being spoiled and going for long runs with Grover and Monty."

The doorbell rang, and the oafs ran to the front part of

the house. I pushed past the noisy beasts and opened the little glass window.

"Hey!" Jim said.

I opened the door, the dogs smothered him with affection and he eventually made his way inside.

I tried to be nonchalant. "Is your friend expecting you back soon?"

"No, my "friend" is gone, and won't be returning."

"Oh ... she seemed so happy to see you."

Jim moved into the living room. "An explanation is in order, shall we sit?"

I followed him to the couch, Faro jumped between us, and plopped his slobbery self down.

Jim studied my face. "Sherry is an ex-girlfriend and somehow found where I was living. She wanted to get back together, really sorry about what happened, it had been a huge mistake and so on and so forth."

I rubbed my hand across Faro's head. "... and now the gorgeous Sherry is ..."

"... on her way back to Santa Clarita or wherever else she decides to go, just as long as it's away from me."

I could now let myself breathe normally. "But she drives such a swell car."

He snickered. "I should have introduced her to the dogs, you know, let them meet and greet a guest."

"She doesn't like dogs?"

"Not really, much to smelly and dirty."

I laughed, and patted Hallie who was sitting on my foot, which was becoming numb.

Jim reached for my hand. "Do you still want to celebrate, go out to dinner?"

"Absolutely, and when we return I have just the thing to finish off the evening."

That devilish grin spread across his face. "Great minds think alike."

"I think the actual quote is *'Great minds think alike, fools seldom differ.'* Gives a little different spin on the meaning."

Jim smirked. "Saints preserve me from English teachers!"

We never made it to dinner. It wasn't intentional, I reminded the guy that he left his guitar and went to fetch it from the bedroom. He followed me down the hall and leaned against the wall across from my room.

Then took the guitar, strummed a few chords and softly sang.

"Stay, lady, stay ... stay with your man awhile. Why wait any longer for the one you love when he's standing in front of you. Stay, lady, stay ... stay while the night is still ahead."

He held out his hand and drew me inside and closed the door. We ignored the dogs that whiffled and burbled outside.

The beach was great, the kids got a little sunburned. Adam and Sandy's boys, Joey and David, ran amok, flew kites, played with Frisbees and generally found things to keep themselves occupied. They even wandered around with Nicole to find shells and pretty rocks.

Penny managed to have an encounter with a jellyfish ... most unpleasant. The raised red welt erupted in a line with small white lesions across her thigh.

Christian, the dear man, offered to pee on it. He'd heard that was the best way to treat a sting, another incorrect "old wives' tale".

The treatment is to rinse with vinegar, and soak in hot water for about twenty minutes.

After a dose of ibuprofen and a liberal slather of lidocaine cream the burning pain lessened considerably.

Jim and Steve came for a day, which was lovely ... long walks on the beach really are wonderful, despite the cliché.

The men grilled steaks, corn on the cob and potatoes, while we women relaxed on the deck, drank margaritas and watched. The whole concept of beachfront living could become addictive.

I tried not to think that school would be starting soon and I'd have to deal with the Witch, Bitch and the Blob once again. Never had many problems with the students, they were usually fun.

Dad called said he had some very interesting news, but it could wait until I got back, the dogs were fine, he thought Hallie had a crush on Percival, the pig. I hoped that wasn't the case, didn't need a pot-bellied critter wandering around the house.

⌘

The CBI had been busy. It took several days for Jason Tanner to recover enough for an interview. He was reluctant to say anything except he wanted a lawyer and to speak with Jay.

Everything changed after searching the Coverdale Retreat. The two back areas were quite revealing. The white van was stashed inside one storage unit and a small operating room was located behind a wall of shelves in the other.

The van had been painted, but the doorjambs revealed a tan color in places. Crime Scene Investigators scoured the vehicle and the operating room. Tiny fragments of physical evidence such as hair, blood and fibers were found in both places.

The small white car was brought in from the side of the road. It was registered to Ashley Heath, a name found in Tanner's phone contacts that turned out to be his girlfriend.

The license plate belonged to another car; two other plates were located in the trunk and the whole car examined for fingerprints.

Even though Jason had nothing to say, Ashley was a

fund of information when the agents informed her she would be held for murder. The first suspect who named names and told the whole sordid tale would be in a much better situation.

Jan Stottler, and a guy named Carl Prosser did the removal of the kidneys. Ashley and Jason Tanner snatched the young victims, mostly from bus stations. The teenagers were injected with Propofol as soon as they got into the car, and kept knocked out until they were delivered to the hotel room.

Ashley and Jason, wearing a disguise, procured hotel rooms beforehand, used stolen credit cards and license plates on her car when registering.

After the surgeries, the victims were transported by van to the motel in the early hours of the morning and left in the room.

Jan Stottler accessed Dr. Coverdale's files, making sure the young people had no health problems or relatives that would miss them. Easy enough to find out when they were expected to arrive at their group home, and of course a recent picture for identification.

Unfortunately, Jan Stottler had the day off when the Retreat was searched, and a nervous staff member notified her what was taking place. So for the time being, Jan, or Jay as her brother called her, was gone. Hopefully it wouldn't take too long to find the greedy predator and her boyfriend, Carl.

Ashley had no idea who purchased the kidneys, it was Jan and Carl who knew that information, all the more reason to locate the couple.

⌘

I read the single page letter one more time before handing it back to my Dad. It was an offer to purchase the coins for the going rate of fifty-eight thousand dollars ... each.

Of course this price was dependent on the coins being in the uncirculated condition as the one presented.

"It's the best deal yet, Maris."

I was finding it difficult to process the information. "Not bad at all, it's just so unbelievable. I still wish to share this good fortune."

⌘

My mother stopped rocking and looked over the pasture. "We don't need much of anything, the ranch has been free of debt for years. Your father has an excellent retirement and I make a nice salary. In a couple of years I plan to stop working and will draw a very satisfactory income as well."

"Not to mention our investments that have accumulated over the years. No, these treasures are all yours," my father exclaimed.

"Okay, the first thing I want to do is to preserve the alphabet sampler and locks of hair, have them mounted and framed. I'm sure the museum can point me in the right direction to have it done correctly.

I would like to donate a small display cabinet and loan the contents to the museum from the Connelly-Johansson families. We have several items that have been passed down from generation to generation. The beautiful porcelain doll and cradle, great grandma's silver vanity and manicure set, the silver buttonhook and the vintage lariat should be good company for the alphabet sampler and locks of hair.

I wish to keep the necklace; it's too delicate and beautiful to sell. Have no idea where I'd wear such an elegant piece of jewelry, but it gives me great pleasure to look at it.

With the proceeds from the sale of the coins I want to establish a college fund for the nephews, pay off the duplex, and build a garage on the side of the house for my bit of extravagance."

Dad chuckled. "And what would that be?"

"A beautifully restored 1957 Chevrolet. Bobby Estrada is just about ready to sell, and I want to buy."

"Then do it, no reason not to self-indulge. So, shall I contact this dealer?"

"Yes please, but I want to keep one coin ... just to have, maybe bestow it as a gift to someone special."

My dad studied me for a moment. "I would venture to guess this person might be Jim Hayden?"

"One might say we're moving in that direction ... sorta-kinda."

"Your mother and I think he's a fine young man, you could do a lot worse."

Good to know the folks liked the guy, always a plus in my book.

Before going home there was a stop to make ... the museum. I had put it off, not knowing if I should tempt fate, as Jim had mentioned.

I waited while a couple of visitors admired the contents of the display case next to the paintings.

When they left I approached the three pictures and addressed the cowboys. "Isabella's needlework and the locks of hair are in good hands, the necklace too. The gold coins were probably acquired while engaged in unashamed thievery, so no sentimental attachment is accorded. Selling them won't be emotionally upsetting."

I looked around the room to see if anyone was overtly watching or listening to a nut-case converse with a painting.

"*La paz sea contigo mi amigo,*" I whispered. No harm in wishing the troublesome legend a little peace. Nothing changed, the faces remained a blur, perhaps a mere suggestion of smile on the face of the last vaquero ... or not.

I should have a T-shirt created with the words from the classic movie *The Man Who Shot Liberty Valance.*

When the legend becomes fact, print the legend.

Jim's truck was parked in the carport when I got home. I knocked on his door.

It didn't take long for him to answer.

"I require a favor."

He leaned on the doorframe and grinned. "Your wish is my command."

"Then I command you to accompany me into town,"

"Okay, you need a milkshake or something?"

"Just put on your shoes, this little task won't take long."

A few blocks from the house we spotted Ryan McAllister sitting at the light, coming in the opposite direction. His car was rather distinctive, a silver Audi A4.

Jim sighed loudly. "Well, well if it isn't your boyfriend, Rufus McCluck, you can flag him down, I'll take the drool mobile back to your place if you want."

I smirked slightly. "Ryan was never my boyfriend, and that budding relationship wilted a while ago."

Jim inhaled. "So in the scheme of things, you're stuck with me?"

"Looks like ... unless that's a problem?"

He grinned. "No problem at all. Where are we going?"

"You'll find out soon enough."

Bobby Estrada was waiting at the garage. He was going to let me take possession of the 57 right now. I handed him a check for the down payment, with the rest due by the end of the month.

Jim wanted to drive the flying 57 and even promised to be extra careful when parking under the carport. I muttered that if the metallic blue paint job were dinged, there would be hell to pay.

The pathetic, but sturdy Honda would be relegated to the street until the new garage was built.

⌘

Jim knocked on my door a little after ten that night. I usually waited up for him when he was on the evening shift.

After the dogs mauled and slobbered on him, he settled at the kitchen island. "Robinson called me into his office today."

I handed him a beer. "Oh, what did the Sherriff want with your fine self?"

"Wanted to give me this," and handed over an official looking document.

I carefully read the paper that proclaimed Jim Hayden was now a permanent member of Sendero de Robles Sherriff's Department, which caused my heart to flutter.

"So why didn't you tell me, I thought you were still thinking about things ... relationships and commitments and whatever."

He rose and came around the island and stood so close that I was sure he could hear my heart racing out of control.

"I did think ... the result is printed on that piece of paper, I'm not going anywhere unless you have other ideas."

I set the paper on the counter. "Since you're sticking around I have a little something for you."

I hurried to the bedroom and returned with a small box and placed it in his hand.

His eyes grew wide in surprise after he pried off the lid and saw the gold coin. "You didn't have to do this, I would have been happy with a lock of your hair," he said softly.

I placed my arms around his neck. "This calls for a celebration."

"I couldn't agree more ... but it's too late to go for a pineapple milkshake, and the almond champagne is gone."

I sighed. "That is disappointing ... we shall have to think of something else."

END

About the Author

A college professor and administrator, Jeninne Taylor made the San Joaquin Valley in Southern California her home for many years. After she retired, she moved to the Big Island of Hawaii, outside of Hilo. Here, she says, she can enjoy the vivid colors of green, fresh air, rain, and the many visitors who make her laugh as well as broadening her horizons.

What makes Taylor's books special? "My female characters are very independent," she said. "Plus they're talented in something unusual. As a writer, applying ideas such as martial arts, facility as a sniper, and or the ability to profile in Victorian terms can be a challenge. And I also love to add a touch of the mystical just for fun."

Taylor has two rescue dogs who keep her company. "They're both kind of special ed," she said, something she's familiar with having been a special education specialist for many years.

As for the rest: "I have travelled the world, love England and try not to get thrown out of foreign countries. I collect yard art flamingos, the more tasteless the better. Even though I'm not brave enough to display them in the front of my house, my friends can't wait to see what godawful *objet d'art* I might find next!"

"As I have mentioned before, I have three goals in life: move to Hawaii, write something other than school curriculum, and marry Johnny Depp. Two out of three ain't bad!"

Jeninne Taylor's books can be found on Amazon.
Search by title or author.

Never Star Crossed

After the untimely death of her father, Juliette finds herself shouldering the responsibility of a vast business enterprise stretching from England to the Americas. She soon discovers that she must fight for her survival, for there are greedy men intent upon taking advantage of her youth and inexperience. In this fascinating tale spanning the globe from Barbados to London, Juliette finds more then she expected; not only does she manage to salvage her father's empire, but she finds the one man who can see her for herself.

Watch for Me

The widowed Arabaya, Viscountess Westbrook, has no intention of sitting idly watching the world pass her by. Outwardly conforming to the role required of her by Victorian Society, Arabaya adopts the persona of Madam Paradis, a reader of Nordic Runes, and finds herself involved in also the quest to solve a mystery, a puzzle that has eluded treasure hunters for more than two hundred years. Here is a fascinating tale of romance, espionage, and murder.

Looking Through Time

Jordis Azgard has the ability to see into the past whenever she touches an antique. When her client is sold a fake instead of the real piece, however, Jordis has to find out who made this million-dollar switch and make it right before the reputation of her family's business is ruined. Here is an adventure and romance spanning two continents.

Listen to The Wind

Life for a female orphan child in Victorian England can be dismal beyond belief. And so, when Alyse is dropped at the home of her distant relatives, she is more than happy to agree with a proposal that she marry her cousin James. While her husband travels in America, hoping to replenish the family coffers, she comes to know her reserved grandfather-in-law, as well as other inhabitants of the ancestral home including the down to earth housekeeper and her talented, street wise, husband who teaches Alyse the art of pickpocketing. The years pass and eventually Alyse must make a decision: does she accept an exciting, yet forbidden romance, or continue to honor the family name and the bargain she struck when little more than a desperate child?

Step into The Light

In mid-century Victorian England, Shaleen Brandon is finding it difficult to secure employment, until she is hired as a secretary for an Inquiry Agency. Soon, however, she is caught up in the more active aspect of the work, and pleasantly surprised at how much she enjoys it. That is until they take on a horrific case A mad man is murdering young women and leaving their bodies in the squalid and shabby areas of London. He also leaves cryptic notes attached to each victim. Solving the bizarre messages takes time and intuition, and even more danger when the search eventually leads to a member of the upper echelons of society.

Circle of Fire

Mary-Corinne Aldridge experiences a sudden tragedy when her father and brother are brutally murdered. The killers are known, members of a ruthless mob that is the scourge of East End, London. When she begs the authorities for help, however, they're not interested. Mary-Corinne discovers that she is going to have to find a resolution herself. This leads her down a very unusual path.

Trained by her best friend's uncle, Mary- Corrine eventually becomes a master of an ancient Asian philosophy and
martial art. At last sure of herself and no longer defenseless,
she becomes the hunter ... only to run into the one official
from the Home Office who decided to look into the situation himself. Now working with Andrew Preston, Mary-
Corinne discover that this investigation is taking them far
beyond an East End mob.

Right Side of The Moon

Joanna Mallory has a knack for finding ancient relics, and
uses this talent to uncover items long hidden, a profession
that is surprisingly lucrative. During her travels, she meets
Ethan, a young archeologist excavating the ruins of a Ro-
man fort. While she is not the typical Victorian lady, Ethan
is yet delighted by the unusual, surprising, and occasionally
nonsensical lady. But Joanna is being stalked by a vicious
malefactor. Soon this mix of unconventional characters find
themselves wrapped up in a mystery, contributing to a clev-
er tale of discovery, danger, and of course, romance.

Slightly Different

A perfect Victorian lady, Mrs. Colfax's time is spent serving tea with impeccable style. That is when she isn't pursuing bad guys, saving the kingdom from terrorists, or
loving a secret agent. Yes, the widow Colfax appears to
be the perfect picture of a well-bred Victorian lady, but
her unique family and unusual friends have no idea that
she's leading a double life, the recipe for either disaster or
for some hilarious situations. How does she balance such
disparate facets of her complicated personality? Carefully.
Very carefully!

www.ingramcontent.com/pod-product-compliance
Lightning Source LLC
Chambersburg PA
CBHW061555170626
46811CB00001B/217